RAVEN'S REVENGE

BOOK THREE IN THE

JIM HAWKINS SERIES

With:

THE DESTINY OF JIM HAWKINS

DISCOVERY

RICHARD A. YACH

Happy Jack Publishing

Cover design by Tina Lampe

DEDICATION

To Linda: for her inspiration, encouragement, and support.

ACKNOWLEDGMENTS

I want to acknowledge the help I received from readers of early drafts of this novel, including Linda Yach and my editor Beth Burgmeyer. Without her professionalism, publishing, and editing excellence, this novel could not have been possible.

.

When asked his name, he said it was Raven. He took the bird's name associated with ill omens and mythological legends of dead and lost souls to remind him of the dark revenge he sought. Already a damned soul, his quest was to murder those who had betrayed him.

Prison turns a man one way or the other. There is no in between. Either he comes utterly and resolutely submissive to the tyrannical, despotic will of brutal guards, or he finds the deepest, darkest evil in his soul and uses it to plot his revenge.

If his soul turns black, he employs that evil—a spirit penetrating evil—and relentlessly plots to escape and seek horrifying revenge on those who betrayed him, testified against him, and imprisoned him in a waiting room to hell.

PROLOGUE

From Discovery: The Second Book in the Jim Hawkins Series

In the fall of 1770 in Portsmouth, England, the jury found the dock rat Bobby Axe guilty of kidnapping, and his employer, Dr. Herman Franks, guilty of conspiracy to kidnap and sell into slavery free-born Jamaican, Angeline, and her mother, Dominique. Bobby Axe's partner in the execution of the crime, Julie Gore, was dead, shot by Sergeant Reynolds on the isle of Cowes across from Portsmouth on the Solent River.

Franks had planned and paid for the kidnapping and was facing the death penalty. Franks' partner in this plot (and a lucrative long-running kickback scheme with medical equipment and pharmaceutical supplier LongAcre Supply at Haslar Royal Naval Hospital) was Dr. Q.J. Shaikh. Shaikh was a cohort he'd met in India, who had provided testimony against Franks in his attempt to kidnap Dominique and Angeline, the mother and daughter who had worked for the previous hospital administer.

Shaikh was also the Crown's key witness and accessory before the fact against Franks in his upcoming trial on the second, more serious charge—the attempted murder of Dr. Jim Hawkins. The prosecutor had allowed Shaikh to hire a separate solicitor and arranged to have Shaikh tried separately on the aiding and abetting the kidnapping charge against him. Because his testimony was crucial for this trial against Franks, the prosecutor and judge agreed to an outcome that was pre-ordained to be lenient.

Eli Williams, the new hospital administrator (after the sudden departure of the opium-addicted Dr. Duncan, the former hospital head), and Q.J. Shaikh's testimonies were the primary witnesses in the attempted murder case against Franks. The court wasn't going to try that case until the following February. Although Williams' evidence was necessary to convict Franks, Shaikh's was absolutely essential, and Shaikh had to be kept from fleeing the country and returning to India. The prosecuting solicitor had Shaikh's deposition naming Franks as the poisoner of Jim Hawkins, but Shaikh's actual testimony at trial would damn Franks to the gallows and a quick descent to hell. As acting director, Williams had the authority to keep Shaikh in the hospital under "house arrest" until the trial date, and that's exactly what he did. Everywhere Shaikh went, a soldier with a musket followed him. The soldiers even went so far as to lock him in his sleeping quarters at night and sleep outside the door.

No one had evidence against Franks for the poisoning death of the surgeon whom Jim Hawkins had replaced. Williams was sure Franks had done this as well, but they had no proof on which to hang the crime on Franks. The most serious charge they could bring was the attempted murder of Dr. Jim Hawkins. Conviction on this charge would likely merit the gallows—a public death by hanging. Franks had no family, no friends or clergy who would speak on his behalf. And despite his service to the Admiralty at Haslar for over ten years, the "Bloody Code" of the English law demanded the death penalty for over 220 crimes and would likely rule the day and take his life. This was the fate that Franks thought was certain as they threw him into the hulk of a rotting ship used as a prison in the Portsmouth Harbor. He obsessed about killing Axe, Shaikh, Williams, and of course Jim Hawkins, to whom he swore ultimate vengeance.

CHAPTER 1

Franks had nothing to look forward to but a loathsome three months in the bottom of a prison hulk in Portsmouth Harbor. These old, rotten ships had their masts, iron, and anything else valuable and usable stripped and repurposed, such was the frugality of His Majesty's Admiralty. All that was left of any of the prison hulk ships were rotting keels and planks. The prison system had used these old ships as prisons for some time. Since they were available, and cheap, they forestalled the need to build new prisons. Franks was roughly hauled from the Portsmouth constabulary to the prison hulk, given a wooden bowl and wooden spoon for his daily thin oatmeal gruel, and dropped rudely down the hatch to join his fellow prisoners.

"You're number twenty-one," the jailer screamed at him when he opened the hatch and pushed Franks down the eight-foot drop to the hold. "You're to answer to that if and when we calls you!" The guard snickered and added his aside to a fellow jailer, "That's if we do." With a laugh, he covered the iron hatch.

It didn't matter to the prison jailers who Franks was. He might have served the Navy as a doctor at Haslar hospital for ten years, saved some sailors' lives even though he was personally responsible for killing or maiming many others with his bizarre brain surgeries.

But to them he was just another criminal to be tossed down in the ship's hold to await trial in February. Since the "Bloody Code" of English law prevailed, he—along with others sitting in the stench of the prison hulk—would most likely be hung in the new year, so the jailers' casual, almost brutal indifference to the basic needs of these men came naturally. If one or more died before sentencing, no one in the entire legal system, including the jailers, would face rebuke. They could do whatever they wanted to the prisoners without retribution.

It was every man for himself in the darkened, minimally ventilated, boarded-up hold. Franks' only personal possessions were his clothes, a topcoat, and his fancy monogrammed boots.

His boots were his trademark, and everyone that knew him at Haslar was aware of this personal vanity. These calf length boots were specially made for him in London when he made trips to secure payment from LongAcre Supply in his kickback scheme. Made by Faulkner's luxury boots in London, they were fitted perfectly to his feet, and had special thick three-layer soles that raised his medium personal height a full inch. Although normal leather boots wore out and required replacement every year or earlier, these were of the finest, strongest leather. He'd paid close to ten times more than the going rate for a pair of production-line stock, ill-fitting shoes. As an added touch of self-importance, Franks had "HF" embossed on the side of each heel.

In the bottom of the prison hulk, however, his coat and the boots presented an immediate problem. They marked him among his fellow prisoners. Once they saw him in the entrenched darkness of the ship's hold, it was obvious from the tailoring of his topcoat and the expensive boots that he had money. They viciously coveted anything Franks had. Franks saw their envious eyes in the dim-lit hold and knew he needed immediate protection. That protection had to come from his own innate savagery, since neither the jailers above nor the prisoners below cared who lived or died in the stench of the prison ship.

During his first hours in the prison ship, Franks took stock of his situation. There were about twenty men packed against the walls of the smelly hold on this part of the deck, each sitting on an old, wet, rat-eaten straw mattress. No one had a blanket to ward off the sea-drenched cold of a Portsmouth Bay winter. All anyone had as personal possessions were the clothes on their backs.

Franks couldn't make out the faces of anyone clearly since the only light came from a cross-ironed hatch ten-feet away and eight–feet up to the next deck that provided minimal light and air. All the gun portholes were solidly boarded up so there was no escape to the sea. These prison hulks were grounded at high tide and were not going anywhere. At low tide, they were firmly sunk into the river bank.

He had to protect himself. Getting a hold of a blade, any blade was a first priority to save himself from being strangled or mauled by any of the prisoners. His coat, his boots, were worth more to these brigands than a life, and he had to act quickly.

Although he couldn't see much in the darkness, he heard the grunts, coughing, and deep chest wheezing from some of the men. The raw cold of early November was setting in, and in this wet, dank pit, those were unmistakable sounds that some were sure to die before their trials.

"Hey, you, number twenty-one, fancy boots," a rough voice from the other side of the hull called. "We got rules."

Franks didn't respond. He'd wait to decide whether he wanted to or not.

"Since you're new, you're the last one to eat when they lower the oatmeal bucket down the hatch. We go by the numbers. Got that? We calls out our numbers and fills our bowl. You also get to haul the slop bucket over to the hatch so's the guards can haul it up, toss the insides overboard, and send it back down empty. You get it and put it back in the corner. Got all that?"

Franks didn't say anything.

"I says… you got that?" The voice grew more demanding.

Since Franks wasn't ready to fight yet, he knew he had to answer or face a confrontation he couldn't win. "Got it," he said in a rough voice.

He wanted a weapon, preferably a blade. He knew how to use a knife. He knew where the most lethal parts of a body were. As a surgeon, he had carved into dozens of men at Haslar looking for unknown answers to unfathomable questions. Now he was a prisoner, a weaponless prisoner. He had to act as quickly as possible. He wasn't about to find a knife laying about the deck floor. All he had was his wooden bowl and a wooden spoon.

It came to him quickly. The handle end of the spoon would have to be sharpened to make something he could stab with. He would never be able to cut with the side of it, but maybe he could sharpen the tip and fend off any attackers. From the sounds of the deep, mucus laden coughing and wheezing, many of the twenty in this section of the hulk were weak, too weak to mount an attack at him, and take his life, his clothes, and his boots. But since they were probably dock rats condemned to die for assault or worse, with nothing left to lose, he assumed that some had superior physical strength that he could only overcome with a sharp blade.

In the darkness, he looked for anything metal that he could use to sharpen his spoon's edge. He knew his fellow rule-making prisoner across the deck was eyeing his every move, so he had to be careful. In the semi-darkness, he strained his eyes and saw to his upper right an iron ring still embedded into the wall of the ship. It was an iron ring previously used to hold cannon ropes to the bulkhead. They hadn't removed it when the ship was stripped of its valuable assets. Old and rusty, it had been ignored as useless. But it would be useful to him. He just had to wait until people were asleep to make a move for it.

After a few hours, the hatch covering opened and the oatmeal bucket came down in a rope. The men called their numbers out in turn and stumbled to fill up their bowls. Franks took note that number nine didn't call out. That meant there must be an unused mattress, an empty bowl, and unused spoon somewhere to sharpen. He wanted a backup spoon to work into a knife. There also could be a dead body lying on a sodden mattress down the way that none of these men could smell right away. If a body needed to be hauled over to the hatch so that ropes could be lowered to take a dead body out, it wasn't his job. Let someone else tell the guards. All he wanted was that spoon as a potential second weapon. Such were the venal nature of survival instincts that swept over him.

He waited patiently for number twenty to sing out, then went to fill his bowl of the cheap meal. Before he ate what he could of the awful, tasteless, nautical loblolly, he dutifully did as he had been instructed and dragged the prisoners' slop bucket to the hatch to be attached and slung skyward to the upper deck for the guards to empty.

As he waited for the slop bucket to be thrown down, Franks took a big breath of fresh air. When the bucket was tossed down, it barely missed him, as the guards had a bit of fun trying to hit the new guy with it. This was his chance to make a move closer to the iron ring. It was a good five feet to the right of his previous position, but no one noticed that he had pulled his piece of mattress underneath the iron ring. As the hours passed, and the darkness of the night swallowed any remaining light, Franks heard the snoring of the others, and carefully pulled himself onto his knees facing the ring and started the sharpening process of his spoon tip on the iron-rusted metal. He covered his entire body with his topcoat, not only for warmth but for concealment. At the moment, he was only concerned about the one tough who'd given him his orders when he first arrived, but there were probably others who wanted to kill him.

He worked feverishly through the night, often stopping to look back to see if anyone was awake and watching. His loss of sleep was nothing compared to the danger he faced when the other prisoners were awake. Throughout the night, he listened carefully for any movement. Even if his visual sense was blocked, his acute inner fear amplified his hearing.

He wanted a katar, a dual-edged blade he once possessed in

India, when he worked in the Bengal province with Dr. Q.J. Shaikh, his betrayer. All he could possibly fashion from this wooden spoon was a five-inch pointed stick that could break when he used it. He needed a blade of steel, but that wasn't going to happen. Not now, anyway.

By morning, he had a sharpened top of his spoon. He tested it against his forearm and thought it could puncture up to four inches if the thrust was strong enough. Made of oak, the spoon might hold up, even after it was used as a weapon, but he couldn't be sure. If it snapped, he would need another, and it would be much tougher to conceal the sharpening of a second spoon in the full view of the fellow prisoners in his immediate vicinity. If prisoner number nine was dead, his spoon might be lying about. Someone else would take the bowl, to try and get an extra helping of the oatmeal, but the spoon might be somewhere. The other alternative—one that entered his vicious mind almost immediately—was that if someone attacked him, and he was successful in killing him with his sharpened weapon, he could take the attacker's spoon and make a second weapon. He had spent just one night in this hellhole, and he was ready to commit murder to stay alive.

They came for him in the morning. Franks hadn't slept, but as the daylight crept from the cross-hatch down to the hole, he heard the footsteps on the upper deck of the guards sliding the cross-hatch open just enough to lower the oatmeal bucket to the hungry men. Franks wasn't sure how they would attack him, but unless they also had a sharp weapon, they would probably try and hold him, strangle him, or beat his head against the bulkhead until he was dead. Franks kept his sharp spoon under his coat and grasped it firmly, the rounded edge of the spoon fitting into the cup of his palm.

He heard number twenty called out, and a man walked bent over to fill his bowl with the thin oatmeal gruel. When he stepped away from the bucket, Franks shouted, "twenty-one" and rose to go to the bucket, his back turned to the rest of the prisoners. Franks looked over his shoulder and saw two of the men move. His icy stare briefly halted their movements, and he continued toward the oatmeal to fill his bowl, all the while raising his head up to see if the two had moved. They hadn't.

He was taking longer than usual to fill his bowl and the guard on the upper deck yelled, "Hey you, twenty-one! Be quick about it. And be lively with the slop bucket. We'll not stand at your service all morning!"

Franks moved his filled bowl of oatmeal aside. As quickly as he could, he turned his back to the others, grabbed the slop bucket from the corner, and quickly came back to the area below the open hatch and secured the bucket to the rope. As the guards pulled the slop bucket up, Franks moved to the side and pretended to eat his watery breakfast. When the guards flung the bucket down at him and closed the hatch, Franks didn't move but continued to feign eating.

"Twenty-one, put the slop bucket back in the corner where it belongs before you eat," a voice from the darkness said. "You eat when your chores are done!"

And with that self-amused crack, the voice cackled with a dry, throaty laugh as did a couple others. Franks put down his bowl and moved to fetch the empty slop bucket which had careened off the bulkhead. When he stooped to pick it up, his back was turned for a moment, and one of the prisoners came at him. He felt a strong arm around his neck.

Someone's hot breath beat against the base of his skull, and an angry voice said, "Give me your coat."

Prepared for the onslaught, he had his sharpened spoon in his right hand. As he pulled it from underneath his topcoat, he looked down and stomped as hard as he could on his attacker's foot. When the man yelped in pain, and his stranglehold relaxed for a second, Franks freed himself enough to turn around, take the wooden blade, and shove it as hard as he could straight into the attacker's chest, penetrating the thug's heart from right underneath the sternum. It was a perfect strike only a surgeon could do.

Franks held the blade tightly as he stared directly into the man's face which was quickly draining of life. They stood eye to eye, with the attacker looking shocked, his mouth agape, blood dripping from his lips. The thug struggled for one final life-exhausting moment, then slumped to the floor. No one else said a word.

The attacker's companion had come up from behind him, probably to help subdue Franks. It wasn't going to happen. With the first man's sudden and immediate death, the second scurried like a frightened cat back to his place against the wall. Franks had the unfocused, almost dazed look of a killer in his eyes.

Standing as tall as he could in the cramped quarters, and filled with blood-lust, said to all and to no one in particular, "He tried to kill me and look what it got him. You saw it. It was self-defense. If the guards want to know what happened, you tell them that and nothing else. You hear me? Or you'll get the same!"

Franks looked down and saw the broken spoon in his hand, covered with blood. He needed another weapon and soon. Shaken at the sight of a killing right in front of them, these prisoners would remain docile for an hour or two, but no more than that.

Franks went to the place where the murdered prisoner had been sitting, knelt, and gathered up his newly acquired bowl and spoon. "These are mine now," he growled. "He won't be needing them. Someone else will be dragging the slop bucket out—it won't be me. I'll leave it to the rest of you to decide who does it." He pointed to another prisoner. "You there, move that man's body out of the way."

One of the others rose and dragged the now dead rule-making prisoner's body to a corner. Even though the guards on the deck didn't care who lived or died, later in the day one of the prisoners yelled up that there were dead bodies that needed to be removed. Number nine certainly needed to be removed. His remains smelled so bad, they overpowered the other disgusting smells in the prison hold. This newly dead one would start to reek as well. They would have to be hauled up to the deck for the guards to dispose of.

Franks knew that for record keeping purposes, they would need to know the numbers of the prisoners so the names could be crossed off a list in order to tell anyone who might come looking for them. But beyond that, they didn't care who lived or died. Most of these sorrowful souls in this prisoner hulk would hang in the new year anyway and would not likely have kith or kin coming to their hanging or to their cheap burial.

With the rest of the prisoners cowed for the moment, Franks took a risk, and rather than eat, he made straight for the iron ring to sharpen his new spoon. He turned as much sideways as he could to keep an eye on anyone who might come after him. It was a calculated move but a successful one. In a few hours, Franks had a newly sharpened spoon and a newly acquired reputation as a killer. Those two assets kept him alive for the time being.

◆ ◆ ◆

The days passed with a mind-numbing, soul-searing monotony. Franks kept track of the days by scratching a mark on the bulkhead where he was perched. He slept fitfully, listening to any sound that might be another attacker. It must have been a Sunday, when a few hours after breakfast, one of the guards yelled down, "Prisoner twenty-one come to the hatch!"

Franks moved to a spot under the iron grating. "You have a visitor. It's your solicitor come to have a chat. We'll throw a rope down. You place it under your arms and we will pull you up. Don't even think of running. We'll have a musket or two aimed straight at you and we'll shoot you dead if you make a move. You hear me?"

"I hear you," Franks responded. What he really wanted was fresh air. He could tell that there was a late November chill, but he'd lacked fresh air for almost a week now. Any chance to breathe in open space would be relished.

Franks put the rope around his body and was pulled ten feet or so to the deck, his newly honed spoon tucked in his boot. He hoped he wouldn't be searched by the guards. He needed that weapon.

When he was on deck, he saw Bentley, his solicitor, over near the capstan. Two guards stood with muskets pointed at Franks. One of them motioned him to go over to the lawyer.

"You've got one hour. Then we puts you down in the hold," one of the guards growled.

Bentley was Franks' lawyer during his trial for the kidnapping of the two Jamaican women and would presumably present his case at the upcoming attempted murder trial in February. He was a small man in his fifties, a lifelong resident of Portsmouth, and had practiced law in the Portsmouth courts long enough to have established mutually beneficial relationships with fellow solicitors and magistrates. His skills in court were matched only by his avarice. He had a reputation for getting people reduced sentences if the price was right and the defendant had the means to buy his cooperation and that of the officials. Franks knew this when he hired him and was gambling his life that this corrupt lawyer could buy his escape from the gallows. Franks didn't want to part with any of the large amount of money he had stashed away, but he would have to pay this crook to work for him.

"I brought some bread and dried fish for you," Bentley said, and handed over a small parcel to Franks. "The guards inspected it to make sure I didn't hide a weapon in the bread."

As Franks looked at it, Bentley added, "I gave the guards a few pence so they would let me give it to you. Most of these officials have a price for bending the rules. These guards come cheap."

Franks took the bread and hungrily ate both the bread and fish in animal-like fashion, barely stopping to breathe as he inhaled the food.

"We have only a few minutes, so let's get straight to what we have to do." Bentley was direct and firm. "I need your money— you'll have to tell me where it is and how to get it. You owe me for what I have done already. The money is also to retain my services before and during your trial. Anything extra is to try and get acquiescence from the prosecuting solicitor and a reduced sentence from the magistrate. They will not come as cheap as these guards did. I make no promises."

It didn't matter that Franks was gobbling down the first decent, if stale, food he'd had in days, and that he hadn't slept but for a small few hours; his mind was racing. He'd be damned if he would give this crooked lawyer all the money he had hidden away at Haslar Hospital. He had two caches where he kept it. Ever suspicious, he never wanted to keep it all in one place. Over the years of running his kickback scheme with LongAcre Supply, he had accumulated almost £7,000. He split it between two separate hiding places, but it wasn't doing him any good now. If Bentley could buy a reduced sentence with some of it, that would be desirable. If Bentley could get him out of this stinking hellhole of a prison hulk, that would be ideal. But he knew lawyers, and everything was always a negotiation. He didn't want to give him everything he had. Everything was brinksmanship. Franks could play that game as well as this solicitor.

"How much will it take?" Franks asked.

Franks could see Bentley's mind working. Bentley would surely ask for as much as he thought he could get. Between now and the trial in February, Franks could die in this prison hulk or get the gallows despite his efforts. Bentley would want his money regardless if Franks lived or died.

"It depends on what the prosecutor wants in return for a more lenient sentence and what the magistrate will accept for granting it."

"You've done this before. How much, damn it?"

"How much do you have to offer? Tell me where it is and I'll tell you if it's enough."

"Get to it. How much do you need?" He spit this last question out through his teeth, trying not to let the nearby prison guards hear what he was saying.

Bentley was more interested in knowing where Franks hid his money than getting an agreement as to the exact amount of a bribe. Franks was sure that Bentley fully intended to take all of it, regardless of the amount Franks agreed to. When Franks had been arrested, there were rumors of a kickback scheme, so Bentley most likely knew that Franks had the means to help himself.

"Two-thousand pounds," said Bentley. "These officials don't come cheap and neither do I."

"That's too high."

"It's your life, Franks. You're facing the gallows. Think about that."

"What sort of reduced sentence can you get me?"

"I can't say. I haven't—" Bentley tried to say, but Franks interrupted him.

"Come on. You know the rules in these courts. That's why I hired you. What can you get me?"

"I haven't spoken to the prosecutor as yet. You've only been here a few days. First, I get paid, then with your money in my hand, I can more easily secure these officials' compliance with our...request."

"One thousand pounds. That should be enough." If Franks could bribe his way to freedom, he would take the remainder of his cash, go back to India, and live like a minor rajah.

"The number, my good sir, is two thousand. You are not in a very good position to bargain with me. I am the only one standing between you and the hangman's noose."

That last pointed argument of Bentley's hit Franks hard. Bentley was right. Franks didn't have anyone else on the outside to fight for him. If Bentley walked away, Franks would be hard pressed to find another solicitor who would take his case and be able to win his freedom from the gallows at a lower price.

"What kind of reduced sentence can you get me?"

"Perhaps, a short prison sentence, perhaps transportation to the colonies."

"Transportation to the colonies!"

"Our courts have been doing it for years. It's a forced indenture. Depends if there are buyers who want your skills. But, let me repeat. No promises. They might very well take your money and still hang you. It's your only chance."

"All right, two thousand it is," said Franks reluctantly.

"Now tell me where I can find it. I have been in written correspondence with Dr. Williams at Haslar and he said I would be allowed to make one trip without interference to your former quarters to fetch personal belongings for you."

Franks paused before he spoke again. All he wanted right now was to escape, get back to his rooms at Haslar, get his money, exact his revenge on Shaikh, Bobby Axe, and Hawkins, and buy passage on a boat to India. But this was wishful thinking born of too many sleepless nights and the fear of death at the hands of the prisoners below. He would have to gamble on this crooked lawyer. Finally, he relented. "I have two rooms at Haslar. Or rather, I had two rooms. I lived in them for almost ten years. You'll find the money box under a floorboard behind the headboard of the bed."

"Is there enough?"

"It's all I have," Franks lied, staring straight at the lawyer. "Take it and get me the best deal you can. When will I find out what you've been able to accomplish?"

"It may take a while. They won't move your trial date up if that's what you're angling for. You'll be here until February fifth, the trial date. If I find out anything before then, I'll come and tell you. Meanwhile, try and stay alive. It could be a rough winter."

Franks already knew that the upcoming months in this hellhole would be terrible. He wanted one more thing from Bentley. "Get me my knife from the upper drawer of the bureau dresser in my bedroom. I need to protect myself."

"Not a chance. If the guards found me bringing a weapon on board this boat, not only would I be tossed into jail, but I would lose my court privileges for smuggling contraband. They might let me bring a bit of food, but that's all. Listen, I will be searched just like every other visitor. There's no way I will even try to do that."

Franks wondered if the scheming lawyer wanted him dead and that's why he didn't want to help Franks arm himself.

Bentley rose from where he was sitting and called out, "Guards! We're done here."

"Come back next week and bring some more food. For what I'm paying you, you owe me that much," Franks barked out as one of the guards poked him with the musket and prodded him to start moving back to the hatch.

Bentley didn't say a word in response but continued walking to the gangplank that led him across the muddy tidal basin to shore. Franks got the feeling, there was a good chance Bentley wouldn't be back.

CHAPTER 2

T he next morning, Bentley went down to the docks at Portsmouth and paid for a ticket on the hourly ferry ride across the bay to Gosport to get Franks' money at Haslar Naval Hospital. He engaged a carriage ride from the Gosport dock to the hospital, and when they arrived after the short half mile trip, Bentley asked the driver to stay and wait. The guards at the hospital's gate kept him waiting while they took a message and his calling card to Dr. Williams, the hospital administrator. He waited at the gate the better part of a half hour in the cold, damp wind until the soldier came back and escorted him to Williams' office.

Because he was a witness against Franks at the upcoming attempted murder trial, Williams wouldn't see the lawyer. He didn't want to explain away an interaction with a defense attorney should a question be raised by a magistrate about what was said or even implied at such a meeting. To Williams, Franks was a murderer and needed to be hanged. He didn't want to taint any of his own testimony or have a word-twisting attorney have any ammunition against what he was going to say.

When Bentley arrived at Williams' office, his secretary told him that Dr. Williams was busy and could not see him but had left word that Bentley would be escorted by armed guard to Franks' former quarters and be allowed a half hour alone in Franks' rooms.

Bentley readily agreed to the stipulations and marched with the guard in the large, multi-tiered hospital to the D ward where Franks had his rooms. Bentley carefully cradled his satchel which hid an iron pry bar he needed to get under the floorboard.

When they arrived at the rooms, the guard opened the locked door and left Bentley alone. Working as quickly as he could, Bentley stripped off his outer topcoat, then his suit jacket, and pulled the bed away from the wall. Testing the various floorboards with his feet, he located the board that seemed a bit looser than the other ones nearby. He tore a blanket off the bed, muffled his pry bar with it, and carefully and as quietly as he could, jabbed the end of the pry bar between the boards and slowly levered the nails up. He stopped midway through this operation and looked towards the door to make sure the guard didn't interrupt him.

Bentley followed this careful pattern until the board was completely loosened with the nails intact for reinsertion once he finished. He took the cloth-wrapped gray metal box from its hiding place and opened it. He saw a wad of notes and greedily counted them. He hoped it was substantially more than the two thousand pounds Franks had agreed to pay.

"God damn it!" he exclaimed under his breath. "Only two thousand. That's why he agreed to it. But he must have more. He has to."

Sweat ran down his forehead as he stuffed the money in his satchel. Thinking fast, since he only had a few minutes left of his allotted time in the room, he thought Franks must have another hiding place. He got off his knees and walked the floor boards next to the wall in back of the headboard of the bed. Nothing! He pulled the dresser away from the wall and found a tell-tale creak of a loose floorboard. Quickly grabbing the blanket-wrapped pry bar, he didn't try to be especially careful or quiet as he yanked the nails up that held the loose board. It took longer than he expected. His heart raced for fear of being found out by the guard. He faced two choices. Either hurry and risk making too much noise, or go out and ask for more time. He stopped and listened for any steps outside the door, then he chose the first option. He hurriedly pulled up the last nails and found what he was looking for. There was another metal box. It was locked.

"Damn," he snorted a bit too loudly. He didn't have enough time to pry it open. He shoved the metal box and the pry bar into his satchel. There was barely room for both. He stood and put the dresser and bed back into place, wiped his face with the blanket, and tried to put the room back to how he had found it.

Putting his suit coat on and carrying his topcoat so it concealed the bulging satchel, he abruptly opened the door only to find the guard had walked fifty paces down the long hallway to talk with another guard. Perhaps, they hadn't heard anything.

"I'm done in there," he yelled to the guard.

"What did you take?" the guard asked pointedly as he came close to the lawyer. You got that satchel stuffed I see."

"Just a couple of shirts and a pair of pants," Bentley lied. "Bulky, aren't they?"

"Well, Franks won't be needing them where he is going. Unless of, course, he wants to dress up special for the hangman." The guard chortled at his crude joke.

Bentley was escorted from the building and didn't put his top coat on until he was outside and headed for his waiting carriage. It was a short ride to the docks, so he didn't attempt to open the locked cash box. He could get a proper tool at his place and explore its contents in the privacy of his carriage house in Portsmouth. So far it had been a successful trip.

When he got home and pried open the cash box, he delighted to see almost £5,000 in various size bills. It was a lot of money, and it would set him and his family up for the rest of his life. He wanted to keep all of it but thought carefully as what to do. If Franks died in prison over the winter, no one would care, least of all the justice officials who viewed him as just one more case to try in February. But if Franks survived the winter, he would be brought to trial and Bentley would have to be there to represent him as the court had already been apprised of his engagement.

He could renege on his effort to get the opposing prosecutor and magistrate to lighten Franks' sentence, but the scene at court might be dicey since Franks would yell holy hell and blame him if the sentence was the gallows. Bentley pictured a scene that would have Franks yelling to the rafters that he had paid Bentley to influence the courts. The people in the court room, the magistrate, the barristers, and worst of all the newspaper reporters who covered the courts might not believe Franks, but then, they might. So, even if Franks was hanged, the sniff of a bribery scandal would jeopardize Bentley's standing and sully his reputation.

Facing this unpleasant outcome, he didn't like the dilemma it put him in, so he decided to follow through with a meeting with the prosecuting attorney to see what accommodations could be made, and what was the minimum price to pay for the bribe.

CHAPTER 3

"**B**ut, Jack, you have to find a pathway to leniency. He's a doctor, a surgeon. He served 10 years at Haslar Hospital caring for his Majesty's wounded. Yes, I admit, he may be deranged. But who's to say that you or I wouldn't be that way if we had treated the twisted and insane at Haslar for so many years. Who are we to judge what it did to him? That daily grind might have encouraged in him a twisted view of human kind, a perverse aspect on reality."

Bentley sat across from Jack Lawson, the prosecutor assigned to bring charges against Franks in the upcoming trial for the attempted murder. It was the week before Christmas and it had taken Bentley a couple of weeks to get a meeting. Bentley was making as plaintive an argument as he could to Lawson to ask for a lighter sentence, without paying for it. His pockets held Franks' cash, and he was prepared to hand some of it over if that's what it took, but he wanted to pay as little as he could.

Lawson was a busy man, an underpaid solicitor for the court, faced with a stack of cases on his desk. Most of them dealt with assaults and thievery. Just the variety of cases you would expect to find in a seaport like Portsmouth. This case was something out of the ordinary. Franks' cases involved attempted murder of another surgeon at the hospital, one Dr. Jim Hawkins. The papers he had on his desk argued for the gallows.

"Look, I have sworn statements from Dr. Hawkins, Dr. Williams, Dr. McLaughlin, and Dr. Shaikh. I have the box from LongAcre Supply that shipped the belladonna to Franks. Shaikh was his partner in the kidnapping, and his testimony especially puts Franks in the hangman's noose. You surely don't want leniency for a killer."

"Hawkins is still alive and living in Bristol, Jack. He's not dead."

"Lucky for him, I'd say."

"What about lowering the sentence to transportation to the colonies? These planters could use some medical help to keep the slaves alive."

Bentley had a hidden motive to asking for transportation to the colonies. Franks could die on one of these "black-bird" ships during a slow three-month voyage, die in the colonies, or after his indenture period, continue to live out his life there. Any one of these options would be a safer outcome for Bentley and his family. If all Franks got was a reduced sentence in a British jail, then he would eventually come looking for him since he now had all or most of Franks' money.

Bentley continued with his plea. "What about transportation? It's common knowledge that England has been shipping convicts to planters in Maryland and Virginia for decades. You've been sending mostly unskilled, brainless labor. This man is a doctor. Some planter or iron mine owner would pay a good price to have him for... what is it now...?"

Lawson responded, thinking it over, "It's still seven or fourteen years."

"Make it fourteen for this one then, considering the nature of the crime. Everyone can win."

"We're being told by the Crown that transportation may end soon."

"Why's that? I thought it was working well."

Lawson looked like he was pondering the transportation sentencing option. "Well, we've already sent close to twenty-thousand men since 1720. They've worked alongside slaves in the tobacco fields, in the iron mines, in the shipyards. But we can't send too many more. The rebels in the colonies are making a lot of trouble every spring and summer. Tax commissioners have been killed, tarred, run out of town. Massachusetts and other states are cauldrons of rebellion. The Crown doesn't want more men angry at us joining forces with them."

"But you're still doing it this spring, aren't you?

"Yes, until we're told to stop."

"Then make it a fourteen-year forced indenture," Bentley persisted. "If he escapes the colonies and comes back, it's a punishable crime, yes?"

"If caught, he would be summarily executed. It's the law. All right, Bentley, I can try to get transportation. But I have to get the magistrate who hears this case to go along with any recommendation. It might be expensive—for him and for me. We won't do this out of the kindness of our hearts."

"Think of a number."

"Two hundred pounds for me, four hundred for the magistrate. No bargaining, Bentley, not this time."

Bentley paused. He was comfortable with what Lawson asked for, but didn't want to agree too readily. Lawson might think he was eager to settle and come up with a reason for more money.

"Ah, Jack...you ask for the sky. That's a lot of money."

"I said, no bargaining, Bentley. Take it or leave it. We can hang Franks with this evidence, remember that."

"I see your point and the position you have my client in. Yes, yes...I agree to those amounts. Can you assure me the magistrate will accept? If he turns your sentencing request down, he could put us both in a lot of trouble. Who's the magistrate on this case by the way?"

"It's Benjamin Warner. He and I have worked together on other situations like this. He'll go along. The springtime schedule is full. He has no time to waste and he has mouths to feed just like me. Christmas is coming soon, and he has a big family. Do you have the money? If I go to the magistrate with cash rather than a promise, I can more easily get his acceptance."

Bentley reached down to his satchel and pulled out a handful of bills. He counted out six hundred worth of pound notes and slid them across the desk to Lawson who quickly put the money in his desk drawer.

"For that kind of money, Jack, I expect you to have a 'convict broker' present at the trial who would have already agreed to sell Franks' indenture rights to a planter or merchant. If that deal is done beforehand, we can get him on a ship to Virginia as soon as possible."

"Yes, I'll do that. Finding one won't be a problem, not for a surgeon. Not for this Franks fellow. That concludes our business, Bentley. I'll have the secretary show you out."

"Will we meet again before the trial so I can tell my client what the expected outcome will be?"

"No. You will have to take your chances. Too many meetings prior to a trial, especially given this transaction, might raise suspicions. I'll get word to you of what the magistrate's decision is beforehand. I won't keep you in suspense, that much I promise you. Once I know anything, I'll leave a note for you with my secretary that will say either yes or no. Don't expect it until the last week of January."

◆ ◆ ◆

"Bring the prisoner Franks forward!" commanded Magistrate Benjamin Warner at the trial the first week of February 1772. Franks was haggard and exhausted. He had survived the last month and a half in the prison hulk but was a skeleton of his former self. Unwashed through the entire winter, he had eaten only the mealy oatmeal mush twice a day. His beard hadn't been cut or combed, and his hair was uncut as well. He felt terrible except for his inner spirit, which had been buoyed by his attorney who had given him the good news a week ago that his life had been bargained for a few pound notes. Bentley had told him that the "arrangement" cost the full two thousand pounds he'd agreed to. Bentley wouldn't tell him who got how much, but Franks suspected that Bentley probably got the lion's share. He was a snake in a suit, but if he saved Franks' life, the money was worth it.

The iron shackles around his feet and hands were tight and chafed against his wrists and ankles. As the dozen or so people in the hearing room got settled, Franks looked around at all the well-fed barristers, reporters, and court snoops and thought about how good a real meal would be. But he quickly put that thought out of his mind as he saw the bailiff stoking the open coal fire in the corner. The fire warmed the chilly room a bit, but there were iron bars sticking in the fire.

"Your solicitor and the prosecuting attorney have come to a settlement in your case, Dr. Franks," said Benjamin Warner from his slightly elevated chair at the front of the room. "That settlement has saved the Crown the expense and time of a trial. And I agree with the prosecuting attorney's recommendation for sentencing."

With that, the magistrate gave a quick look over to where Lawson sat, and the two exchanged slight nods of agreement. The magistrate avoided looking at Bentley. This was to be a very fast hearing with a fast sentence pronounced, and the prisoner escorted back to the prison hulk.

"The case against you is for the attempted murder of a fellow physician at Haslar Hospital," continued Warner at length. "I have been told by the prosecutor that this Dr. Jim Hawkins is alive and has recovered from this attempted poisoning. This is a heinous act, Dr. Franks. If we were to have a trial, perhaps the court and the public would learn of your motives, what you could possibly have gained from Dr. Hawkins's death. But whatever your motives, it was a deed that should merit the gallows.

"However, the court has been persuaded that you shall be worth more to the Crown alive rather than dead. It is the sentence of this court, therefore, that you be indentured to a British citizen in the American colonies for no less, nor no more, than fourteen years. You shall be transported to said colonies at the first opportunity. If you escape and return to England before your term in the colonies is completed, you will be shot on sight. I hope you understand that. You have the right to speak before we execute the sentence. Since you have been placed before this court by your solicitor without benefit of clergy to speak for you, do you have anything to say?"

Franks thought for a minute. If his hatred boiled over and he condemned this court for the indignity of even being there or for throwing him in that prison hulk, he would only make it worse for himself. Instead, he slowly turned, his foot shackles rustling against the wooden floor, and shared a look of revenge in his black eyes, a look no one in that room would ever forget.

As he wheeled to face the magistrate, he quietly said," I have nothing to say that would change the sentence."

Without any prior indication of what he was to do, the magistrate raised both of his arms and motioned to two guards to surround Franks.

Warner then stood and spoke severely to Franks, who was no more than ten-feet from the magistrate. "There are some here who will privately and publicly criticize the sentence of this court. I assure all of you that this is not a lenient court. Dr. Franks, you will carry with you a reminder of your evil deed and a reminder that the English Crown condemns your actions. Guards, secure the prisoner. Bailiff, bring the iron."

As the two guards grabbed a firm hold on Franks, he looked at Bentley who showed his surprise, and the shrug of his shoulders implied that he knew nothing of what was to transpire. Bentley shot a look at Lawson, who returned his raised-eyebrows incredulous stare.

Even though, Franks struggled, they were able to move him a few feet closer to the stove. Thieves were often branded with a "T" on the thumb to remind them of their crime, but also to alert anyone who came across them that this person was a thief. It was a scar for life, a harsh relic from English medieval days. However barbaric and inhuman, the branding was still used by some magistrates. Certainly, he had paid these court officers enough so they wouldn't brand him.

As the guards held him, one of them had both of his hands and held Franks' left hand down flat on the rough table. When the bailiff got the nod from the magistrate, he applied the burning hot brand on the palm of Franks hand. Franks belched out a terrible, loud, unearthly scream. The iron was quickly pulled away and the guards shoved Franks' hand into a bucket of water to cool the burn. Franks continued to scream, and his cursing from the depths of hell could be heard out in the hallway. The deep anger in his voice was the voice of vengeance.

"Take the prisoner back to the prison," the magistrate bellowed above the screams. "This hearing is adjourned."

The two guards who held Franks ushered him out of the hearing room as fast as they could. He yelled obscenities all the while, cursing the magistrate, the Crown, his solicitor, and the prosecuting attorney. No one escaped his wrath. But since he addressed everyone with his violent screams, no one paid attention to his exact words that included the payment he thought he had made to secure his lenient sentence.

At the end of the hall, the guards had heard enough and shoved a gag in his mouth, then secured his hand shackles to his foot shackles so he couldn't reach the mouth gag. He was rudely thrown into a constabulary wagon and driven back to the prison hulk, where nobody paid any attention to his muffled wailing.

Bentley caught up with Lawson in the hallway as the court reporters scurried out to catch the wailing of the prisoner as he was loaded into the prison wagon.

"You didn't tell me that branding was going to be administered. I promised Franks the transportation sentence. That's all."

"I didn't know for sure what Warner was going to do. I got his acceptance of the transportation decree, didn't I. You should be glad Franks isn't headed for the gallows."

"All the same. You better hope he dies on the transportation ship or in the colonies. If he ever gets back here, we're both dead men. He won't forget."

◆ ◆ ◆

In March, having spent one last month in the prison hulk beached in Portsmouth's Harbor, Franks was chained and hauled to the *Jonathan*, a prison transport ship that hauled slaves from Africa—and English prisoners—to the so-called New World. A broker on the Portsmouth dock had put a bid in for £50 for Franks' indenture and secured the rights to sell his labor in Virginia where the *Jonathan* was headed.

There was an iron-mine owner by the name of Taylor who had engaged the broker to find skilled or unskilled labor for his tobacco fields and his iron mine. Taylor had established a banking relationship with a London bank that would pay the broker upon receipt of healthy people who were to be his indentured slaves for fourteen years. He would have none of the seven-year types. Their service would be over too soon to be profitable. What was risky was the voyage across the Atlantic.

The *Jonathan* and ships like her were older, slower, and more rotted than any of the other ships that sailed the sea for England. The *Jonathan,* as her captain would say, was the oldest, slowest, most ill manned, filthy ship that still floated. It's bilge pumps had to be constantly manned to pump out leakage.

Pure and simple, it was a convict slave ship. The air below was putrid, and rank, smelling of urine and feces. It was the home of rotten food, lice, rats—and worst of all—typhus.

This was Franks' home for the next three months as he was shipped to the Chesapeake Bay and a new life as a slave.

CHAPTER 4

CHAPTER 4

BRISTOL, ENGLAND: SPRING 1771
LIVESEY ACRES

D r. Jim Hawkins and his wife, Livian, took up residence with Dr. Robert Livesey, his wife, Elizabeth, and their three-year old daughter, Margaret, at Dr. Livesey's ten-acre farm outside Bristol. This was home when Jim apprenticed with Dr. Livesey following the magnificent, and highly successful voyage to Treasure Island. Jim had hidden his share of Captain Flint's gold at Livesey Farms and had fostered a lifetime friendship with his mentor and benefactor, Dr. Livesey. Jim had learned much of herbal medicine in his time with Dr. Livesey and had gone on to medical school in London because of him. Livesey Farms was also special since he'd met Livian at Livesey Acres, his wife of almost two years whom he cherished even above his own life, and the mother of his sweet daughter, Belle.

Ever resolute, persistent, and resourceful, Livian was adjusting to hearing in one ear after receiving a small miracle from God when Jim, Mac, and Daniel Foreman successfully employed their electrostatic generator at Haslar to spark life back into Livian's left ear. Although the men wanted to work on her right ear as well,

Livian chose at that time not to suffer any more of their electrostatic treatment since their daughter would soon be born.

When Belle the beautiful was born in March of 1771, the joy in the Livesey household was felt by everyone. Belle had her mom's auburn hair and her greenish-blue eyes and fair skin. She was a sight to behold. Livian's parents, Arnold and May Adams—who were caretakers of the Livesey farm operation—were there to celebrate along with Jim's mother, Sara, and her sister, Maddy. Sara and Maddy had taken time off from running the Admiral Benbow Inn to come and see the newborn, who by her very presence, sent waves of happiness through all who saw her. It was almost as if she could feel the power she had over the cooing adults who fawned over her every move and giggle. The grandparents, Arnold and May, found many reasons to leave their chores on the farm and drop in to see Belle and feel the love of new life in the household.

With Livian's left ear getting increasingly better, she could sometimes hear Belle's cries and cooing without the aid of the ear horn. It was awkward to hold the ear horn and her baby, so in the early days after the birth, and for a month afterwards, Elizabeth and even the small toddler, Margaret, helped Livian with the basics of baby care.

The most difficult task facing Livian was learning to speak. The fever had taken her hearing when she had been but three years old. Although she had been able to speak quite well at that age, having been robbed of her hearing for the past twenty-plus years prevented her from speaking clearly. Her words came out haltingly, and her lips and tongue muscles needed to be exercised to correctly speak the English language.

But ever the strong-willed and determined woman, she used her excellent lip-reading skills—which she had honed to a fine art—to purse out the sounds she now could faintly hear from others. She was the one who would be teaching Belle to speak, and she wanted desperately to give her baby girl the best mother she could be. Livian had been the best linen maker in Bristol, a superb cotton-sheet weaver in Gosport, and defender of her husband when the odds were against him. She had belted Ozzy with a clay pot, hit Bobby Axe with a brick, and was ready to use a mooring rope iron to send Bobby's soul to the bottom of the Solent when he and his partner, Julie Gore, had attacked them. This set of tasks was just another challenge to be overcome and conquered.

She was the best possible partner for Dr. Jim Hawkins. Although a success at many things already in his 25 years, Jim could have a failing of spirit when his medical practice or his experiments didn't go well. He was never a great book learner, but was an iterative scientist always depending on practical tests to learn what worked and what didn't. His lack of theoretical knowledge was a weakness overcome only by his internal persistence, which could ebb in dark times. Throughout their almost two-year marriage it had been Livian's steadfast, stubborn will to overcome that often gave Jim the added inherent strength he needed.

Livian had grown up on the farm at Livesey Acres. It was a real home to her. She had lived with Jim in Gosport when he worked at Haslar Hospital, but was happy to be nesting, as she put it, in her own environment.

Jim and Livian had depended on a chalkboard for communication before the God-given miracle of her reawakened hearing in one ear. Since Livian was just learning to speak again, the two of them still relied on the chalkboard when they needed to communicate. Using that chalkboard, they had put before them a two-year plan to establish the medical practice with Dr. Livesey, then build a house on land that Dr. Livesey would sell to them. The ten-acre farm had some very pretty sections, and since Livian had been raised on the property, she knew exactly where she wanted the house to be built. They had the dreams of young married couples, star bright and star lit, filled with love for each other and for their daughter. While Jim was away in Bristol, Livian and Elizabeth would often take pen and paper and draw up imaginary plans for the home they wanted to build.

When they left Haslar Hospital in Gosport for their new life in Bristol, Jim and Livian were accompanied on the trip by Dr. David McLaughlin, Jim's working partner at Haslar. Jim and David had agreed to be medical partners with the intention of practicing with Dr. Livesey at his surgery in downtown Bristol. Dr. Livesey had agreed to the three of them working together before Jim and David ever traveled back to Bristol, the previous December. It was a partnership that he thought would suit them all.

Early in January, soon after they had arrived in Bristol, Dr. David McLaughlin decided to rent sleeping quarters in downtown Bristol. Initially, he had slept in Livesey's house, but soon moved to the spare sleeping room at Livesey's surgery in Bristol that Dr. Livesey and Jim had used when Jim apprenticed in Bristol. That arrangement worked out well for a month or so. McLaughlin could stay at the surgery and see to any patients who came in for medical help when Dr. Livesey or Jim weren't there. But McLaughlin needed some time and space to himself, and eventually took separate rooms in Bristol discovered for him by Squire Trelawney, the wealthy wine merchant who had been a partner in the great Treasure Island adventure.

When the baby was born in March, Jim wanted to spend as much time as possible with Livian and Belle. With McLaughlin in Bristol, he could afford to spend a long weekend at Livesey Acres and work but Monday through Thursday at the surgery.

Dr. Livesey readily accepted the rotation the three of them set up. Now in his early fifties, he liked having the young doctors take care of the increasing volume of patients. He had set up the surgery when Jim spent four years at medical school, had shipped with His Majesty's Navy for two years, and spent a full year toiling at Haslar Hospital in Gosport. Over that seven-year period, Livesey's reputation for excellence had brought many patients to him.

Many of his patients came from the well-to-do parishioners from his church. His practice grew despite Livesey's strong anti-slavery position that differed markedly from that of his true friend, Squire

Trelawney, and many of the Tories who attended St. Nicolas and who had benefited richly from Bristol's part in the English slave trade.

To help with the increasing work load and to handle more minor treatments, he hired a nursing staff of two women in town who were willing to leave the Bristol Royal Infirmary to work for him. But there were plenty of decisions that the three men had to make if they were to work successfully as partners and grow the one-man Livesey Surgery into a full-sized medical clinic.

◆ ◆ ◆

It was a cold, windy day in mid-March with the wind blowing briskly up the Avon River from the sea when Drs. Livesey, Hawkins, and McLaughlin were in the surgery's office discussing the steps they needed to take. They spent the entire afternoon in front of the office's warm fireplace assessing how the previous two months had worked out. Changes needed to be made. Without any rancor, the three made plans to buy more equipment, arrange working hours for the three of them, and agreeing in spirit on a partnership on which they would share expenses and revenue.

Dr. Livesey said he wanted to be sure the three men understood one another. "We should make a partnership agreement in writing. As the medical practice grows, we'll need that to compensate everyone fairly. As your role expands and mine diminishes over time, you need to be partners in any changes. But for now, you should know that we will have to take into consideration the practice I have built up over the past eight years. It reads Livesey Surgery on the shingle outside the door."

"Right sir, and I'm sure Dr. McLaughlin and I will always respect the fact that we are joining your medical business and that we would do nothing to jeopardize your patients or their loyalty to you."

"Well stated, Jim. What I want to say is that our partnership agreement should never come in the way of our friendships. That's too important.

"We do have a major deficiency in this operation because of the potential growth of our medical practice," Livesey continued. "We can't rely on the produce from my herb garden. It's too much work for Arnold, Maye, or even Livian who is pre-occupied now with Belle, and she should be."

"Have you a local source like the apothecaries?" asked McLaughlin.

"Sometimes I have relied on them. However, there's some animosity between them and the surgeons in town. They think we're in competition with them and they have withheld supplies at different times. I can't rely on them. In an emergency, they've charged me many times more than what's warranted. When it has been a seller's market, and they know it, they've taken advantage of me and other surgeons in Bristol. It's well known among us."

"We have to go to a large supplier," said McLaughlin.

Jim and Mac exchanged knowing glances with each other, pausing to see who would be first to mention the medical supply firm that had been the source of the belladonna that almost killed Jim.

Jim exchanged a knowing nod with Mac and went first. "At Haslar, we ordered everything from LongAcre Supply of London." He thought about all the trouble dealing with LongAcre had brought them at Haslar with Franks ordering belladonna to kill him. Then there was the kickback scheme that LongAcre had agreed to with their sworn enemy, Franks.

"The administrators we worked for at Haslar didn't even think of preparing medicines by themselves. Orders were made and delivered, by my recollection, in a week's time," Jim suggested.

"Given what you told me about what Franks was up to with them, doesn't make them sound like a reputable company," said Livesey with a strong degree of doubt in his voice.

"I understand your skepticism, Dr. Livesey," chimed in McLaughlin. "But they are the biggest in England and they have large quantities of herbs, medicines, and equipment that we need and can order from one source. Seems to me that efficiency is of paramount importance here."

"All right, Mac. With caution, I'll go along with LongAcre. But you two will do the ordering and make the contract with them. You have to buy smart. I don't want them to overcharge us like they probably did Haslar. We're not the Admiralty with an unlimited budget."

The three of them shared a small chuckle, but knew this was serious business they were contemplating.

"Here, here to that," said Mac. "As far as new equipment goes, we need to buy a Robertson microscope. I can't operate without one."

"That would be a major expense," said Dr. Livesey, looking like he was bracing himself for the technical equipment that would change the way the Livesey Surgery would practice medicine. "What would that cost?"

"I think Haslar bought theirs for £100 each," said McLaughlin. I can get them to accept a third of it as down payment."

"Not inexpensive," piped in Dr. Livesey. "But I agree that it is absolutely necessary. Especially because of the steady income stream I have secured for us."

"Steady income stream?" asked Jim.

Livesey explained. "The head of Naval Administration is a friend of mine from church, and since you two are joining this surgery, we have the manpower to accommodate his request. He came to me after services and broached the idea of having our surgery check out all of his seamen once they come ashore, and also give sailors a pre-sailing checkup to ensure they are not carrying anything aboard that would jeopardize the health of the crew. At his suggestion, we could bill the Naval Administration a monthly fixed fee and stand ready to assess the health of these disembarking sailors and assess the health of those going on board for a voyage. You had to do something similar, didn't you, Jim, when you embarked on the *HMS Romney* a couple of years ago?"

"Yes, sir. I did. Although it was merely a perfunctory exam. They didn't take much time with it, to be sure."

"Well, if we're to do justice to the Admiralty's goal, we'll have to do our best," stressed Dr. Livesey.

Jim answered eagerly, "We'll need that microscope sooner, I believe. Just the thought of taking small blood samples and seeing what these sailors have brought with them from the ends of the British Empire is exciting."

"I did a fair amount of tissue, blood, and urine sampling in Edinburgh where I went at medical college, and at Haslar," chimed in Mac. Jim knew Mac was eager to put his education to work. Haslar Hospital was a testing environment, but one that didn't give him enough time to use his considerable Scottish medical education.

"I'd attest to Mac's work with the microscope, Dr. Livesey. He kept an organized filing of all the samples we ever used for comparison."

"Oh, my God, Jim, I had to leave my sample collection at Haslar. I had over two years of samples collected, labeled, organized!" Mac said in a moment of despair.

Jim wanted to be helpful. He and Mac knew that there were no books with benchmark blood or organ samples. The collection samples were at Haslar. But it was a big problem. They couldn't drive down to Haslar or up to Edinburgh or even over to London every time they wanted to compare a new patient blood sample.

"Wait a minute, Mac. Didn't you have duplicates of anything in your tissue sample drawers?"

"Yes. In many cases, there were duplicates," answered Mac. "What are you thinking, Jim?"

"Dr. Eli Williams would let you part with duplicates, if you asked."

Mac nodded, looking relieved. "Yes. Maybe he would."

Dr. Livesey jumped into what the two young doctors were dealing with. "Maybe you won't have to go all the way to Haslar, Mac," said Dr. Livesey. "The British Royal Infirmary has urine color code charts for visually matching urine results with a standard color for certain diseases. These have been codified for many years. Maybe they have other things to share. But, Mac, if you have duplicate blood samples at Haslar, perhaps you could write a letter to your friend Williams and have him send them here. Saves all of us time."

"I'll write the letter today," answered McLaughlin.

"Good, then we're agreed. Oh, not to spread out all the ideas I have been thinking about, but if the sailor checkup plan works out well with the Admiralty, perhaps, we may want to offer the same medical checkup plan to the Merchant Ship Association. Squire Trelawney and I had dinner not too long ago and he mentioned that more merchant ship captains were concerned about starting out their voyages with as healthy a crew as possible. They always hire the minimum size crew, and if more than a couple are ill, the entire voyage suffers."

"That sounds perfect. My head is spinning with the possibility of having revenue for an entire building for our medical practice," said Jim.

"That's plenty for now, gentlemen. Let's tend to our respective tasks and then to dinner. I'm already getting hungry and I have a list of medicines to prepare for our order, and you two have to list equipment needs."

"You're right Dr. Livesey." said Jim.

But before he could continue, Livesey interrupted. "You know, fellows, I think when we're together like this, we should use our Christian names, but when we're in the company of patients, we use our formal appellations? What say you David? Call me Robert?"

"I prefer Mac. It reminds me of my Scottish heritage. But, yes, Robert it will be."

"Right it is, Mac. And Jim?"

"It's too hard to call you Robert, Dr. Livesey. I have been calling you Dr. Livesey for a decade or more that I have known you. You've done more for me than I can ever repay. No, I can't do that. It must be Dr. Livesey. I feel very odd calling you Robert."

With that, their meeting was over. Jim was already thinking about all of the possibilities that might come out of their shared medical practice.

CHAPTER 5

Franks was in hand shackles deep in the hold of the *Jonathan*, an aged, heavy, decrepit "black-bird" ship of the slave trade that the British justice system employed to haul prisoners to the colonies. Outfitted for carrying slaves from Africa to Jamaica, and then convicts to Virginia, this ship was as ill-maintained as any vessel in the sea. It stayed afloat only because the prisoners were forced to man the bilge pumps twenty-four hours a day, pumping out the seawater that leaked into her lowest decks. Since many of the convicts were forced to live in the lower decks, it was in their own self-preservation interests to keep pumping. How they divided up the work was up to them.

The *Jonathan* managed about six knots an hour even at full sail. With that slow speed, it was expected to take almost three months to make it to Virginia and disgorge her cargo of indentured servants. The Captain of the *Jonathan*, Campbell Eliot, had a minimal crew aboard. He and his crew hadn't been able to ship on regular merchant ships due to their sullied reputations as sotted drunks, so they had to settle for this cargo—men they despised yet were cut of the same canvas. Eliot and his crew were just one more bar fight, and an alleyway stabbing away from getting the same fate as these men in the hold.

Eliot was under orders from the Judiciary to get these convicts to Virginia alive. Unless there were extraordinary circumstances that he could prove, he would be financially responsible to the English Judiciary and to the transportation brokers for any deaths that occurred aboard ship. He had made this "transportation" run to Virginia before, often bringing back iron ore and tobacco, deerskins, some cotton bales, and molasses. He knew the minimum he could get by with and how to cut costs on the prison ship. One of the biggest expenses was food for the prisoners.

Each prisoner had a wooden spoon and bowl and was fed thin oatmeal twice a day for six days. Usually on Sunday, each would be brought up individually, hosed down to wash the stench off their bodies, given a dry linen shirt, and fed a special meal of dried fish and some hardtack biscuits from the barrel. There would be no citrus, no fresh meat, and no vegetables for the three-month voyage. The dry clothes were important since conditions below were liable to breed typhus from the urine, human feces, rats, mice, and lice that ran wild in the ship's hold. The two cats Eliot had brought aboard couldn't keep up with the volume of vermin on the old ship.

The monotony of life aboard the *Jonathan* was stultifying. The prisoners scratched the passing days on the bulkhead near their wooden bunks. The crew above did the least they could get away with while Eliot drank rum and beer back in his cabin starting often at noon and continuing through the early evening. His second in command, Army Neville, ran the ship, and along with a first mate, navigated according to the readings he made on his sextant. As they passed the Azores and made their way to the mid-Atlantic trade winds, Neville harbored a special dislike for Eliot since the Captain would receive the bulk of any money paid for the trip, and in this case, assume very little of the responsibility.

Neville had set his heading for a landing near the western shore of Chesapeake Bay, a place called Northern Neck, Virginia. Planters or their representatives would meet the ship, and the convicts would be transferred in chains to whomever had purchased their indenture contracts for either seven or fourteen years. If he was sober enough, Eliot would certify the name of the convict, present papers for each, and obtain signatures that would release funds back in London banks to the brokers who had 'fronted' the indenture payments to the Judiciary.

As Eliot perused the papers for each of the 100 convicts he was transporting and the amount that was owed by the planter or miner for each, he saw Franks' name, and the relatively high amount paid by the Portsmouth broker. The papers also identified his trade as surgeon. *This man could be useful*, Eliot thought. *He has skills far above the unskilled dock hands that have found their way below and on their way to heavy farm or mine work alongside the black slaves of Africa.*

◆ ◆ ◆

Below, Franks had long since sharpened his wooden spoon into a prison shank like he had done in the Portsmouth Harbor prison hulk. The shank was shoved into his fancy boot ready to be used. He was among men who had nothing to lose. They had escaped hanging but were being shipped like cattle to a life of drudgery with a daily whip at their backs to ensure they did the boss man's bidding. He was now into the sixth month of his imprisonment, and his survival instincts were increased to a virulent aggressive edge. The hatred he carried for those who had led him to this place had taken over his black soul. He would not be denied revenge.

Franks was forced by the others below to take his hourly turn at the bilge pump. Deep in the hold, the convicts often used the bilge as a latrine. Added to this was the accumulation of filth and garbage in the hold that polluted the bilges, leading to a smelly, hazardous living environment.

The *Jonathan* had an older bilge pump system. Made from bored-out tree trunks, tubes stretched from the lowest point to a hole on the side elevated six to eight feet above the heads of the men. Raw muscle power turned a windlass causing metal rubber discs to pull water up one of the tubes. As each disc reached the top, the water would spill over the top of the elm trunk, and into channels that directed it overboard. There were no slackers allowed since water from the sea constantly leaked into the bilge. The enforcement of "pumpers" fell to everyone, and no convict who wanted to escape a beating shirked his turn.

The biggest danger aboard was typhus. Over a three month voyage it was common for men to take sick especially as the weather in the spring turned warm near the southern section of the trip. The air below was hot, humid, and the smells were rancid despite the weekly "shower" on deck. Those Sundays were looked forward to just because of the fresh air if nothing else. It didn't matter to a convict that he was chained and rudely stripped of his clothes and hosed down. Breathing the ocean air, feeling the wind was worth the humiliation.

♦ ♦ ♦

As Eliot, Neville, and the first mate plotted their final leg to the Virginia coast, Eliot reminded Neville that they had to land the ship at Northern Neck without any typhus aboard.

"It was passed only six years ago, but we've been sailing under this particular English Law that bans typhus ships from landing," said Eliot to the two men. "This is the first time you've sailed with me, so let me spell out what we have to do."

"What's that, Captain?"

"If anyone aboard has the 'gaol fever'—the typhus, we could be quarantined by the naval officers at the port harbor. That would delay us considerably, and I don't want that. When we drop anchor, and before we can unload this sorry lot of convicts, officers will row out to meet us and I will have to swear an oath that no one on board has typhus. If I make a false oath, I could be fined £50 per man who is sick. That's the law, and these naval officers know it and will enforce it. So your job now is to haul every god-forsaken man up here one by one and have him checked out by this Franks fellow."

"Franks? Who is Franks?" Neville asked.

"I'll point him out to you. You know that black-eyed, black-bearded, surly prisoner with the fancy boots the court let him keep."

"I know the one now. Yes. I know who he is."

"Well, I didn't mean to keep this from you, but his papers say he is a surgeon. We'll use him to identify and heal anyone who is sick with the 'gaol fever' before we land."

"Will he know what to do? Will he do it?" Neville asked.

"He will, or I'll throw his arse into the Atlantic." Eliot's voice boomed with drunken conviction.

◆ ◆ ◆

It was two weeks before landing. Coming close to Northern Neck, Virginia, Eliot had Franks hauled up to the deck in chains early in the morning. It wasn't even a Sunday by Franks' count, but he could guess they were getting close to their destination. The heat of the southern clime had abated as the ship swung to a northern direction toward the Virginia coast. Franks could tell by the height of the sun in the sky that they had swung north.

Both Eliot and Neville grilled Franks, who was forced to kneel on the deck surrounded by two guards with muskets and their ever-present clubs which they delighted in using on reluctant or disobedient convicts.

"Listen carefully, Franks," said Eliot, with a snarl in his voice. "We can't land with typhus. It's as clear as that. You've seen it before and don't tell me you haven't. You have a simple task. You get to breathe fresh air for two weeks and you'll get some extra food. That's the privilege you get. We will bring each of the 100 convicts to you. Examine these prisoners and cure the typhus if they have it, or I'll kill you, bury you overboard, pay the broker for your sorry soul, and pay the typhus fine, if I'm damned to do so. You need to cure anyone who's carrying it and I need to land this ship. Do you understand me, Franks? That's your name isn't it?" Eliot's voice rose in anger as his anxiety over the typhus problem seemed heightened.

"Yes. I understand you plainly. Sometimes, there is just so much that can be done. And yes, that is my name. For now. That's what your paper reads doesn't it?"

Eliot nodded. "Is there anyone down there now you suspect of having the typhus?"

With the small privilege of being able to breathe fresh air, Franks quickly weighed his limited options and decided to do the captain's bidding. He didn't have many choices. "Well, there is a lot of coughing, wheezing…but I don't walk around other than to man the bilge pump and get my grub. I can't say for certain who has the lice bites, fever, rash, muscle pains and who doesn't. It's too damn dark down there!" Franks barked, showing his teeth.

With a nod from Eliot to the guard, that last remark got Franks a solid poke in the kidney with the butt end of a club. Franks grunted in pain and fell to the deck, but he muffled his reaction as best he could. He would have loved to take the sharpened wooden spoon from his boot and shove it into this guard's throat, but since he was outnumbered and had his wrists chained, a rash move like that would likely be his last.

As the guard yanked Franks back to his knees, Eliot said bluntly, "You'll get more than that if you don't do as I say and do it well, Franks."

"Then bring out the sickest ones first. If they can be helped, they'll need the most time."

"No, we're not doing that. We'll take each man in turn. That way, Neville here can mark him off the list. We must go in that order. We have to account for every one of the convicts. Neville here will have someone get you what you require." And with that, Elliot did an about face, and walked haughtily back to his cabin.

Franks was left with the guards and Neville, who he had to assume would get him what he needed.

"I'll need my hands unchained."

"Nothing doing," said, Neville. "We have the crew to carry out any manual work. You'll be guarded at all times. We won't take any risks, so don't even think about escape. It's a long swim." With that sick attempt at humor, Neville and the two guards had a good laugh.

"Bring one up at a time, if you don't want to go down yourself," responded Franks with a sneer in his voice. "I'll check each one over and you can mark down their name as being looked at."

While two other guards went to the hatch and lowered a rope to bring up the first convict, Franks thought about what he had to do. He had to save his own life first, and that meant doing the exams. He didn't feel an ounce of compassion toward any of the other prisoners. But if one had typhus, and he suspected that some did, he had to treat any typhus, or the irascible, drunken captain would follow through on his threats and throw Franks overboard.

He went over in his mind what to look for in the sailors. There were certainly enough feces for lice to develop in the hold. The stench in the hold would prove that to any fresh nose that sniffed down there. Lice would infect a human with a bite. The chain of events after that was fast enough. The prisoner would scratch the bite and rub feces into the wound. With an incubation period of one to two weeks, a severe headache, muscle pain, a rash on the chest, cough, and high fever could occur. If the normal disease fighting system of a man was weak, and the typhus spread through the body, the victim could fall into delirium, stupor, often vomit, and produce a stink of rotting flesh. He had seen the typhus in sailors at Haslar Hospital the Admiralty had dumped on them. Some made it, others didn't.

Franks turned to Neville while the first man was hauled up through the hatch. No guard wanted to go down to fetch a convict so the prisoners had to help fasten the looped rope under a man's arms so the guards could pull him up. It was often a painful way to get on deck, but they had done it ten Sundays in a row and had the procedure down pat. This exam and possible treatment process could take a week or two for the 100 men in the hold since they were being checked individually.

"I'll need a few things if I find anyone with the typhus," Franks said to Neville. "You should have someone get them ready."

"What are they?" asked Neville.

"Sheets, clean sheets if you have them. Mustard paste, or

mustard seed from the infirmary with some way to warm up water and flour so I can make a mustard paste. I may need to wrap someone up with a clean sheet and mustard paste to relieve any rash or swelling. I'll also need more clean shirts and cold water and cloths so I can place it on the man's heart. You got all that?"

Neville motioned to one of the guards to start fetching. "Mustard seeds! You fool. We don't have mustard seeds. There are no surgeon's quarters on this ship and no infirmary. This is not a regular merchant ship, or haven't you noticed?"

◆ ◆ ◆

One by one, Franks inspected the skin of every man the guards brought to him. Without mustard paste to relieve swelling, he hoped that hosing down with water, and supplying clean shirts would benefit any prisoner who had spent almost three months below in chains. He spotted some with a small numbers of lice bites and he cautioned each man not to scratch the bites. It would only get worse, he told them. It may have been the only truthful medically wise thing he ever said to any other convict in the ship's hold the entire trip.

It was near the end of the first day of these examinations when the guards brought a young man up who was severely stricken with typhus. The guards mentioned to Franks that the lad was badly bitten all over his body and was very weak. The prisoners below had a difficult time stretching the haul rope around him. He was certainly dead weight when the guards pulled him to the deck.

When he was laid down in front of them, Neville leaned close and asked the young man his name. From his parched lips came the name "Cairnes…Joey Cairnes from Kingswood," he murmured.

Neville found the name on his list and crossed it off.

The words came slurred, uneven, raspy, and Franks had a hard time hearing the boy.

"He has a bad fever," said Franks. He took a cloth drenched in the bucket of cold water, squeezed out the excess, and padded the forehead of the stricken prisoner. Franks opened the young man's shirt and saw that the lice bites had been scratched, almost torn open multiple times and scarred over only to be ripped open again. Franks put a cold-water cloth on the sick lad's chest to try and cool his heart. From the boy's sallow face and burning skin, it was clear he wasn't going to live much longer.

"We had 'em, didn't we boys! We had 'em," gasped, Joey. "We got everything the buggers had. Clean as a whistle we got away. What a night!"

As Franks continue to put cold water on the patient's forehead, he tried to listen to the rantings that were clearly that of a fatally sick man. With that mumbling from Cairnes came a rumbling from his gut and he spewed out oatmeal vomit that reeked of dying flesh. The crew member with the hose washed it away as soon as he could, but the smell lingered. It didn't make Franks any more eager to treat the boy.

"Get me a sheet and throw the cold water on it. That's right. Throw the whole bucket on it. Help me put the wet sheet around him. He has the fever and the delirium. He may go any minute. Quick about you," barked Franks.

As the wet sheet was wrapped around him, Joey Cairnes kept mumbling. It was barely discernible, but since Franks hovered over him, he could catch the main parts. As the boy kept ranting, Franks motioned for more water to be continuously poured on the sheet that now cover the boy.

"Nobody messes with us," Joey exclaimed to no one in particular. "We're the Rooster Road Gang."

"Where's that?" said Franks wanting to engage the delirious lad to keep his mind occupied.

"Near Bristol. We own Kingswood, we do," stammered Joey as his head slumped on the deck. It was as if he was using his last breath to shout his bandit heroics to the sky above. His strength was diminishing and Franks, who had seen many dying men at Haslar, knew this man would soon join them across the river of no return.

"We took Mrs. Prigg for everything she had, the rich snot." Although Joey was delirious, somewhere in that delirium he had to get his story to someone. He grabbed Franks' collar, pulled him tight in a dying man's grasp. "We had pistols, we had swords. I held the edge of a sword at her throat. Made her tell me where she kept the money and silver—a silver punch-ladle it was, and silver spoons. We ate her food, drank her beer. Had a good time we did," belched Joey. Joey turned his head from Franks' face and gave up another stomach-retching vomit that the guard hosed down the as soon as he could.

"See this locket around me neck? Pretty ain't it? Me brothers gave it to me. When the constables raided me home the night they carted the four of us away, they didn't take the locket." Joey wheezed and coughed from deep in his chest. He didn't have much more time.

"If I dies, take the locket and tell me brothers what happened to me, will you mister, will you? Tell me you'd do that. Go ahead, take it. It's all I have left," gasped Joey. With that dying request, Joey's eyes opened wide and the deep death rattle came from deep within his chest and he died.

During his ten years at Haslar, Franks had seen many men die and looked at them as research specimens and not much else. Some were useful when they were alive, some were of value when they were dead. This convict was no different to him. He felt nothing. But his brain worked to see what he could take.

Franks took the locket from Joey's neck and put it in his pocket. It was too bad the kid died, but maybe Franks could use the locket. If ever he got back to Bristol to hunt down Hawkins, he could use the locket to get help from the kid's brothers…maybe to find Hawkins, maybe to help kill him. *Even in death, the young man can be useful*, Franks thought. *Useful to me.*

CHAPTER 6

BRISTOL, ENGLAND: LATE SPRING AND SUMMER 1771
LIVESEY ACRES

D r. Livesey and his two young associates, Dr. Jim Hawkins
and Dr. David McLaughlin did everything they could to
build their medical practice throughout late spring and
summer of 1771. Given the weather conditions and rough roads in
spring, neither Mac, Dr. Livesey, nor Jim wanted to travel to London
to secure a separate agreement with LongAcre Supply. But it was
more than the weather that led to another arrangement.

Both Jim and Mac knew that the board at Haslar Hospital was
reconstructing its relationship with LongAcre Supply due to the
years-long kickback scheme engineered by their enemy, Franks. So
when Dr. Livesey suggested they order through the local hospital,
the British Royal Infirmary, they readily agreed. It was best to keep
their names and faces away from LongAcre until Livesey's Surgery
was large enough to have purchasing clout with the giant medical
supply firm.

With the BRI's help, they successfully ordered medical
equipment and supplies from LongAcre Supply, and even obtained
quantity purchase pricing shared with the British Royal Infirmary.
Because of Dr. Livesey's connections, the local hospital had agreed

48

to go along with letting Livesey's smaller clinic order medicines, herbs, ointments, and materials through them.

Jim and Mac did their best to help at Dr. Livesey's surgery. Mac lived close by in rented quarters with sleeping rooms, so all three doctors could have a place to stay if all three happened to be in town. Mac put in long hours helping Dr. Livesey and the two nurses, Gwen and Mary. Jim came into town Monday noon through Thursday evenings, and left for Livesey farms for a long weekend so he could relieve Livian of some of the child-care of baby Belle. In truth, he wanted to spend as much time with Livian and baby Belle as he could. As spring stretched into early summer, and the English countryside was alive with greenery and flowers, Jim and Livian discussed the shared child-care openly.

I want you to work with Mac and Dr. Livesey as much as you want, Livian wrote on the chalkboard. *I can tell you want to be there more.* Although her speech was getting better every day, sometimes she still relied on the chalkboard communication to get more complicated ideas across. Jim in turn, spoke directly to Livian as he had always done, because her lip-reading skills were excellent. The ear horn Livian braced against her left ear was cumbersome. Sometimes people who wanted to speak to Livian, including Jim, had to speak directly into the horn, thus eliminating Livian's lip-reading skills since her face was turned. She often missed the nuances of facial expressions that accompanied the words. It wasn't easy, but the two young parents were very patient with each other. And their love transcended any difficulties.

"What do you mean?" Jim said, speaking distinctly into the ear horn. They both knew the more she heard words, no matter how faint, the more she would pick up, repeat, and increase her own halting, stammering diction that had been dormant for so many years. It had been almost six months since her ear-awakening miracle and she was speaking better with each passing day. "I like being with you and Belle. Are you sending me to Bristol to live in Mac's rented quarters?" asked Jim.

"No, silly," Livian said, her words not as fully formed as she would like. Livian scribbled quickly on the blackboard, *Do your share. Don't make Mac work so hard. I can see you feel guilty.*

That written comment made Jim think. Perhaps, by spending long weekends at Livesey Farms, he was acting selfishly. But he thought balancing his work with his obligations at home was what Livian wanted. "I can work two more days a week at the surgery, Livian. Is this what you want?" Jim spoke into the ear horn.

It took a few minutes for Livian to write the sentences on the chalkboard. She often alternated using it with trying to speak. *Yes, Jim my love. Belle and I are fine. Elizabeth and Margaret help. Build your business. Be successful. Don't use 'chest of gold' to build our house. Save it. Elizabeth is not at all anxious for us to leave the main house.*

"Always the practical one, aren't you? Practical and self-sacrificing. I do have some ideas that will need time at the surgery."

"Go with my blessing," said Livian directly to Jim, enunciating her words carefully. Then she wrote, *We will revisit this at the end of the year.*

"What about your right ear?" said Jim into the ear horn. "Should we build the generator here in Bristol?"

If you want to, wrote Livian. *Help others first. I can get by.*

◆◆◆

On a Monday afternoon, Dr. Livesey and Jim had ridden in together from Livesey Farms. Dr. Livesey left Jim at the surgery while he had lunch with the Naval Administrator to check on the account set up for the Livesey surgery the two of them had arranged. When Jim arrived, Mac was with a patient. When the patient left, Jim told Mac what Livian had said to him.

"Livian has persuaded me to spend more time in Bristol with the surgery and to help build the business. She's a practical, frugal woman and she can be very convincing."

Mac smiled. "I remember how convincing she can be with an iron rope gaff in her hand threatening that little scum, Bobby Axe, on our trip back to Portsmouth."

"She didn't need the iron gaff this time," said Jim with a laugh.

The two of them chuckled at the memory of Axe and his now very dead partner, Julie Gore, attacking them in the middle of a summer lightening storm on the Solent. Livian had scared Axe into jumping overboard to save himself from her.

"She wasn't that frightening this time, Mac. But she did say I could spend as much time as I needed with the surgery, help do whatever we could to build the business, and take some of the load off you and Dr. Livesey. I realize that my Tuesday through Thursday routine hasn't been helpful, and that you've had to cover all weekends. I'm in full time now."

Mac looked relieved. "I could use a couple of Saturdays off. As you know, I've had to stitch up a few Friday night cut-up dock fighters lately. I was thinking we shouldn't even be available on Saturday mornings. Let the Friday night drunks get patched up at the hospital."

"That's certainly a thought. Let's run it by Dr. Livesey. But until we change our hours, we need to work out a rotation. It all brings in money."

Just then Dr. Livesey entered the surgery and joined the two men. "Gentlemen, a bright and good afternoon to you both. I see from our patient scheduling book that we have a full week ahead of us. That's not counting walk-ins from the Admiralty. As you know, I just had lunch with the Naval Administrator and he is quite pleased with the pre-board checkup system we've provided for his sailors. Simply put, he can guarantee his captains healthier crews, at least on the start of a voyage, than he could before. And the Admiralty pays its bills, which I like to see. We don't have to rely on patient reimbursement. Unfortunately, some of our patients tend to forget us when they're feeling better."

Dr. Livesey paused for a moment as if to consider what he wanted to say next. "There's something new I want to talk to you about. It's a way to get more business and it will make it easier for us to work harmoniously with the local hospital. But it also means that all of us will have slightly less time at the Livesey Surgery."

"Less time?" asked Mac.

"Just slightly less time. I've volunteered the three of us to make rounds at the Bristol Royal Infirmary. Each of us will take three hours in the morning, one day a week. I'll take Tuesday. Mac, you get Wednesday, and Jim gets Thursday. We can rotate if need be. It's a way of paying back the cost of the slides they'll be providing us, the quantity discounts we're receiving from LongAcre by ordering through the BRI, and the good relations we want if we need to place a patient of ours in one of their beds for an extended stay. We give a little, perhaps, but we get back many benefits. What say you, Jim?"

Jim thought about it for a moment. "So you made this offer to the hospital administrator? And we're to work there without pay?"

"Correct. It's a volunteer job for the time being. If all parties agree, we might change the arrangement next year. I told him I would be there at 7:00 a.m. tomorrow. You two can open the surgery at 9:00 in the morning as usual. I'll just be an hour later. I would have told you over the weekend, Jim, but I wanted to tell you both at the same time.

"They're seriously understaffed over there. It's only one morning a week for each of us and you'll have a nurse at your side. You won't be given a ward of responsibility. It's not that kind of a burden. Of course, you'll have to coordinate any treatment regimens with the staff, but the administrator said he would welcome the manpower. They have such a variety of cases. If something gets serious, they would call on us anyway, and this way we would have a relationship established."

"What do you mean, if something gets serious?" asked Jim.

"There have been outbreaks of infectious diseases that have claimed many victims," explained Dr. Livesey. "That hospital could get overcrowded in a day under those circumstances. Face it, the sewage disposal system in this town is terrible. People's hygiene is pathetic. There have been outbreaks of cholera and typhoid fever. They don't wash or bathe nearly as often as they should.

"And don't get me started on the sea dogs who come off the merchant ships and the black- birders that bring fevers from all parts of the southern climates. The holds on those ships are filthy. Not to mention the emptying of piss-pots in the middle of the city streets. All sorts of diseases are spread. The children who are born in the squalor of the poor section are undernourished to the point of getting weak bones or rickets. And then there's always the threat of an epidemic of smallpox."

"There are cities in England that have built controlled sewage systems," offered Mac.

"Then bring those systems to the attention of the city council. We need a complete change on attitude toward cleanliness," said Dr. Livesey. "See if you can get someone to voluntarily pay for clean water and a sewage control system. Just try."

With that disparaging note, the three separated and went to their respective patients that had come into the surgery.

Jim was really bothered by Dr. Livesey's assessment of the population's need for better hygiene. It could be such an upward struggle to educate an illiterate population. Scientific miracles were the same as magic to many of these people. They didn't have a knowledge of science. Even after four years at the London Company of Surgeons, two years practicing at sea, and a year and a half at Haslar Hospital, Jim still felt inadequate. Mac was more educated than he was.

If they went ahead with the electrostatic generator, the country folk would hear of a miracle machine. Who could predict what they would call it? They clung to the past—alchemy, pagan worship, magic fairy dust, blessed spring water, and unicorns. When mixed with their ignorance and residual fear of science, Jim and Mac might be branded as warlocks or witches and burned at the stake. The resistance of a stirred-up mob could be a disaster. But, there were so many scientific discoveries that lay on the horizon, if they were just allowed to find ways to prove their worth.

While pondering these twin obstacles of fear and doubt, Jim

made up his mind that his medical knowledge, and that of Mac, Dr. Livesey, and anyone else in the region needed to be brought to the public's attention. Jim wanted to press on with educating the people of the area. He didn't want people to stay stuck on their farms, stuck to their old fairytales, especially if they got sick and died while there was a cure available that might save a life. Didn't he have a sworn duty to help get that information to them? Maybe it wouldn't be the electrostatic generator and the potential to cure deafness that needed to be made public, but simple everyday hygiene and established curative medicine.

People needed new simple cures that would be helpful. His mind was spinning now. This was a publishing job. Maybe he could write an article a week, maybe Dr. Livesey could write one every two weeks, and Mac, too. If Jim could get the other doctors in town together—many of them drawn by their egos—they might submit information. Their vanity would propel them to write something of their successes, and once a month there could be a forum to openly look at the pros and cons of the various treatments offered by each. This forum could get rid of the insular nature in which the various practitioners worked. What would he call it? Why not The Bristol Medical Group? Pretty fancy name for a group of men sharing ideas.

Maybe he could get Dr. John Shelton at the London Company of Surgeons and the curator of the Hunter Brothers Museum of Natural History to write about what was happening in London and put that into the publication. He would need payments from everyone to keep it going, but to start it, maybe, just maybe, Squire Trelawney would front the money for the first publication. He could advertise his wines. Now that would appeal to the mercantilist in him, for sure.

◆ ◆ ◆

A letter came from Eli Williams back at Haslar, along with the duplicate slides that were available. What disturbed Jim was what Eli said about Dr. Herman Franks. Jim and Mac had assumed that Franks would be dealt swift justice by the British courts. With the hard evidence against him, including Shaikh and Williams's testimonies, they thought Franks would be dead now at the end of a rope. When Williams wrote that Franks had been branded on the palm of his hand and been given transportation to the American colonies, Jim and Mac looked at each other with astonishment, and not just a little fear.

"He's in the colonies, Jim. The chances that we'll ever see him again are next to nothing," Mac offered, seeing the look on Jim's face. They both thought they were through with the demon forever.

"I'm not so sure. What did Williams say? He was there for fourteen years? That's not enough. If he ever gets back to England, he'll come looking for me. I know that. I feel it. He swore he'd get me. He's just the kind of maniac who will stop at nothing to get those he thinks wronged him.

"America is an ocean away," said Mac as he tried to calm Jim's fear. "It's a world away."

◆ ◆ ◆

Throughout the summer, the three doctors were busy with the growing population of Bristol. At St. Nicolas Church, the vicar had persuaded Dr. Livesey to use church donations to help the medical needs of the poor in Bristol. What little money there was helped in these months as Dr. Livesey and Dr. Jim Hawkins agreed to treat patients in the poor sections on Saturday mornings in the summer, looking especially for children who were ailing. The two men set up a couple of tables in an apothecary shop. In return for the use of the space, Dr. Livesey agreed to use the church funds to purchase the herbal wares sold by the owner.

The crowded, high density living quarters of the poor sections of Bristol were right next to the industrial manufacturing operations which belched out toxic fumes of sulfur, mercury, arsenic, and coal soot from their smokestacks as they made artifacts of brass, tin, ceramics, and textiles. Bristol was booming, and the manufacturers considered the poor squalid tenements as acceptable garbage pits for the toxic run-off from these businesses as well as from the processing of sugar, whale oil, and hides in the tanneries. Kids walked in the polluted streets and breathed the foul air which often blocked out the midday sun.

It was no wonder that Dr. Livesey saw young children under the age of five who coughed, wheezed, and were short of breath from pleurisy. Many of the children they saw on these Saturday mornings suffered from vomiting, cramps, fevers, coughs, deep chest congestion, mouth sores, and lice. The two doctors correctly diagnosed that these illnesses came directly from the children drinking contaminated water, playing in the industrial run-off in the streets, living in the unhygienic homes, and breathing the foul air of the increasingly industrialized city.

Many of these illnesses couldn't be completely cured in the Saturday morning visits, but both Dr. Livesey and Dr. Hawkins did what they could. The kids with diarrhea were given garlic with a little bit of cinnamon to chew. They bought some expensive myrrh oil from the apothecary and swabbed the children's mouth sores. They used thyme oil, some ginger tea, and honey for the ones with deep chest congestion. This oil was known to break up the congestion. They made some mullein tea for the children with ear infections and chest congestion. They also mixed ginger tea and honey for the kids to drink along with flax seed and honey to chew. They tried to leave the ingredients with the children's mothers, hoping the parents would continue the treatment for a week, since herbal treatments took at least that long to have any effect.

They used some of the church's money to buy milk for children whose legs and arms showed lack of proper bone growth. It made Jim angry to see children with less than adequate nutrition. His beautiful baby, Belle, was growing strong at Livesey Farms with Livian tending to her every need. It was obvious these children were not so blessed.

The two of them made a half dozen trips on Saturday mornings during the summer before they drove back to Livesey Farms for a couple of days rest. Jim and Dr. Livesey knew that what they did on

Saturdays wasn't enough. They needed their fellow practitioners to band together to try and prevent outbreaks of diseases in Bristol. Their experience with their Saturday morning clinics convinced them that the conditions in the city were a breeding ground for rapidly spreading epidemics.

◆◆◆

During the summer months, Jim convinced Dr. Livesey and Mac that starting the Bristol Medical Group was a solid idea that should be pursued. With Dr. Livesey's standing in town and with the support of Squire Trelawney to front the costs of the printing, Dr. Livesey wrote letters to his fellow physicians and invited them to an introductory meeting of the Bristol Medical Group.

The first meeting of the group was at Squire Trelawney's house up the hill in Bristol. He had his country estate where he spent weekends, but he stayed in town during the week where he kept his warehouses. He was accompanied by his household staff of Monica Browne from Gloucestershire, his free-born Jamaican cook, Olivia Newsome, and Abraham Gray, his assistant and fierce bodyguard.

Twelve doctors enjoyed the squire's hospitality at the first meeting, sampling the Squire's wines before, during, and after dinner. The squire was the largest wine merchant in the Bristol area that stretched all the way up to Liverpool. He imported wine from Spain and Portugal, and financed many a merchant ship with his outsized profits. When Jim and Dr. Livesey had approached the squire with the idea of publishing common sense hygiene ideas for the growing Bristol population, he saw the benefit immediately.

After dinner, he addressed the group. "Gentlemen, all learned members of the Bristol medical community, I welcome you to our first, inaugural meeting of the Bristol Medical Group. You have already heard the plan outlined by Dr. Livesey. Let it be my pleasure to fund the first couple of publications until we can build the readership. We can meet here the first few times if you like, but eventually, you'll have to find another home. I believe if we continue to meet here, you'd run my wine cellar dry." The squire laughed at his own humorous directive, a directive that had a truth laced within it.

"Young Doctor Hawkins has accepted the job of collecting your written insights into the various diseases you have run up against, the cures you have prescribed, and prevention steps. You can drop them off at the Livesey Surgery by the end of this week where he will sort them and get them to the printer. Now the next step is for your dues, gentlemen. You knew I would get around to the money sooner or later." The Squire laughed again at his own dry joke, as if trying to keep the air in the room as light as possible.

"For our dues, you will all get free copies to distribute to your patients. The Royal Bristol Infirmary and the Naval Administration will get free copies as well. After the first two publications, we'll rely on your dues to pay for the next few printings. If we're successful, we'll get subscriptions that pay for the BMG News, as I am calling it for now. What say you to this title, Dr. Hawkins?"

"Sounds good for a start, Squire. Whatever you say."

"If I may interrupt, Squire?" asked Dr. Livesey. "I appreciate your jocularity and your support in broaching this venture. But I maintain that the information these men provide is more important than the financing of it. If I may."

"Certainly, Dr. Livesey, the floor is yours."

"There are so many diseases transmitted in this city because of the foul stench that many live under. You are all aware of it, I'm sure. We must get simple cleanliness and hygiene practices to the people. I often fear an epidemic, like the one recorded around the turn of the last century when thousands perished. We'll be on the front line trying to stem it. Prevention, gentlemen, prevention is the answer, and this publication is meant first and foremost to make as many people possible aware of what they can do to prevent disease."

A voice came from the assembled medical men. "What about the illiterate? If they can't read, what good is a printing?"

Another voice echoed the same concern. "We can't very well stand on a street corner and howl into the night."

Yet another voice expressed the concern many had. "We can only treat the people who come to us. You're asking for city-wide announcements on a regular basis."

Dr. Livesey tried to halt the growing criticism and negative comments. "Yes... Yes... We can only do what we can. But prevention is worth the effort. If you like, we can distribute these pamphlets to the churches, to businesses—"

"Aye and then the pubs. That would reach a lot of them." The last remark got a hoot of derisive laughter from a couple of the hypocritical doctors who had imbibed much of Squire Trelawney's wine.

A couple of the more serious attendees to the Squire's dinner ended the criticisms by saying it was a good start, and anything that improved the health of the citizenry was a positive step. They added that they would send their notes to Livesey's surgery and leave distribution of the information to Hawkins.

A certain practitioner from the BRI stood and said, "Assume for a moment that we are members of the Bristol Medical Group. If this is published under the banner of the group, do we all have to agree upon the prescribed treatments that are contained in it? I, for one, may do things differently, if only by a degree. Do we all have to agree that there is one best solution for a given medical problem?"

A voice from the back blurted, "We could be here weeks trying to come to a consensus. I don't have the will or the time for that."

Dr. Livesey spoke up. "The writer of the problem and the treatment will have his name at the end of the article. He stands by it. The group does not have to. Simple as that. The writer gets the publicity and perhaps the new business that comes from his written description in the... what did you call it, Squire?"

"The Bristol Medical Group News, I believe."

Jim Hawkins stood and was recognized with a nod from Dr. Livesey. "The information in this newsletter does not necessarily have to come only from you gentlemen. I'll be traveling to London next week. I'll be meeting with Dr. John Shelton, the current curator of the Hunter Brothers Museum and newly elected headmaster for the London Company of Surgeons where I attended school. The intent of my visit is to arrange for him to send us information on a regular basis from what his current and former instructors and students are relaying to him about any advancements in the medical field.

"The two-day journey can seem like a half-a-country away when there are advancements we need to hear about. All of you, I would assume, exchange letters with fellow doctors in the outlying districts. You get that information personally. That's fine. But we need as much information as we can get, and we need it on a regular basis for all to share. My intent is to ask Dr. Shelton to regularly send information and systematically alert us."

The meeting broke up soon afterwards. Jim, Dr. Livesey, and Mac retired to their quarters. "I think we received full support for the general intent of the group," said Dr. Livesey. "It helps that the squire is funding the first few publications. Otherwise, I'm not sure it would ever get started."

"Quite a few parsimonious folks in that group. It will be hard to get them to part with any money. They may offer some helpful written tips, but money, that's another thing," mentioned Mac. "Jim, do you want me to go to London with you?"

"You're needed here, Mac," interrupted Dr. Livesey. "Let Jim make the trip. We all can't be gone at the same time."

"I've already engaged the coach for the trip," said Jim. "I wish I could bring Livian, but Belle is but five months old and the trip would be a burden for them. I intend to leave Monday morning and be back by Saturday night. That should be enough time with Shelton. Who knows what I'll find out."

◆ ◆ ◆

Before Jim left Livesey Farms early Monday morning, he packed his clothes and was careful to carry the minimal amount of bank notes for food and lodging. He placed a couple of gold pieces in a separate place in case the coach was robbed on the way.

Highwaymen were everywhere in the countryside. The coach wouldn't be carrying anyone else, so there would only be the driver and Jim to ward off any attackers. He expected the driver to have a musket for protection, but he wanted more, so he loaded his pistol and took extra shot and powder along, then carefully tucked them away. No use taking chances.

The two-horse driven coach could travel at seven miles an hour, and he expected to be on the road for at least six to seven hours the first day. The horses would either have to be changed out or rested for a time each day, which ate into any travel time. The one-hundred and twenty-mile trip would take two-and a-half days. He had to make the most of the time he had with Shelton.

◆◆◆

He arrived at the London Company of Surgeons midday on his third day of travel. The coachman and his rig would spend two days resting before taking Jim back to Bristol. Going alone was expensive travel, but Jim thought it worth the investment.

Dr. John Shelton, the best and brightest of Jim's class at the London Company of Surgeons had been granted a curatorship for the past three years at the Hunter Brothers huge museum of fourteen thousand animal exhibits that were used for research purposes. Having proved his management capabilities, along with his brilliant intellect and passion for medical science, he was then appointed as the youngest surgeon ever to run the medical school. When Jim entered, he could see there was one other man in the office.

"How was your trip, Jim?" John asked, shaking Jim's hand. "No problems, I hope. Roads rough enough for you?"

"I asked for as much speed as the driver could give me, and I was bounced around," Jim answered, massaging his aching back. "It's good to see you, John. Moving up in the world, I see."

John nodded. "It's a heavy responsibility, but one the board believes I can handle. Hope to do the job and the school justice. Let me introduce you to the man who took my place at Hunter Museum as chief researcher. This is Dr. Edward Jenner. Dr. Jenner, Dr. Jim

Hawkins now of Bristol, one of my classmates at the Company. Jim, Edward here was apprenticed to the surgeon George Hardwick in Sodbury. That's near Bristol, isn't it?"

"Not twenty miles away almost directly to the east. A solid three hours travel time by carriage or horseback. I know those roads to be poor. Almost as rough as going cross country," answered Jim.

"Edward was almost exactly four years behind you in school," offered Shelton. "He was head of his class and is completing his advanced medical training in record time at St. Georges here in London. John Hunter picked him out to succeed me at their museum and took him on as a private student. I don't believe I was awarded that honor, and certainly not at so young an age."

"You flatter me, Dr. Shelton," said, Jenner. He directed his next comment to Jim. "I hope to be done with my studies by the middle of next year and return to set up practice in Berkeley, near where I came from. I come from the country and my heart is there, and frankly speaking, not in London."

"Berkley is close to us as well—to the Northeast of Bristol. We look forward to having you in the area. My wife, Livian, and I live with Dr. Robert Livesey at Livesey Acres to the southwest of the city. He and I share a medical practice with our partner, Dr. David McLaughlin in Bristol. When you come back to the area, please stop in. We'll show you around Bristol. Help get you started, if you need any help, that is."

"That would be much appreciated, Dr. Hawkins," said Jenner.

"Please, call me Jim, everybody does. You will certainly be welcome to join our newly formed Bristol Medical Group, which is the main reason for my barging into Dr. Shelton's office today."

"Bristol Medical Group? What's that?" asked Shelton.

"With Dr. Livesey's leadership, we are asking the practicing physicians in the area to submit treatments and cures for common illnesses and basic disease prevention. We'll take what they've written, print it, and distribute it around Bristol. The city is growing, and in certain industrial areas, there is a decided lack of basic cleanliness—basic hygiene. Dr. Livesey and I made several visits to the poor sections of the city and found the living conditions to be deplorable with many sick and undernourished children. Hopefully, our publication will help."

"How can I help?" asked Shelton.

"I'd like you to write us as often as you can and send information about any medical breakthroughs, medical treatments, preventative steps, or anything of value that we in the country can blend into our own practices. Communication by letter alone to one doctor or another isn't spreading the word fast enough. Heavens, there must be things happening in hospitals in other parts of the country and in the city, that you know about. We can't just pop up to London—or in my case travel back to Haslar Hospital in Gosport—where I spent a year and a half just to pick up research news."

Shelton looked deep in thought. "That sounds like a good idea, Jim. I'll be glad to help. Perhaps I can ask some of our instructors, like the great Hunter brothers, to pen something and send it along. We have something like your group here in London. But oftentimes, it's just a gabfest over wine without any structure at all. There are a lot of strong personalities here. These men and the hospitals they work at get a bit proprietary about what they know. Sometimes, I think they want a monopoly position whenever they can establish a foothold. But, I will admit that cooperation rather than competition would make us better off."

Jim nodded. "Yes, I'm aware that each of us has a passion for something, some illness in particular. You already know my goals deal with deafness."

"Of course, I can see why you have that passion."

"I'd like to tell you a lot more about that over dinner," Jim said. "Dr. McLaughlin and I have made some progress in that area. So has Livian."

"Progress, you say. Well, I will love to hear of it. I should tell you before we go any further that Dr. Jenner here has already identified his mission, and that is to save people from smallpox."

"Smallpox!" exclaimed Jim. "That's a worthy ambition. If we get an epidemic... if we... it can be no good at all."

"There have been some advances, some setbacks, to be sure. But, Edward has written up the status of the research and advances that have been forwarded by any number of people. He has looked into cases that have real promise. Edward, tell Jim how you came to make smallpox your passionate interest."

Edward Jenner motioned to them to sit in the office chairs and told them of his obsession with stopping smallpox.

"When I was eight, I was inoculated with a small amount of cowpox from an infected animal."

"Excuse me for interrupting, Dr. Jenner, but inoculated? What's that?" asked Jim.

"Ah, Jim, ever the Latin student," kidded John Shelton, knowing that Jim had struggled with Latin in his medical studies when he was a student at the London Company of Surgeons. "It comes from the Latin inoculare, meaning 'to graft.' It's the subcutaneous placement of a cowpox or smallpox virus into a non-immune individual. The doctor takes a lancet and obtains the wet material from the ripe pustule of a person who has the smallpox. He places it under the skin of the patient."

"We also use the term variolation," added Dr. Jenner. "Anyway, I was inoculated. I developed a mild form of the disease and have been immune ever since."

"Immune you say. Why hasn't this been widely disseminated and practiced?"

"You touch on a very important yet sensitive area there, Jim. We all ask why? Why indeed? The answers are as varied as human nature itself and the unwillingness to try something that on its surface seems risky. When I was apprenticing with George Hardwick, he had in his possession a paper written in 1765."

"Almost seven full years ago?" asked Jim, confirming for himself that the Bristol Medical News was more and more important.

"That's right. News travels slowly doesn't it. The paper was written by Dr. John Fewster and presented to the Medical Society of London. It was entitled: 'Cowpox and Its Ability to Prevent Smallpox.'"

"Do you know of this paper, John?" queried Jim of his friend.

"Now I do," replied Shelton with a sense of shame. "Unfortunately, sometimes new ideas somehow get buried without proper promotion. Fewster was a country doctor. Many London physicians disdain anything that doesn't come from them."

Jenner continued. "Yes, indeed. I have run into that bias. But that is another matter. As you may know, smallpox has brought terrible epidemics in England. Yet Fewster wrote that in the dairy farming areas in the southwest of the country, the milkmaids and other workers who contracted cowpox from handling cows and udders, were afterwards immune to smallpox. Such people were able to nurse smallpox victims without fear of contracting the disease themselves."

"I have heard of this," said Jim. "But I thought it was merely country folklore…a legend…a myth, like so many fairytales country folks hold on. No offense meant."

"None taken, but what if there was a scientific basis for this, Jim? What if we could replicate the tests…replicate the results? Establish a pattern. Would you believe it then?" Jenner's passion was rising. Jim guessed it rose every time he heard the cowpox story disputed or dismissed as an old wives' tale.

"Let me give you another story that John and I heard about from a newspaper in Dorset, down in the southwestern part of the country," Jenner said. "Benjamin Jesty has a farm in Yetminister near Dorset. Last year, two of his female milkmaids were infected with cowpox. When an epidemic of smallpox came, Jesty decided to give his two eldest sons immunity by infecting them with cowpox. He took his family to a cow at a farm that had the disease, and using a darning needle, transferred pustular material from the cow to his sons by scratching their arms. The boys had mild local reactions and quickly recovered and did not catch the smallpox. I have to study this further. There has to be something there. If we can inoculate people and save them from smallpox…"

Jenner's passion for the problem and a possible solution showed in his voice and animated gestures. But Jim was naturally skeptical. "Edward, I can appreciate your passion for this, but it sounds risky. Would you inoculate your children like this man Jesty did?"

"I don't know. I'm not married as yet. I do not have children as yet. But what is science without experimentation?"

Jim had no answer for that. He had risked his own beautiful wife's life by running the electrical spark from the electrostatic generator through her skull to reawaken her hearing. The risks were ever present. The danger was immense. He was a practical man of science, where repetition and replication were the only proofs. How could he doubt the passion of a young man who wanted to save people?

Shelton spoke into the tense silence that followed. "As you can see, Edward has a passion for this. Very similar to yours, I might add. I have a suggestion. As a first contribution to your medical group's journal, why not have Dr. Jenner write up a short synopsis of what he's just told you. You can put it in your Bristol Medical Group News and see what the reaction is among your peers at Bristol. It will be our first contribution."

Shelton stood. "Listen, I'm starved. Why don't the three of us go to dinner. I want to hear about that electrostatic generator. Electricity is all the rage in London these days."

"Electricity?" Jim wondered. "Why Electricity?"

"I guess you wouldn't have any way of knowing," answered Shelton. "The American, Ben Franklin is in London."

CHAPTER 7

VIRGINIA: FALL OF 1771

The British Naval officers boarded the *Jonathan* at Quantico, Virginia. At a depth of 24 feet, the harbor could handle ocean going ships. The river was increasingly being silted in farther north by run-off from the slash and burn technique on the tobacco fields, so this was as far north up the Potomac River as the *Jonathan* could get.

As was their custom with ships with this kind of cargo, they immediately asked the captain of the convict ship whether there was any typhus aboard. If there was any, the ship would be quarantined in the harbor until the sick were cleansed sufficiently to land, which could take weeks if not longer.

"No typhus aboard this ship," claimed Eliot who was sober this morning. He'd put on his best face for the inquiring and often nosy officers. He had been through this inspection a number of times before.

"You will not land this cargo if there is any typhus aboard," one of the officers said. "You know that don't you? As we inspect every god-forsaken man you try to unload, and we find any typhus, you will pay a fine for every lie you tell. You are clear on that, Mister Eliot?"

"That's Captain Eliot to you, and yes, I know the rules. I've done this before."

"Well then, be straight with me. What is your answer?"

"We had one die. Here is a surgeon named Franks, ask him. He examined every man in the hold." He pointed to Franks who had been brought in chains to the deck to answer questions for the British Naval officers inspecting the *Jonathan*. Franks had been told to give minimal answers and to give the ship a clean bill of health or he would be thrown down in the hold and beaten.

"A surgeon you say? You have a surgeon as a convict? Well speak up, man," said one of the officers. "Was there typhus?"

"Yes, and he died," muttered Franks.

"And the rest of the cargo of convicted transports?"

"They are well enough with no obvious signs," answered Franks. He knew the answer he was supposed to give. The convicts below were in terrible physical shape, having barely survived the trip across the Atlantic and up the Chesapeake Bay. But he had not seen the dreaded typhus breakout among the convicts.

"No obvious signs?" barked the naval officer in charge.

Franks answered, glancing at Eliot and Neville who were carefully watching and listening to what Franks said. He knew they would give him the butt of the gun if he didn't give the expected response.

"See for yourself as they are brought up. I examined every one of them over the past two weeks. I saw a few rat bites, some lice, but no typhus except the man who died." Franks had taken to wearing Joey Cairnes' locket around his neck to remind him of his mission to get back to England and complete his mission of revenge.

The convicts were brought up one by one as they had been on Sundays for the past three months during the slow, tortuous journey to the Virginia shoreline. Some may have thought this was the toughest part of their lives to this point, but they had no idea of the brutality they would be subjected to in the next seven or fourteen years of their slavery to the colonists.

The naval officers looked over each man as he was brought up to the deck and passed on the lot of them. The captain was allowed to bring them to their new owners on the dock, sign them away, and receive paperwork that would reimburse their brokers back in Portsmouth. Eliot would transport the papers back to England on his slow route home. The transaction would take months to accomplish, but it would be the grease that kept the wheels of the convict transport trade alive for at least a few more years. These 100 men would be a small part of the 52,000 British convicts who been shipped to the colonies in the 18th century.

◆ ◆ ◆

Most of the convicts would labor in the rapidly expanding tobacco and grain fields of Prince William County, Virginia. But there were other industries that demanded labor. The manufacture of iron ore was a large industry in Virginia and Maryland. Franks' indenturement was purchased by a prosperous, wealthy Virginia land owner named John Tayloe. His estates included the Neabsco Iron Works, which were the first iron works in Northern Virginia, established in 1737. Tayloe had been sending close to 700 tons of pig iron each year to England for the past 35 years, and along with his tobacco crop, was earning close to £2,000 sterling every year. He was one of the wealthiest men in the colonies and was determined to stay that way.

Iron made in the colonies was typically of low grade, but England took as much as the colonies could produce. There were 50 ironworks throughout the Chesapeake region at the time producing one-third of the new world's iron. Most of it had a ready market across the Atlantic.

Tayloe's land included almost 5,000 acres of trees which the convicts and slaves cut and brought to the mill to manufacture charcoal to heat the blast furnaces. Tayloe's land had plenty of running water and large deposits of iron rich ore. Tayloe needed labor to mine and transport the ore, cut the trees, make the charcoal, operate the furnaces, and forge the iron. He currently had 100 men in his labor pool. Some of the men were white wage workers and overseers. Some were company-owned slaves, while others were slaves hired from nearby farmers. Convict labor from England made up the rest.

The actual iron works consisted of an 18-acre complex separated by Neabsco Creek. The site had two blast furnaces, a water powered grist mill, sawmill, pit mines, forge, and storage areas for iron ore and coal. It also had room for forging with two smithies, and workers' quarters. The rest of the acreage was wooded, which Tayloe exploited to the fullest. But Tayloe was frugal and prudent. He also had land allocated to tobacco production since it was a cash crop that helped finance the iron ore operation. Tayloe had the land. He needed plenty of labor for all his operations, and he needed it to be cheap.

His Neabsco Ironworks transferred newly blasted pig iron by boat less than a mile downstream to Neabsco Harbor on the Potomac River. At high tide, the iron could then be transferred by his own sloops to ocean going vessels at Quantico. It was also close to a Major road—the Kings Highway.

This was a 1,300-mile road laid out from 1650 to 1735 in the American colonies. It was built on the order of Charles the Second of England who directed his colonial governors to link Charleston, South Carolina to Boston, Massachusetts.

Tayloe and his son had no naïve illusions about the forced labor he was buying from the English judiciary. These men wanted to be free. They wanted to be free of their shackles and free to ship back to their homes—however wretched—in England. These two land barons knew that the convicts and slaves they bought had to be kept under a steady and firm hand. Tayloe's two main enforcers were men named Mercian and his brutal assistant, Shruggs. The two of them directed more white low-wage overseers for each work crew. All these men had free rein to do whatever they wanted, short of murder, to keep the labor force in line.

◆◆◆

As Franks was physically shoved into a caged wagon that would cart him up river to the ironworks, he kept note of where the docks were, the number of naval harbor guards, and where their quarters were. He fully intended to escape as soon as he could. And since this was a deep enough harbor for convict ships, it was also a harbor for the prized tobacco and iron shipments that would leave this region and head back to England. His vengeance-ridden soul was set on going back. He wanted to get back as soon as he could, but he needed to find the right time. He had to get on one of the outgoing ships, most likely under another sailor's identity since his own was permanently labeled as a criminal, just like his scarred palm.

As the caged wagon made its way up the road, Franks thought about a new name for himself. His spirit was black, his murderous intentions most certainly black as well. He had given medical help of a sort to Captain Eliot on the wretched *Jonathan*, but not willingly. He needed to survive here in Virginia, but he didn't care who had to die to achieve his ends of getting back to England. Nobody mattered that much.

As the wagon stopped at a creek so the driver could water the four horses that hauled the fifteen men to Tayloe's ironworks, Franks saw a couple of ravens feeding on the dead carcass of a possum. *That's who I am*, thought Franks. *I am a raven who will kill and find strength from the carcasses of others*. When he was a medical student, Franks had once read that the raven was considered to be a bird of ill omen. It had a mythological legend of being associated with dead and lost souls. It had biblical connections— even Leviticus in the bible forbade the eating of crows. *That's it*, he decided. *When asked my name, I will say it is Raven. It will be a constant reminder that I am already a damned soul and my quest will be to send to hell those who have betrayed me*.

After driving all afternoon, the wagon arrived at Tayloe's works in the early evening. That timing gave Franks an idea of how far away the harbor was from the ironworks. This heavy wagon with fifteen caged men couldn't have been traveling more than five, maybe six miles an hour. The group had been loaded in shackles and chained to the wagon around one in the afternoon. It had to be seven or eight at night, very close to sunset. *At our speed, we had to be no more than twenty-five miles upriver.* As the sun set in the west, Franks made a mental note as to his location relative to the road they had traveled and the expected distance back to the harbor. *I must remember these things. I will need them, and the sooner the better.*

When the wagon reached the ironworks, the men were unchained from the wagon and stood with their feet and hands shackled in a line. They were fed a corn porridge, then Tayloe's roughneck boss man, Mercian, addressed them.

"I am Mercian. My name might suggest that I will show mercy towards you convicts, but I assure you I will not. Mr. Tayloe has paid for your labor. Your labor belongs to us. For the length of time you'll be with us, never forget that. You will work in the tobacco fields, you will cut trees and haul them to the furnaces, you will mine and haul limestone, you will mine and haul iron ore if we tell you to. You will make charcoal if we tell you to.

"You will be chained to your beds every night. You will be taken to the fields or to the mines every day, and unchained so you can work. But there are overseers who have the authority to deliver the lash and the boot if necessary. We will provide you with food, clothing as needed, and sleeping quarters with blankets for the winter.

"We have our own farm here, so you will eat better than you did on that prison ship. But, never forget that you are outlaws from society's rules, and that we can do whatever we want to keep you working and obedient. You see Shruggs here?" He nodded to the man beside him. "He is my assistant. He and his overseers have the authority to beat you, whip you, and keep you in an iron collar that will spike your neck if you get out of line. I rather think he enjoys it."

Shruggs was six-feet tall and weighed 250 pounds. His other distinguishing physical characteristic is that he only had one ear. Mercian felt the need to tell the group about that lost ear. Shruggs walked in front of the men and pulled up his hair so all could see his missing appendage.

Mercian continued with a snarly glint of humor in his voice. "You may have noticed, my good man Shruggs has only one ear. The other ear having been bit off by a now-dead prisoner who claimed he was hungry. When Shruggs denied him more rations in the field, the man jumped on Shruggs' back and bit his ear off. Shruggs threw him off and shot him on the spot. Shruggs enjoys using the boot and the butt of a musket and his whip to teach prisoners their place. Do I need to tell you more me fellows?"

Just to get everyone's attention, Shruggs uncoiled the bullwhip he had roped around his shoulder and set a withering sharp lash to one of the prisoner's stomach. The convict cried out in pain, but it set the mood of the group to one that was decidedly more obedient.

Entering the convicts' field of vision was an overseer holding a group of hounds at bay. The hounds strained at their leashes and yelped like crazy. It took the overseer's full strength to keep them back.

Mercian nodded in the direction of the hounds and continued his short harangue of rules and expectations. "Oh, yes. You may think about escaping. We expect that, and we want you to know today that we are within our rights to shoot you like the mad dog you are if you try to escape. We've had a few. Tim Carpenter, William Simms and Tyrie Roach come to mind. All are dead now. Tyrie almost made it as far as the port on the Rappahannock before we caught up to him.

"The last escaped convict was a man named James whom we sent the hounds after. He tried to run to Quantico. He was an easy catch. The hounds found him, they did, and held him at bay until we arrived. As a lesson to those who worked for us then, we brought him back and hung him from that tall oak tree over there with everybody watching him squeal his last breath. Yep, cost Mr. Tayloe money but he felt a need to set an example. You might take heed of this story. The hounds know this area and we do too, almost as well as they do. You escape, and we will find you." He glanced at the oak tree. "And we might hang you."

Mercian's tone of voice shifted as he finished his speech. "You will rest on Sunday, for Mr. Tayloe is a Christian and wants to observe the Lord's Day. We aren't inhuman, after all. Sundays, there is usually plenty of chicken. But do not challenge us. If you malinger, you will not get fed. If you disobey one of the guards, he will call Shruggs over and you will be delivered righteous punishment.

"Well, then, my fine fellows, there will be no more rules tonight. The guards will show you to your quarters and chain you to the beds. Sleep tonight. Tomorrow you will rise early and be sent to your jobs."

◆◆◆

In the morning, the job allocation came early—right after the prisoners lined up without leg irons for the morning serving of a corn porridge that was thicker than the thin gruel they had been fed on the *Jonathan*. Eight of the fifteen new convicts were assigned to the woodcutting crew. They were put aboard a wagon that would take them to the woodcutting sites. Three of the men went with another overseer who would take them to the ore mines across the Potomac in Maryland. Tayloe's low grade iron ore in Virginia was playing out and he was bringing iron ore in flat boats across the river from mines he had purchased in Maryland. Those men would likely stay over in Maryland and prevent any crowding back in the cabin at the Neabsco iron works.

Tayloe had another ironworks north of Neabsco at Occoquan which used the Maryland iron ore. The four remaining men were walked to the ironworks up the hill from their sleeping quarters. This included Franks, who was always looking at how many were guarding him and what weapons they had.

As he walked, he felt the sharpened wooden spoon hidden in his boot. It was a weak weapon and wouldn't be much good to him in a fight with overseers armed with muskets, bayonets, and knives most likely crafted in Tayloe's forge. Franks longed for one of those knives. As they were walked to the ironworks, he kept thinking about what he could do to avoid the manual labor that would exhaust him and take away the energy he needed to escape.

Escape seemed almost hopeless. Not only were armed guards watching him, but the Potomac river port at Quantico was twenty-five miles away. On top of that, England was a three-month voyage across the Atlantic. These people had guns and hounds in the wooded country of Virginia. Even if he could run, how could he make it on a ship that would transport him? This dim prospect had bothered him last night before he could nod off to sleep. Now that he was at the ironworks, the prospect of successful escape seemed even bleaker. He could possibly kill a guard, steal a weapon, and make a run for it in the woods. But then what? How long could he escape the hounds?

As the small group got to the top of the hill, Franks saw a shed that stored wheelbarrows and shovels which he and others would use to haul material to the furnace. It was explained to him that piles of iron ore, charcoal, and limestone were there waiting for a command from the ironworks supervisor. Franks and the other 'fillers' would shovel the material into wheelbarrows and cart them across the walkway, then layer the three components into the blast furnace that formed the basis for the pig iron the furnace would produce. There were two furnaces that needed to be fed. Since it was now July, the Virginia heat was starting to rise, and as they got closer to the furnace, Franks felt the heat both furnaces produced. *This is going to be like Vulcan's hell*, he thought.

Once started, each of the furnaces would produce pig iron for a 24-hour run and needed to be fed the three basic materials on an ongoing basis. Shoveling and hauling the materials and dumping the ingredients was hard work, and if the run was going to last 24 hours, fillers like Franks had to be there. The overseers had two crews for two rotating shifts of 12-hours. The overseer told the fillers to stay alive and to be ready to shovel the limestone, charcoal, or iron ore into the wheelbarrows on his command. The only small benefit to being a filler was that the overseer and the two guards took off the wrist shackles so the men could handle the wheelbarrows. He was shackle free. It felt good after being chained daily for the past three months.

Down the hill, Franks saw large bellows that puffed up and down controlled by the lifting mechanism powered by a water wheel. The bellows fed hot air into the base of each furnace and kept the charcoal white hot to melt the iron ore. Every eight hours or so, the fillers could take a break while the men at the base of the furnace took the molten pig iron out and shaped it into casting beds that created rectangular pieces of the pig iron six-inches wide and four feet long. The shapes from the casting beds resembled little piglets nursing at the mother sow, hence the name.

CHAPTER 8

F ranks did what he was told the first week until he could get his bearing around the land. He hated the manual labor—it was exhausting and ran against his haughty nature that he was better and smarter than the other uneducated morons that grunted their way through the work. The overseer kept a close watch on the new men to see if anyone of them had escape tendencies. For sure Franks was one of them. But Franks' big break came at the end of the first Sunday as he was fed his first real meal in over seven months. It consisted of hot corn meal, green beans, corn bread, and all the fried chicken he wanted.

As he gobbled down his meal, he heard Mercian's distinctive voice. "You, black beard, over here."

Franks put down his bowl and ambled over to where Mercian and another overseer stood.

"What's your name?" asked Mercian.

"I call myself Raven," Franks said, feeling completely worn out after a long week of shoveling and dumping iron ore into the furnaces. "Just Raven."

"Well, Raven, the manager, Tom Lawson, wants to talk with you. Come this way."

Franks and Mercian walked to a shed with Franks leading and

Mercian following with his musket strapped on his shoulder and one hand placed on the loaded pistol in his belt.

"This is the man who calls himself...what was that again?" asked Mercian.

"Raven," said Franks.

"I'm Tom Lawson, the manager of the ironworks. We have your name down here on the rolls as Franks from Portsmouth, purchased by Mr. Tayloe for a fourteen-year indenture period. Is that right?"

"If you say it is, it must be."

"And I do say it is," responded Lawson. "The records don't indicate what you did to get this transportation sentence, but I would imagine it was pretty serious. The overseer at the filler says you keep looking around, as if you are looking for a way to escape. Well, are you?"

"No," said Franks, not wanting to take the bait dropped at his feet. It would mean a sharp butt of the rifle from Mercian, who stood behind Franks as he was addressed by the ironworks manager.

"Then what is it?" said Lawson.

"It's only been a week. Just trying to get my bearings."

"That's a phony answer if I ever heard one," said Lawson laughing, he and Mercian enjoying the small joke.

"Says here on our records from the captain of the *Jonathan* that you are a surgeon. Is that right?"

"Served at Haslar Naval Hospital in Portsmouth for over ten years."

"Ten years a surgeon and now here you are, shoveling iron ore. Quite a come down, I must say."

Franks stood silent. He didn't have to be reminded of his fall in status.

"Well, I have a need which you may be able to fill. But I won't even explore the subject if I think you would abuse it and run from us. Besides, Mr. Raven or Franks or whatever you want to call yourself, there is a great big wide ocean between you and your native country. Think of it. You do your term with us, establish your freedom after your indenture, and you can make a home in this country, even practice medicine, rise again in the stature of your community. Think about that. Many people who have been indentured to us never went back to England. They're here in the colonies, making a life, raising a family."

Mercian interrupted Lawson. "Listen to what Mr. Lawson says, Raven. He runs this operation. He can make your life here a lot easier."

"I'm listening," said Franks.

"Good. We have over 100 people working on this side of the Potomac here, at the Occoquan ironworks, and another fifty mining ore on the Maryland side. People get sick, and given the often hazardous nature of the work, they get hurt. The tree cutting is especially dangerous. The iron ore mining is dangerous. We don't have a physician. I'd offer you the job if I thought you'd do it, wouldn't run from us, and could keep these people well. If they're bedridden, they're of no use to us. Your job would be to treat the workers at this location, travel to the Occoquan works once a week, and get over to the Maryland side on a rotating schedule. All of this with an armed guard, I would add. You will not be alone. Not for a minute."

"I don't have any equipment. I don't have any medicine, herbs, oils and ointments, bandages, splints.

"You know how to make these oils and ointments?"

"Yes, of course."

Then, I'll see you get a space in one of the sheds to make the things you need. But I still don't trust you. Mercian, I want Shruggs to watch him. Get him from the tobacco fields tomorrow and have him or another guard watch him at all times. Keep an eye on, uh... Raven here as he gets his boxes of herbs and ointments together. Raven, you can start examining the workers as they present problems. But I refuse to accept any malingering. If you are complicit in any malingering, such as saying a man is hurt when he isn't so he can get bed rest, I'll have you both lashed, and this medical experiment will come to an end very quickly. Have I made myself clear?"

"You have. Very clear," said Franks, who was looking at easier duty, walking and working without shackles, and perhaps a chance, in the future…of a real chance to escape.

◆ ◆ ◆

Franks needed to put together a small medicine chest of herbs, oils and ointments that he would need. At Haslar Hospital, he had relied on LongAcre Supply to send the hospital everything they needed. It was different out here in the colonies.

He asked Mercian if he could buy medical supplies from the nearest apothecary. He didn't want to go walking in the woods to try and locate the proper herbs and plants. He was granted permission to travel to the small village of Woodbridge where he went with an armed guard the very next Monday to buy some of what he needed from an apothecary there.

The trip itself took half the morning in a slow-moving one-horse buckboard. The road took them to the east towards the Potomac. Franks tried to memorize every huge tree and bend in the road for his escape plan. He had to get out of here. His life would be ruined if he didn't get back to England. His armed guard for this trip was a trustee black man named Caylor who had his musket handy as Raven handled the reins with his shackled hands on their way to and from the village.

He was able to pick out a few known herbs from the apothecary shop, although there weren't many. The storeowner agreed to send Lawson the bill, so he didn't need any colonial currency.

On the way back, Caylor spoke for the first time. "I am just making talk with you, Mister Raven, to pass the time. So you gonna be a doctor for all of us?"

"That's right." He wasn't much interested in what his guard had to say. Small talk didn't interest him unless he could find out something he really needed to know. Like did he know of a boat he could steal at the small river port of Woodbridge, or when high tide was so he wouldn't get stuck on a sand bar? His mind worked towards what he needed to know when his time for escape came. What could Caylor know that would be of benefit? He didn't want to act too nosy less Caylor report back to Shruggs, a report that might strip him of his newly appointed position and get him the boot or a whipping.

"You need medicines, eh, that right?"

"Yes. More than what that apothecary shop has to offer."

"You should talk to my wife."

"Why?"

"She knows what flowers and plants are around here. We black folks have been treating our own for some time. She could tell you where to find the plants and tell you which flowers do what and such."

"Tayloe has a herb garden?"

"Not that I knows of. My wife fetches plants and flowers in the wild. Squeezes the juice out of them sometimes."

"Stop there before we get back to the ironworks."

Caylor was a slave of Tayloe's and had been for fifteen years. He and many of the other African slaves worked the tobacco fields and tended the Tayloe farm that produced the chickens, corn, and other vegetables for the Tayloe family and for the labor force. It was not a small operation by any means. Foodstuffs needed to be grown, harvested, gathered, and stored for future use.

As they entered the small one room shack, Franks could see the dried flowers hanging from the rafters. Dried roots were up on a shelf.

"This is Millie. This here is Raven. Mister Lawson made him a doctor for the workers here," said Caylor.

Millie looked at the black-bearded, black-haired man standing gruffly in front of her. "What do you want?" she asked with apprehension.

"Caylor says you know where the medicine plants and flowers are. I need you to show me. I need to collect them to make oils and ointments for illnesses and injuries the men suffer."

Millie directed her next question to her husband. "Do I have to help him? We takes care of our own. We don't get no help from Lawson or Tayloe when one of us suffers."

"Hush woman," said Caylor. "Just show him where they are. You don't have to collect them, if you don't want to."

"Yes, just show me where to find them."

"You can take some, Mister Raven. You don't take them all. I needs them."

"I'll take only what I need."

"All right. Follow me. Grab that gunny sack over there. You gonna need it."

The three of them collected plants that Millie Caylor had cultivated in the wild for the past fifteen years. They were spread out in the fields and hedges that surrounded the black quarters and were not contained in some tidy English herb garden. Millie knew them like they were her children and could tell whether one or another was ripe for harvesting. Since Franks had not grown any of his own, but had relied on LongAcre Supply for the ten years he was at Haslar, Millie's help was valuable.

Over the next month, even while he was guarded by one of Shruggs' men, Franks took the yarrow root, southernwood, feverfew, basil, mint, catnip, chamomile, hyssop, rosemary, sage, and thyme and processed them. Some he merely cut up to be used as leaves in different teas. Some he distilled in a small distillery unit that he constructed to extract the steam and produce oils for a couple of different herbs.

His desire to escape had not waned. It was late in the summer and the Virginia countryside slowly turned to autumn. The fall equinox was upon them. Crops were being harvested while the blast furnaces were being fed and pig iron produced. He knew that soon there would be no ocean going merchant ships headed back to England. Winter travel on the Atlantic was a certain trip to disaster and death. If he was going to make a break for England, he had to do it without a guard looking over his shoulder. Shruggs or his guards weren't always with him, but he could tell that Shruggs and

Mercian didn't trust him at all. The guards they rotated to guard him couldn't care less about the assignment, only that they would suffer a life-threatening beating if Franks escaped under their watch. He quickly came to the realization that he would have to wait for spring to make his move. It would have to be in March or even April when the merchant ships would come from England to the colonies and be looking to haul back tobacco and pig iron.

He mentally ruled out Quantico as a port to which he would escape. Mercian's speech about the hounds knowing the woods all the way there made him very wary of this port even though it was the closest. He would need to find a way farther south on the Chesapeake to a port large enough for him to change his identity, change his costume, and blend into a much larger port community. At this point however, he didn't know the colonies or where that port was. There were questions he needed answers to, but couldn't be too obvious about.

◆ ◆ ◆

During the next months, Raven became a doctor again. By then, he'd completely let his old name of Franks go, even to himself. Throughout those months, he had to make trips to the blast furnace to bandage burns suffered by the iron men who extracted the hot pig iron from the bottom of the furnace. He made numerous trips to the forests where men had fallen. During the summer, a couple of them actually broke their legs and he had to set the bones and wrap splints around them. Some men on the tree-cutting detail got gashes from saws that slipped. Raven did what he could. His heart wasn't in helping them, but the job kept him from hauling iron ore, and most of the time he worked free of shackles.

Pretty soon, he hoped they would take the guard away. Pretty soon, he hoped they would look at him as a trustee and not expect to see him shackled. He still was shackled at night, but most times during the day, the guard let him work without them. It felt really uncomfortable when they were slapped on him at night before he went to sleep.

He took note that there were always at least two guards in the convict shack. One to point a musket at them and one to set the shackles. As he lay in his bed every night, he could hear the two talking and then silence followed by the soft sound of a single man's footsteps as only one of the guards slowly marched around the perimeter of the convict shacks. The only other sound he heard from the night guard was the unmistakable noise of a cork being pulled from a jug. That made Raven smile as he drifted off to sleep. *Maybe, I can run when the sentry has fallen into a drunken sleep.* But they had even fewer guards across the river in Maryland. Maybe that was where he needed to escape from.

Before the Potomac River froze over across from Woodbridge, Raven and his guard traveled the short distance from the ironworks to Woodbridge, then boated across the Potomac to make one last trip before winter to the Maryland ore mine. At the riverbank they were carted roughly six-miles into Maryland to tend to the needs of the workers stationed there. The usual supply of food stuffs from Tayloe's farm came with them in the boat across the water for them to cook. At the ore mine, the men had fewer guards but a rougher life than the people in Virginia. The shacks were in worse shape, and the work was exhausting and dangerous.

As soon as Raven thought of using Maryland as an escape location, he had to measure time and distances to keep any pursuers separated from him. The distance from the Neabsco ironworks to Woodbridge was five miles. The time it took for an unloaded iron boat to get to Maryland was a good half-hour. It was another six miles or so upland to the Maryland ore mine. He kept this in his head and memorized the time he estimated for the hounds to chase him. If the hounds were on the Virginia side of the Potomac, he had the water between him and the hounds. It became obvious that he needed to flee in the night and gain five hours' head start. He couldn't run across land; he needed a boat to get downriver as fast as possible. He had to keep his scent from the hounds or he was a dead man.

These thoughts were only the beginning of a plan and he knew it. He needed more information. The Potomac would have to be his escape route since the land route on the Virginia side of the river to Quantico, or points south, were known so well by his minders. These watermen had answers.

Each time, Raven and the guard had stayed for three days at the Maryland iron ore mines. Each time they made the trip, Raven paid close attention to the watermen who portered the iron ore across the water to waiting drays that would haul the iron ore to the Occoquan or Neabsco ironworks.

The watermen who rowed us across were freer, thought Raven.

Yes, the watermen held the answers. They knew the current and how to handle the often heavy, ore-laden boats. Even though they were slaves or convicts, they were without shackles so they could manage the boats and steer them without crashing into a dock or accidently dump the ore in the water. They could be useful. His guard told him that some of them who had worked for Tayloe for years were actually paid wages and were granted freedom to move bigger sloops down to Quantico and further to transport pig iron and tobacco to ocean-going merchant ships or to pick up goods the ironworks had ordered from England.

At the Maryland mines, men—including watermen who slept in the worker shacks—sat around during their evening meal eating, talking, and sharing stories they'd heard. It was just like prison. Not all the stories were true, but there was always a kernel of helpful information that Raven would hold onto and keep. On the second night of this last pre-winter trip, the guards were sitting by themselves apart from the others, while the convicts were around a fire finishing their meal before they would be rudely pushed to the shacks and put in their chains.

A waterman named Willow was asked if he knew the river all the way down to where it emptied into the Chesapeake Bay.

"I do, I do. Been there delivering tobacco a number of times," said Willow.

Raven was at the campfire listening intently but did not say a word.

"There are so many creeks and rivers and inlets that empty into the river and into the bay, you cannot count them. I knows a few of them. I knows where the current is. I knows where the sandbars are. When the tide is low, you can get stuck, sure as I am talking here."

"Hell," said one of the convicts, "you could leave here for a trip downriver and find your freedom."

"Find freedom where?" said Willow. "I don't have chains like you do. I work hard, eat well, got a roof over my head. Where would I go that's better than this? I may be a slave, but where would I go where I wasn't? Would I go across the river to Virginia, down to North Carolina? No sir!"

"You could hire yourself out to the deep draft merchant ships as a guide up the Potomac. Keep them from grounding," one of the convicts said gruffly.

"Yes, yes," said Willow. "But as soon as they found out I belonged to Mister Tayloe, I be chained and sent back never to work the boat again. No thank you."

Raven took a chance and spoke. He didn't want to draw attention to himself but needed an answer to an important question. "You ever seen a map of the river?"

Willow answered. He seemed to feel important now, being looked at as someone with answers about the river he knew best. "Nope, never needed one," Willow said proudly. "But I saw one once at Quantico docks. The British naval officers down there had a map, showed the Potomac, the Rappahannock River, The York, and the James. They all empty into Chesapeake Bay, all drawn up like they knows where all the rivers and inlets are. Hell, they don't know half of them like I do."

That was all that Raven would ask this night. He didn't want anyone to think he had plans to escape. If this river, and maybe even this waterman, was going to get him downriver to a merchant ship, he would need a map. His escape would be a long journey, but he had to do it. He would not live and die in the colonies.

At night in Maryland, his guard would shackle him just like the others. But without Shruggs or Mercian to watch over them, the guards often slept or drank and didn't patrol around the perimeter of the shacks of the sleeping men. It was getting cold outside and they wanted their comfort. Raven had the beginnings of his plan for his spring getaway…he would leave from the Maryland side, steal one of the boats, and make his way down the Potomac.

CHAPTER 9

As winter set in, Raven had plenty of herbs and roots to process in his small space in the tool shack. At his request, Caylor had brought his gunny sacks full of various herbs and roots and plants that Millie had harvested in the fall. When the snow fell, and men left the convict shack to haul ore to the ever-burning pig iron furnace, he could stay in the tool shack with the guard and process herbs and plants. He took his time. Why hurry? If he finished early, they might send him to the furnaces again to be a filler. The weeks went by slowly, but his plan for escape was taking shape. He was going to make a run for it in the spring but with a plan that had to succeed.

◆ ◆ ◆

It was the middle of January when one of the smithies at the iron forge burned himself badly. Raven was called over to dress the wound and bandage it. His guard at the time followed him over to the forge shack. When Raven arrived, the smithy, Henson, was mewing like a baby and had his hand stuck in a bucket of cold water. When Raven looked at it, he knew the burn was severe and needed to be treated.

He said to Henson, "I'll have to make you a mitten of a sort with some balm that will help ease the pain." Raven had never visited the forge where the pig iron was heated and shaped into iron bars, but he immediately noticed there were plenty of iron tools around. His quick eyes spied some recently sharpened six-inch hide-skinning knives sitting on a workbench.

"Guard, I need some things. Run and get some cloths and flour paste. I need to make a poultice for this man's burns," Raven said quickly, hoping that the urgency in his voice would lead the guard to leave him.

Without pausing, the guard lurched out the door and went to fetch the cloths and flour. In a quick move while the smithy still had his hand in the bucket, Raven took three steps to the workbench and stealthily took a knife and jammed it inside his boot right aside the wooden one. He had never gotten rid of the wooden shank.

The guard returned a moment later. Raven drenched the cloths in the water and retrieved some marigold leaves and willow bark that he had obtained from the apothecary and some thyme that Millie gave him, then added them to the cloths along with some flour. He made a paste and rubbed it into Henson's wound and tied the cloth so it wouldn't fall off.

The procedure didn't take but five minutes. All the while, Raven kept an eye on the guard and on Henson to see if they noticed the missing knife from the workbench. They hadn't. They both kept their attention on Henson and his yelping. With the poultice in place, Henson felt a little better and said as much.

"The relief won't last long," Raven said. "The herbs mixed with the flour will be but temporary pain relief. You have a bad burn. This dressing will have to be changed almost every hour all day today, maybe even tomorrow."

During the day, Raven and his guard came back to the forge four different times to put a new poultice on Henson's burns. Raven was conscientious about this. But he had an agenda all his own. The more times he went to the forge the more likely they wouldn't pay attention to him. He had his eyes on another knife or two. Backups always came in handy.

◆◆◆

During the winter, Raven treated any number of men. Given the disparity between the falling temperatures outside and the heat of the furnaces, the men were constantly going from very hot conditions to very cold temperatures. Many came down with colds and chest congestion. None of them were dressed warm enough, and the tree cutters frequently complained. Millie provided some mint and sage leaves which he could mix in a tea and give to those who needed it. Some of it helped. Most of it didn't, but it gave Raven an idea.

"I have to go into Woodbridge," he said to Tom Lawson the next Monday.

"What for?" asked Lawson, suspiciously.

"I've run out of mint and yarrow root that Millie gave me to help treat the chest congestion the men have. I also need clove and garlic to give them to ward off illness."

"I'll have Caylor drive you in. Be sure you're back before sunset. Oh, since you are making the trip, check in with the keeper of our stores. He has tannin and iron sulfate which we sell to the Woodbridge printer. He makes ink with it. Make sure to take the invoice for payment with you."

Raven tried to keep eye contact with Lawson, for he knew that although he had spent seven months at Tayloe's ironworks, Lawson had never relinquished his suspicion of Raven. Raven had been in Lawson's office only a few times, but every time he was there he tried to read the map on the wall behind Lawson's head without Lawson catching him.

This time, as Lawson was speaking, Raven's eyes drifted slyly to the map of the Virginia. Raven peered as quickly as he could to see the land and where the rivers were and where they flowed. His eyes couldn't focus quickly enough, and he silently cursed the fact that he couldn't get close enough to see a legend to the map and be able to calculate distances. The last thing he wanted was for Lawson to see what he was looking at. There must be another map like this somewhere.

◆ ◆ ◆

Raven was inside the Apothecary's shop waiting for him to fill the order for the herbs he wanted. Caylor was warming himself at the stove in the corner. *There has to be a map like Lawson has at the courthouse*, Raven thought. Maybe he should create an argument with the apothecary, maybe even hit him. *I can get arrested, be put into the courthouse jail overnight and steal a map from there. No, that won't work. They'll search me in jail, take the map, take my knife, and maybe my boots as well.*

Raven and Caylor finished their business with the apothecary and drove the buckboard down the city block to the printer's shop. Both men walked into the shop, one carrying the tannin and the other the heavy iron sulfate. They set them on the printer's shop floor and immediately Raven thought he had been granted a gift. He spied multiple prints of the map of Virginia drying on a table. He couldn't believe his luck. The maps were identical to the one hanging behind Lawson's head in his office showing the rivers—the Potomac, The Rappahannock, the York, and the James. It showed the major ports and the larger inland towns.

As the printer turned and went to his desk to sign the invoice Caylor had given him, Raven stuck one of the maps in his coat. He thought he was fast, but Caylor saw what he did out of the corner of his eye. Raven brought his finger to his lips, signaling Caylor to be quiet about the theft. He could see the indecision in Caylor's face, and for a moment he thought Caylor would say something. If he did, and the printer was alerted, Raven would be forced to pull his deer-skinning knife. Nothing would end well if that happened. Even if he overpowered them both, he would have to run for it in the middle of winter and would surely be caught or die in the woods of starvation.

Caylor's silence seemed reluctant but he didn't say anything. The printer turned back to them with a signed acceptance of the ink-making supplies and bid the men good day. In the buckboard driving back to the ironworks, Raven kept his silence, but Caylor felt the need to speak.

"What's you want that map for?"

Raven knew he couldn't tell Caylor the real reason, so he made up a phony one.

"I like to know the lay of the land where I live. I've been here seven months—July to the end of January of 1772—and I don't know anything about this country. Lawson said I should settle here after I pay the indenture. I just want to know what Virginia looks like."

"You could have paid for that map. Not steal it."

"Money? Hah. Of course not! What money do I have? They took everything from me back in England. Everything, I mean to tell you, and someday I'll get it back."

CHAPTER 10

Each day in February and early March, Raven studied the map. He had a work space in the shack where he worked cutting herbs and making ointments with the small distillery unit he had. The guard who was assigned to him often left him alone. As the weeks went by, he was increasingly thought to be harmless and less and less of a flight risk. That meant the guard would frequently leave the shack either to relieve himself or smoke a pipe. Those time segments gave Raven time to pull out the map and memorize it.

From the map, Raven knew he had to get downriver as soon as possible, away from the Neabsco ironworks. It couldn't be over land; the hounds would get him. It had to be by boat. The map showed him where Yorktown was, and he decided that he would be able to blend into the dock scene there rather than at a smaller port. Using the legend on the map, he determined that Yorktown was at least one hundred and sixty miles away. Even if he wasn't caught by Lawson and Mercian, it would take him many days and nights. He needed to prepare.

Over the next four Sundays, he stuffed extra chicken from the Sunday dinners under his shirt and took it back to the shack and placed it in an empty gunny sack that the herbs from Millie came in. He only took a little at a time so no one would notice. The food might spoil if it got warm, so he kept the sack in the coldest corner of the shack. He thought about the cold spring nights and decided that he would need a blanket or two from the Maryland operation.

With the spring runoff and melting ice on the Potomac, the Potomac's current would be running strong, propelling him downriver. The only problem with the high spring runoff and the rapid current was the peril of hitting submerged trees. He didn't know the river well enough to take that risk. Willow had said it. Staying in the channel was important. He could get stuck on a sand bar or by a tree and it would be all over for him. Raven decided that he would force Willow to take him as far downriver as he could. If Willow did what he was told, he might save his own life and make it back to the Neabsco people with a story that would throw them off Raven's scent.

◆◆◆

The weather was intermittent rain during the previous day when he was boated over to Maryland in early March as part of his visiting rotation of the camps. He had his gunny sack of herbs covering the food that he had tried to preserve over the last four weeks. At the docks where Willow had landed, he could see other boats other than the slow, heavy flat-bottomed iron ore boats. There were at least two dory boats that had a single mast and sail. He didn't think they would be there. It was his previous intention to force Willow to move one of the slower larger ore boats downriver. Having a smaller boat would be much better and faster.

After the day's work of checking the health of the iron-ore miners, Raven and the workers were fed and retired to the inside of the shack. All of them were leg- shackled but not wrist-chained as was the normal procedure, including Raven. Raven knew which guard had the key.

When nighttime came, Raven moved ever so carefully out of his bunk. He tried to make absolutely no noise. He curled up his gunny sack with his dried chicken, rolled it up in his blanket, and wrapped it around his leg shackles to prevent them from clanging together.

The room was pitch black, and all Raven could hear was snoring from the sleeping men.

Before nightfall, he had determined where Willow slept. He was a trustee, and therefore, wasn't shackled. That would make it easier to get him moving. He knew where the guard slept. One was in the same shack as the convicts, the other two were in a spare shack next door sleeping after tugging at the corn liquor bottle. Raven knew their patterns, and this night, above all nights, he relied on them to follow that same pattern to a heavy sleep. The guard in the convicts' shack had drawn the short straw this night and it would be his last. Raven knew what he had to do to silence the guard and get the key that would unshackle him.

With his chains muffled, Raven shuffled closer to the sleeping guard, and drawing his sharp knife from his boot, positioned himself quietly above the head of the cot where the guard slept. With the deft skill of a surgeon, he quickly and violently slashed the guard's throat, cutting a three-inch deep gash across his entire throat. The guard never made a sound. To make sure, Raven took the man's straw–filled pillow and pushed it hard over the man's mouth so no sound whatsoever would emerge. He held the pillow down hard and listened to the guard's dying breath. In less than a minute, the guard was dead.

Before he moved again, Raven rolled up the guard's blanket and tied it in a bundle. He needed to take it with him. He stealthily tied both blanket rolls around his body.

Raven retrieved the key from the dead guard and quietly undid his leg-irons. He paused carefully to listen if anyone else in the shack had awoken, but heard nothing. With his shackles removed, he took a rag from the guard's pocket, crept across the room, and knelt next to Willow's cot. Willow was asleep until Raven stuck the rag in the man's mouth to keep him quiet. Willow's eyes widened in fear and his hands went for the rag to remove it. Raven stopped him by pointing his bloody knife at Willow's face.

"Leave it be," whispered Raven. "You're coming with me. Quietly, or I'll kill you right here."

Raven gruffly pulled Willow from his cot, and with one hand on the gag in Willow's mouth and the other holding a knife at Willow's back, marched him out the door. He kept moving over to the small stable where two horses were tethered. Raven was still intent on escaping without any noise, so he placed the rein in Willow's hand, and whispered, "Hold on. You pull the horse."

He still wanted to keep the knife at Willow's back until they were safely around the corner and could jump on the back of the horse and trot the six-miles to the boat dock. It was risky, but with the other two guards in their corn liquor-induced sleep, he could feel a bit safer in getting the horse around the corner.

"You make one sound and I'll kill you right here. Killing the guard didn't bother me in the least. You got that, Willow? Keep that rag in your mouth. If you move it, I'll kill you."

Willow did as he was told. The fierceness of Raven's command and the knife at his back convinced him to do what Raven wanted.

As they got far enough from the shacks, Raven motioned for Willow to climb up on the horse. It wasn't easy without saddle or stirrup, but he managed it. Raven followed suit and the two of them trotted off. He didn't want to gallop. The horse had two riders and would move slowly anyway. They just had to make it six-miles to the dock.

As they rode, Raven did the math. It was midnight or later. He couldn't tell for sure. Neither he nor Willow had a time piece. Daybreak would be in four to five hours. He needed to be well down river before daybreak. When the other guards discovered the dead man, Raven's and Willow's empty cots, and the missing horse, they would mount the other horse to a wagon and come tearing to the docks.

◆◆◆

It took less than an hour to arrive at the docks. Raven dismounted first, then pulled Willow from the horse's back. Without a saddle, it had been a rough ride, but the two of them made it this far. If Willow made a dash for it, Raven would make sure he never made it back to tell the story around the campfire.

Raven came straight to Willow's face, and with a threatening growl and the knife at Willow's throat said, "Which of these two dory boats is the one to take?"

Raven yanked the gag from Willow's mouth and could see the fear in his eyes.

"The second one doesn't leak as much."

"Get in it and get the sail ready."

"There's no wind."

"Then you'll row. Get going."

The two of them shoved the dory away from shore and Willow rowed out to the middle of the Potomac. The current was swift with the early spring run-off, and the boat headed downstream with the kind of speed that put the Maryland ore dock at their backs in a hurry. It was a pitch black night outside, and Raven knew that avoiding sand bars and river debris was crucial.

"Avoid the sand bars, Willow. You know the river, keep us from getting stuck."

"How can I do that while I row?"

"You look around as you need to, that's how!" Raven could speak in normal tones, but the river had a way of carrying his voice to the shores of Virginia and Maryland, so he was careful not to yell. No one should be awake at this hour, but he couldn't be sure.

The swift current pushed the boat at eight-knots or higher, and they could see the Quantico shores and the various ships just before daybreak. It was another stroke of luck that dawn had not yet broken, so there was no one at the Quantico dock that would see the two-man dory moving swiftly downriver.

"Put up the sail, Willow. You've rowed enough for a while," said Raven. "Then take the tiller. And mind you avoid the shoals. We have hours to go before I let you off and make my way south."

Raven wanted to put the waterman at ease. He needed Willow's cooperation, even though it would be with reluctance. They had made it this far at night. He had his knife and he held it menacingly at Willow whenever he spoke to remind him that he could end the slave's existence in a fierce, quick, and deadly thrust. He also wanted to let Willow think that they would be traveling down the Potomac. He had another plan he had worked out from his study of the map he stole from the printer.

They had swiftly floated downstream another two hours when Raven told Willow to put to shore. It was daylight now, and even on a cold spring morning with the mist on the river, he needed to get his bearings. He also needed to avoid being spotted by sloops coming up river. They would carry a tale to Quantico that they had seen a single small boat with two men, and the hunt for Raven would be started.

They steered the dory to shore where Raven pulled out the blanket with the gunny sack of food and gave Willow some of the dried meat.

"Here, eat some of this. You'll need it for your walk back."

"Walking? You ain't gonna kill me?" Willow said with a deep sigh of obvious relief.

"No. Either you can walk the twelve miles, or you flag down one of the sloops coming back upstream and get them to let you off back at Quantico. I'm going with the current down the Potomac, and it's on to the Chesapeake all the way to Norfolk. I'll get on a boat there and sail to Jamaica."

Raven wanted the phony story relayed to the naval officers at Quantico just as he told it to Willow. They could sail the Potomac for days looking for the boat and not find him. And he certainly wasn't going to Jamaica. By the time Willow got to Quantico, then carted back to Neabsco ironworks, it would be three days later. By that time, Raven would be far away from Mercian, Shruggs, and the hounds. And once they did set out for him, he would be off the Potomac, headed elsewhere.

Raven left Willow on the bank, who helped shove the dory away from its shoreline mooring. Raven raised the sail and drifted down the river. He worried a bit that by not killing Willow he had made a mistake, but he had to hope that his false story would work and buy him a week's time away from a hunting party.

Once around the corner of the river, Raven kept the boat close to shore. He manned the tiller and kept a sharp eye out for river debris that would snag him, and currents that might warn of a sandbar. The spring runoff had increased the depth of the Potomac to where the sandbars were less of a danger than the moving tree debris, but he couldn't be too careful.

He had studied his map to its finest detail, using the legend to mark expected distances. They wouldn't be perfect, but as daylight increased, he had a better approximation of where he needed to land the boat. According to the map, there was a sandy shore after the turn in the river twelve miles or so south by southeast of Quantico. He was a mile or so downriver of where he had left Willow stranded. When he knew he wouldn't be seen, he took down the sail, manned the oars, and drove the boat into the beach as hard as he could.

By his reckoning he was at Fairview beach. It was a sandy area, so if the map was correct, he could walk inland roughly twelve miles and be at the tip of the Rappahannock river at Port Royal. He was in Virginia, and that was unsettling. But, by his reckoning, from his study of the map, it looked like the shortest distance to the next major river. He hoped that any search crews would be thrown off by Willow's story and he would remain free of the hounds. His map gave him an overland route. There was no pathway to be sure, but if he could walk three-miles an hour, he could reach Port Royal by late afternoon and rest. He had not slept the night before, and he knew his physical limits. Just the act of murdering the guard and escaping made his heart pump faster and used up his available energy. Sleep was important.

He moved the dory as far off the beach as he could, then tore down some bushes to shield it from the prying eyes of anyone looking ashore from a passing boat. He took some of the dried chicken and munched on it as he started his trek. He walked with the blankets strung across his chest and around his back. It was crucial to get as far away from the beach as possible, as soon as he could.

Although he thought he had a comfortable margin of safety, it was noontime—based on the location of the sun—and the alert must have been sounded four hours ago.

Will they float downriver looking for me immediately? Would they first go to the Neabsco ironworks and tell Lawson since there was a dead guard back at the Maryland works? Would they find Willow? Would Willow find them? Would the hounds be searching frantically on the Virginia side of the Potomac? All of this played with his mind as he struggled through the woods, constantly looking for easier ground to walk on. He was glad he had his good boots on. They had held up well.

After three hours, he saw the town of Port Royal in the distance. He had a big decision to make, and it depended on whether the search crew and hounds would travel throughout the night. It was late afternoon and the sun was setting. He needed rest and more food than the few pieces of dried chicken he had left.

He reasoned that any search party would travel over land toward Quantico since it was the first deep water port they'd look at. Then it would take them at least two days to cover the twenty-five miles. They had to rest the dogs, feed them and themselves, and then try to keep going. By the legend on his map, Quantico was at least fifty miles from Port Royal. If they ran into Willow, presumably at Quantico, they might take a sloop and race down the Potomac looking for Raven. That would be the fast way. If they wanted to use the hounds and pursue a land-based search, it would take them five days or more to make it to Port Royal. They would probably take the well-traveled path of the Kings Highway rather than go through the bush, and that would take even longer. He felt more and more at ease despite which path his pursuers chose. As long as they didn't find the dory hidden on the shore.

If he indeed had a week's head start, he could afford to rest. At a hillside above Port Royal, he bedded down for the night, wrapped himself in both blankets, ate the last of his dried food, and slept until morning.

When he got down to the docks at Port Royal in the early morning, he saw the hogsheads of tobacco lined up ready to be loaded onto a barge and floated downstream on the Rappahannock River. From his map he had taken note that the Rappahannock was a major river in Virginia that flowed into the Chesapeake Bay some seventy miles downstream. He wasn't about to walk this distance, so he needed to get on a boat.

He saw a number of men rolling the hogsheads up ramps onto flat bottom scows about twenty-four feet in length. He walked up to one of the men and asked where he could find the overseer.

"He's over there, barking orders," said the tall black man loading a hogshead onto one of the barges. "You can't miss him. He's the one doing all of the talking."

Raven approached the dock boss. "You need someone to help get this tobacco downriver?" asked Raven.

"Yeah, we need some people to pole these boats down to Yorktown. You want the job?"

"Yes," said Raven, allowing the blustering dock boss to have his loud braying way.

"You poled on the Rappahannock before?" the dock boss yelled.

"No, but I have sailed the Potomac."

"Is that right? What's your name?"

Raven didn't want to leave a name that could be traced should Mercian and his hounds make it all this way.

"Henson," said Raven, taking the name of the blacksmith back at the Neabsco ironworks.

"You a runaway, Henson? We get runaways, we have to report them. You got papers?"

"What papers?"

"Sailor protection papers. Shows officials and slave catchers that you're a free man and a citizen so you don't get impressed by the British Navy."

"I worked for John Tayloe up at Woodbridge at the ironworks. Worked in the forge. That's how I got this burn on my hand, grabbed something I shouldn't have." He needed to bluff his way onto the boat, yet not appear too eager.

"Bad burn, Henson."

"I am not a runaway," Raven lied. "And I don't have any papers."

"Well, Henson, I'll take a chance. Pay is a dollar a week. You make it back here, you'll be bringing back foodstuffs and other goods. It will be two dollars in your pocket, payable once you get back. When you get back here, come look for me. Name is Beckett. People know who I am. They'll come and fetch me."

Raven would agree to just about anything to get on that boat and shove off. "Agreed," he said. *Damn, that's the first I've heard about having papers.*

"There's three men on a boat—two polers and a man to help steady the load. You'll rotate the tough poling job. You have eight hogsheads of tobacco on each of the four boats. Each of those hogsheads weighs about 900 pounds and we don't want them to shift or fall overboard. It should take the four boats three, maybe four days to get to Yorktown. Harrison, the head boatman, has money to pay for the entire crew's meals at Tappahannock, Deltaville, and in Yorktown. He knows where to go at the Yorktown docks and where to unload. You follow his commands and that of your own boat leader. You just get the tobacco there. Safe and sound. You get to rest a day and then start back. When you get back, you'll be paid. Understood?"

"Understood."

"Then get aboard and do what they tell you. This tobacco has been curing all winter in a warehouse and needs to get to port. When the last boat is loaded, all of you will shove off together. There's food and fresh water on board for the trip. No drinking until you get to Yorktown. Understood?" he bellowed.

"Got it. No drinking," said Raven masquerading as Henson.

CHAPTER 11

It took all day for the small, slow moving barge-type scows to travel to Tappahannock, about thirty miles downstream. It was easy work managing to keep the hogshead roped together. But poling the heavy load in the old barges was a chore. There were three men aboard each boat, with the extra man relieving the front poler on a rotating basis. Raven didn't expect to ever do the rear poler's job since he was the one who kept the boat straight, off sand bars, and away from floating debris. Even though the barge-type boats were weighed down, with the spring current flowing in the Rappahannock, they made good time. They stopped for the night in Tappahannock. The river was almost a mile wide there, and there were many boats on the river. It was spring and there were a lot of goods—mostly tobacco—moving south.

Eight of the twelve men assigned to this tobacco convoy went off to the Scot's Arms for a pint, a meal, and a bed. They were the old hands and knew that one pint wouldn't get Beckett's ire if he was to find out about it. The new hires, which included Raven, were forced to sleep on board and guard the tobacco. It was a grievous insult, but he was tired after having only a few hours' sleep the night before and working all day on the river. He wanted desperately to be in Yorktown, so he decided not to put up a fight. The four men who drew the undesirable task of guarding the tobacco hogsheads slept in their individual boats. Harrison (the head boatman) and one other of the eight who would have a warm bed for the night brought the tobacco guards slabs of cooked pork and beans which they ate greedily before wrapping themselves in their blankets and falling asleep.

The way that Harrison carried himself made Raven suspicious. Having run a kickback scheme at Haslar Hospital for almost ten years, he had an instinctual feeling that Harrison was pocketing the money set aside for paid lodging for the four tobacco guards. He could pocket eight nights lodging for the four men if they were forced to sleep on the boats. Raven thought Harrison might need to be taught a lesson.

The next night at Deltaville, Raven's suspicions of Harrison were hardened. They were four of only eight other tobacco boats moored that night, and still the four new hires had to sleep in the boats. None of the other tobacco boats had night guards. And to make it worse, it rained hard that night, drenching Raven and the others under their wool blankets. That made Raven definitely want to teach his boat boss some manners.

It was late in the day when they pulled into the docks at Yorktown. Harrison was in the lead boat and the other three followed him to the unloading docks that had been pre-arranged. Harrison had made the trip for five years and knew the people who were buying the tobacco and trans-shipping it to England.

Raven and the other men rolled the heavy hogsheads off the scow and toward the warehouse. When they got one there, they tilted it upright and fetched the next one until the scow was empty. Given the weight of each hogshead, it was hard work and took the better part of two hours. They also had to contend with a lot of traffic on the wharf. There were a lot of boats unloading and loading goods, some river craft, and more than a few ocean going merchant ships.

Harrison gathered the twelve men together on the dock. "We have sleeping quarters at the Swan Inn for all of you. Rest tomorrow, or have yourself a grand old time, whichever it may be. This is a seaman's city and the attractions and pleasures are to be found, that's for sure. We start loading the merchandise at daybreak and take off in the same boats day after tomorrow. If you're not here to make the trip up river, it's too bad for you. We only pay when you come back to Port Royal."

One of the men yelped, "What'll we do for money while we're here?"

"You should have thought of that. If you borrow any from me, there's an interest charge."

With that, the men disbanded except for Raven who borrowed a dollar from Harrison, never intending to collect his other dollar that was owed him in Port Royal, nor pay back any interest to this schemer.

The men walked down the wharf marveling at all the goods being unloaded. Since they had just spent almost four days sharing a boat on the Rappahannock and the Chesapeake, Raven walked with his boat mates. They saw all types of goods on the wharf— hogsheads of rice, tobacco, and turpentine, bales of cotton for outgoing shipment. Incoming goods from England included clothing, wines and liquor, furniture, jewelry and silver plate, riding gear, and magnificent English made coaches, swords, firearms, books, and even a few slaves. Yorktown was a thriving shipping town in spring of 1772.

But Raven's main mission was to find a ship that would get him back to England. But before he did that, he couldn't waste any time waiting to get 'sailor protection papers' that would give him necessary clearance from suspicion.

Raven kept his eyes and ears open that afternoon, and the men found a tavern to get drinks and a meal. It was a boisterous crowd in the tavern. There were merchants, shopkeepers, dock rats begging drinks, an entire cacophony of Yorktown's finest. Seamen who were on the last days of their shore leave were drinking their pay at a record pace. The rum and beer flowed freely, but Raven nursed the small amount he ordered. He was listening to conversations around him, keeping his silence for the main part.

Raven saw a sailor at the bar reeling from his overindulgence in rum and proclaiming loudly that he was going to have a good rip tonight since it was his last night in Yorktown.

"Gonna ship out tomorrow on the *William*," he slurred. "Gonna be at sea for two and a half months. Gotta drink up."

Raven left his seat and sidled up to the sailor.

"Buy you a drink, sailor?" asked Raven.

"Why I would indeed like another, kind sir."

Raven got the bartender's attention and motioned for him to pour another run for the sailor who was obviously drunk.

"What ship did you say you are sailing on?" he asked the drunken sot.

"Tis the *William*, and she's loaded and ready to ship out with the morning tide. It's the first time I've sailed on her. Came over on another English ship and stayed in port through the winter. Had just enough money to see me through."

"What cargo would you be carrying? Which English port are you headed for?"

"Funny you asked me that, Mister," the sailor said slurring his words. "I believe it to be tobacco, rice, and turpentine. Dock men loaded it yesterday. All in hogsheads. All safely stowed. We'll be going to East Coles across from Portsmouth Harbor. That's when I get paid the real money and live well off the land for a month or two."

Raven took a step backward and sized up the sailor. He was about the same height, perhaps an inch taller, and close to the same weight. The sailor had a cap on which covered his unruly, but closely cropped hair. He didn't have a beard but still had a small black mustache.

"They call me Henson," said Raven. "What's your name?"

"My papers call me William Reynolds, but I go by Willy. I am a William sailing on the *William*," the sailor said, loudly laughing at his own joke above the din of the crowded tavern.

"What papers?"

"Why me sailor protection papers. I keep them safe in my billy-bag, I calls it. Proof I am not a runaway…a freeman and not a slave," the sailor bragged.

"You're white. You couldn't be a slave."

"Ah, my friend, that is true, but I could be a runaway. An indentured man. Papers prove I'm not. Port authorities are checking for runaways more and more."

The sailor suddenly lurched and reeled back on his heels, then steadied himself on the shoulder of another drinker who rudely shoved him into Raven.

"Hey, watch who you shove, matey," growled the sailor to the man who pushed him.

"Steady as she goes, yourself, swabbie!"

Raven stepped between the two drunks. "No need to fight. I'll help my friend home."

"All right, keep him outta my sea lane!"

Raven grabbed his new sailor friend under his armpit and directed him towards the door. "Early bell tomorrow, sailor. Let's be getting you to your berth."

"Ah, I guess. Lead me out the door and get me to the boarding house, will ya? I don't have my land-legs anymore tonight," said the drunken sailor as he teetered from one chair to the next while he weaved towards the door.

Outside in the fresh air, Raven asked which way to the boarding house.

The two of them reeled and stumbled down the cobblestone streets of the port town. Raven had the sailor in his grasp, and more than once prevented him from crashing into the window of a shop or stumbling into a passerby. They weren't the only two sailors on the wharf. It was a brisk evening, and because of the relatively large number of strollers finishing up their evening of bar hopping, Raven felt like he was hiding in plain sight. It was good cover for his evil plan.

He helped guide the sailor to the door of his room on the second floor of a stone structure two city blocks from the main wharf. When the door opened, the sailor named Willy fell onto the bed and immediately fell asleep. It only took a minute for Raven to find the drunk sailor's billy-bag. He rifled through its contents and found the 'sailor protection paper' he needed.

He lit an oil lamp and scanned the paper describing William Reynolds. It stated that he was a free American sailor. The document looked legitimate, bearing the imprint of an American eagle at the top. What it didn't do, and Raven was glad to see, was to describe the physical characteristics of this man who called himself William Reynolds—not age, height, or race. This was his ticket on a ship sailing to England.

He thought quickly as the drunken sailor snored loudly, passed out to the world, deep in the arms of Morpheus. He searched the sailor bag and found the man's personal razor. *I may not look exactly like him, but with his cap pulled on my head and a trimmed beard, I'll have as good a likeness as I need.*

He took the lantern to the small table which had a water pitcher, towel, and basin facing a small mirror, then began to trim his long hair and beard using the razor. It was an arduous process. He sharpened the razor every so often on the leather strap that Reynolds had. Within an hour's time, he had his hair trimmed down and his beard shaved to a mere stubble. He took the basin full of his cut hair, opened a window, and tossed the cuttings outside. He glanced down at the sailor who was dead asleep.

He had a decision to make. He could leave with the protection paper and get to the ship before this drunken buffoon did, and try to pass himself off as William Reynolds. He could leave this man alive to sail another day, but that would be foolhardy. The sailor could find the *William* in the morning, and Raven would be found out. It couldn't happen. Not when he was so close to sailing away from this wretched place of his bondage.

Raven pulled his sharp deer-skinning knife from his boot and went slowly to the bed where the sailor lay prone, stomach pressed onto the straw mattress, snoring loudly. He didn't want to attempt to turn him over and possibly wake him. He needed to be as quiet as he could. During his days at Haslar hospital, he had operated on many sailors' brains, both dead and alive. With all of the dissection he'd done, he knew exactly where the brain's connection to the spinal cord was.

He didn't hesitate. He leaned over, braced his knee aside Reynolds, carefully placed the tip of the knife on the back of Reynolds' neck, and with a forceful motion, plunged the sharp knife deep into the sailor's neck. Raven twisted the knife and moved it viciously sideways to sever the spinal cord. Reynolds made an involuntary lurch, but it was his last. He never made a sound.

When he was satisfied the man was dead, Raven got off the bed, pulled the blanket close to him, and sat down against the wall and tried to sleep. He had participated in so many deaths at Haslar hospital, had so many operations that ended in death, that he felt not one small twinge of remorse about ending Reynolds' life. He had killed with cold efficiency before. He would do it again. This man was just an obstacle to his true motivation—to get to England and exact his revenge.

◆◆◆

Raven awoke early after sleeping but a few hours. He quickly packed up Reynolds' billy-bag, and his blanket, then quietly strode out the door of the rooming house. He got to the wharf in a few minutes. There were a half-dozen three-masted sailing ships at the docks. It took him about fifteen minutes to find the *William*. The sun had not yet cleared the horizon, yet there were a dozen men busily milling around the *William*, some hauling trunks aboard, some going aboard the ship. Raven could see that there was two men, one with a musket, checking the papers of the men who wanted to go aboard the ship. Raven pulled out his newly acquired protection papers and boldly got in a line of six men waiting to get clearance to go aboard.

As he got to the top of the gangplank, the naval officer asked for his papers.

Raven produced them without so much as a good morning greeting. The more he appeared to be a sailor with a severe hangover from a rowdy last night ashore the better. This was an easy acting job that he could pull off with ease.

"William Reynolds is it?" the naval officer barked. "Where you from?"

Raven decided to go with his adapted version of the truth. "Neabsco ironworks up at Woodbridge."

"Never heard of it," said the officer. "Let me see your hands."

Raven thought quickly, but he obeyed the command and showed the officer his hands which bore the burn scar. The scar was mostly healed but it was still visible fourteen months after the magistrate in Portsmouth had ordered it before he was transported to the colonies.

"What's this scar?" barked the officer suspiciously.

"I was working in the forge, handled a hot iron," said Raven. "It doesn't prevent me from working on a ship."

"I suppose it doesn't," mulled the officer. "All right, the papers are in order, Reynolds. You can go aboard."

With some relief, Raven—now Reynolds—walked onto the ship and was met by the first mate, Klug.

"I'll show you where to stow your gear, Reynolds, isn't it? I met you a few days ago. How was shore leave?" said Klug with a friendly, bright morning attitude. "You seem a little different today."

"I did my best to drink myself to death," said Raven, now Reynolds, wanting to match the jovial nature of the first mate.

"Oh yeah, didn't we all. Well, stow your gear below and get back on deck, we're pulling out in the next two hours. We'll need everyone once the captain comes out of his cabin and gives the orders. What'll I call you?"

Raven stared for a moment up at the masts that were ready for their sails to be unfurled and carry him home to Portsmouth. Feeling more at ease than he had in months, Raven replied, "Just call me Willy."

CHAPTER 12

BRISTOL: EARLY SPRING 1772

"It's the black slaves from Jamaica, I swear!" said one of the members of the Bristol Medical group, raising his voice to be heard among the heightened tension and chatter in the meeting room.

"It's the India merchant ships. Has to be. It's the equivalent of the plague over there," said another.

"No. No. You both have it all wrong, I say. It's from the cowpox carried by the animals that infest the fairgrounds every weekend! It's animal based!" cried another nervous Bristol doctor, wiping the perspiration from his brow.

"Those people have been eating rotting meat all winter. What do you expect from decomposing pork? They'd eat it if it was green with mold!" yelled another.

"We've had the smallpox before. It was contagious and very dangerous. Lives were lost."

"It's the black-bird slave ships. They come back from the tropics filthy with typhus and the pox!"

The hue and cry were getting noisier and nothing of any value was offered. Only blame and pointing.

"You forget the filth that some of our own Bristol citizens live in. Gentlemen, gentlemen, please, sit down. We need to form a plan of action," said Dr. Robert Livesey, the unelected head of the group, who had help found the BMG.

"How did Dr. Hawkins get the smallpox then? Maybe he brought it back from London?" said one of the doctors with a dark, accusatory tone.

"He didn't bring it back from London. That trip was two months ago. I suspect he caught it during one of our Saturday medical visits to the Bristol poor," said Dr. Livesey, trying to calm the group.

Dr. Livesey continued to explain as calmly as he could, but he was up against the irrational fear of a small pox epidemic, and explanations could only do so much to quell the base fear of the medical men who gathered in Squire Trelawney's Bristol townhome early on a Saturday. Dr. Livesey and Squire Trelawney had hired messengers to contact the BMG and call them to an emergency meeting. This meeting was far from friendly, and rather than sample wines and tell ribald jokes, these men were scared of what might happen.

"Jim, rather Dr. Hawkins, and I were in the Bristol slums two weeks ago treating the sick, and what we saw made us gasp in horror. It wasn't pretty. A mother brought her nine-year old son to us. He was covered with smallpox pustules on his arms, face, legs, and abdomen. The pustules were big, black, and scabby where it was obvious that he had violently scratched them and torn them off. He looked like he was a monster from some other world. We did what we could on-site at the apothecary's shop where we'd set up receiving tables."

Livesey continued after settling himself. Reviewing the awful sight in his mind made him shudder. "I asked the mother when the illness began, and she said a week to ten days earlier. She said when he developed chills and a fever and began to vomit, she kept him in bed away from the other children."

"Well, you damn well better keep Hawkins away from anybody else. This is a most contagious disease," barked one of the physicians at the meeting.

"Of course," said Dr. Livesey. "He has been placed in quarantine at the BRI in a ward far removed from any other patient. I just left him in the care of my nurses and I'll go back before I venture home to tell his wife. He'll be quarantined. You can count on it. But there should be other measures taken. For example—"

"Stop the damn cattle from coming into town!" yelled one of the members of the medical group.

"Stop all incoming ships from docking!" said another.

Squire Trelawney shot back, "You can't stop Bristol's commerce, man. These are valuable goods coming to our docks." Of course, the wines Trelawney was importing from Portugal and Spain were very dear and were a large source of his revenue.

"Stop the blacks from congregating," said another. "They just breed filth among themselves!"

"Keep the poor in the slums. Don't let them roam the streets. They're the ones who are to blame. They have no hygiene whatsoever."

"Now just a minute," shouted Dr. Livesey, who had heard quite enough racist talk. "We cannot panic."

Livesey saw that he had to exert some control over the group. Although educated men, they could behave as a rabid mob just like any other crowd. That's exactly what he wanted to prevent. Somehow, they had to stem panic and have some procedures to forestall any spreading of this virulent disease.

"We don't know the exact starting place of this. All I can tell you is what Dr. Hawkins tried to treat during our trip to the poor of Bristol. It is two weeks since then. He came down with a bad fever and was vomiting yesterday, so I immediately secured him in the hospital room and left my nurses close by."

"What is it you want to do, Dr. Livesey?" asked Squire Trelawney, acceding leadership to Dr. Livesey.

"First, if you all agree, we must print up a warning and distribute it. I realize that it might start a panic, but if people see anyone with a strong fever, they must report it to the hospital so that person is taken out of circulation and quarantined. Do you agree?"

As a group, they all agreed loudly. Information and communication were key at a time like this.

"Secondly, Dr. McLaughlin and I will be going to the Bristol slums once again tomorrow and try to find anyone else who has a fever or any of the other signs. We'll need a coach and coachman to take those individuals to the hospital so they can be quarantined. Two of us can't possibly ferret out all the possible cases in one day. We need some manpower to do this work. Who will help us?" Livesey looked out to the group of twenty or so medical men, but not a one of them volunteered.

"Come now. This is for the survival of Bristol. The sooner we stem this the better. The sooner we quarantine the sick with smallpox the better. You know as well as I do that smallpox will blind or kill many more. Squire, what was the death toll during the epidemic at the turn of the last century?"

Squire Trelawney gravely cited the record. "The death toll was in the thousands. A smallpox outbreak could kill thirty percent of us if we don't stop it. It will kill or blind anyone. It doesn't discriminate—young, old, rich or poor!"

One of the physicians spoke next. "Of course, we need to stop this as soon as possible. Squire, I propose we go to city government and ban the weekend cattle fairs. It is a disease that is contagious in highly crowded conditions. Combine the crowds with any cattle that might be infected, and you have a two-headed monster invading Bristol."

"Will the city fathers ban all congregating? That will surely breed panic," one of the doctors said with a snort.

"If panic leads people to find anyone running a fever and report that person to a hospital and get them out of the general population, then let's have the panic, damn it. Segregation away from others is foremost, is it not!" shouted another.

"Yes, but we must have a thread of treatment that will work! What do you suggest? Dr. Maitland, remember him? He practiced variolation. The induction of active disease into the healthy," offered one of the doctors. "Dr. Charles Maitland successfully inoculated the five-year-old son of the British ambassador to the Turkish court under orders from the ambassador's wife."

"That was in 1718 and it was eventually outlawed!" yelled one of the members.

"No, it was not!" said another with a commanding voice.

The voices rose again, showing the impatience and lack of understanding of what needed to be done.

Once again Dr. Livesey spoke. "Gentlemen, gentlemen, this shouting and confusion is getting us nowhere. Here's what I believe we need to do. The Squire and I will see that the pamphlet is printed immediately. He will talk to the city government about suspending the cattle fairs. Dr. McLaughlin and I will make a trip to the Bristol slums tomorrow when the printing is finished and distribute them.

"But in the meantime, if you have a patient, please let one of the BMG know so we can all be apprised. Next, tell your patient and any nurses to apply a cold compress to the forehead and try to alleviate the fever as much as possible. As the body tries to expunge the toxin, the boils, the pustules will form. They tend to be red and white and hurt like the devil. For heaven's sake, do not allow the patient to scratch the boils and open them up. It will only spread the toxin and make matters worse. Keep the patient warm. If he or she develops chills, it's important to keep them warm."

"How long does the fever last?" asked one of the physicians.

"Maybe a couple of days. Maybe a week. It might kill someone who's not strong. This is a critical time," answered Dr. Livesey.

"How long has Hawkins had the fever?"

"One day by my recollection. I have to go see him now. Oh, and to help us, he recommended we contact Dr. Edward Jenner at the Hunter Museum in London. Jim met him, and he thinks this Jenner fellow can help us. He's devoted his medical studies to smallpox and cowpox. I sent a message yesterday afternoon by courier. Hopefully by Tuesday evening, he can be with us. I'll send word when he gets here so we can reconvene. Until then, if you have a patient who is showing symptoms, get him to a hospital. I've alerted the BRI to set up a segregated ward."

The group disbanded without any one of them volunteering to help Drs. Livesey and McLaughlin work the Bristol slums. Livesey wasn't surprised. He knew all too well these weak-minded, charlatan Christians who had forgotten the Hippocratic oath they had taken.

Dr. Livesey went straight to the BRI and practically ran up the stairs to the ward where Jim Hawkins lay sweating in his bed. Although Dr. Livesey had been with the same patient Jim had contracted the pox from, he felt all right. He thought that maybe it was possible for one person to catch the disease while another, although in the same vicinity, would not.

"How do you feel, Jim?" asked Dr. Livesey. He could tell from Jim's flushed face and his wet, hot forehead that the fever was strong. Jim couldn't be feeling well at all.

Livesey turned to Gwen, one of his nurses, and asked, "Has he vomited recently?"

"Not since yesterday when you brought him in. I don't think the fever has gone."

"Jim, what are your symptoms? I know you don't feel well but take the role of the doctor. Help us understand what is going on with you."

Jim lay flat on his back and his voice was weak, faint even. But he managed to talk if ever so quietly. "The fever is sapping my strength. Please, more water...more water, please."

Dr. Livesey nodded to Gwen and she rose to get Jim some water.

"I am feverish all over my body," said Jim. "I get chills that don't go away. I feel the fever spike sometimes as I lay here and then it goes away for a while. And my back aches as well. I've lost track of time. What day is it? How long have I been here? When did we see the boy with all the smallpox marks?"

"It seems it took about two weeks for this to come on you," said Dr. Livesey. He took the cloth from Jim's forehead, drenched it in the bucket of water near the bed, wrung it out, and placed it back on his forehead.

"Gwen, continue to give Jim the yarrow root tea, will you? More rather than less. Let's see if we can't break this fever as soon as we can. Also, take some apple cider vinegar from the hospital stores and place it on his forehead and stomach. It may help cool him down.

"Jim, do you think you can drink some apple cider vinegar tea? It might be a little tough to get down, but it should complement the yarrow root teas and draw out the fever faster. Gwen will stay with you tonight. I'll be back in the morning."

"What about Livian? What about Belle? Or Elizabeth or Margaret? I'll never forgive myself if I infected one of them when I went home after my visits to the slums."

"I'm leaving for home right now. Don't worry, Jim. Between us, Mac and I will cover this and protect them as best we can."

"Is Edward Jenner coming?" croaked Jim as he turned his head to the side and moaned in discomfort.

"I hired a rider yesterday to race as fast as he could to contact Jenner in London. It was an expensive private courier but there is no time to waste. We all need to know as much as we can, as soon as we can. I have no way of knowing if the smallpox is spreading in the Bristol slums, but I'm not optimistic. Look, whatever you do, if you spot a rash or a pustule, it's a sign that the toxin is leaving your body. Do not under any circumstances scratch the pustule and open it up. It will only spread the disease. You may see them on your arms or chest. Do *not* touch them, even though they burn. Do you understand? You'll be in for a rough time anyway. We'll lick this, Jim."

With that, Jim fell into a groggy, fitful sleep as Gwen rinsed another rag, placed it on Jim's forehead, and went to fetch some yarrow root tea. As she left Jim side, she asked Dr. Livesey the most important question. "Will Jim make it through this? His fever is very high."

"We have to rely on his inner strength, Gwen. Keep doing what you're doing. Thanks for doing this. Jim needs around the clock care if he's to pull through. I want to stay, but I must see to the people he has come into contact with at home. I'll be back as soon as I can. Your partner, Mary, will relieve you in the morning so you can get some rest."

Dr. Livesey bolted into his coach and told the driver to speed back to Livesey Acres as fast as he could safely make it. The roads were dry, as the spring rains had let up for a few days, so the road home wasn't muddy or rutted. Livesey had time to think about how he would break the news to his wife, Elizabeth, and Jim's precious Livian, but those thoughts were distracted by his medical training. He needed to check them for any sign of a fever. He knew that the women's first thoughts would not be of themselves but of their young ones—his own little daughter, Margaret, and the one-year old Belle. Smallpox was especially fatal among the young, and they needed to be protected as much as earthly possible.

A devout Christian, Dr. Livesey took time during the ten-mile journey to say a prayer asking the Almighty to spare the ones he loved. Smallpox wouldn't care if someone had led a physically hygienic life or a saintly one. Royalty or peasant, the killing pox would have no preference. Prayers might not be enough, but God might help them. Just a little bit of Divine help might pull them through this crisis.

When he arrived home, he was greeted by Elizabeth with a warm hug and a kiss. When Dr. Livesey stiffened at Elizabeth's hug, she clearly sensed something was amiss, especially since Jim wasn't with him.

"What's wrong?" she asked plaintively. "Where's Jim?"

"Please go get Livian. I'll tell you both at the same time," said Dr. Livesey, his face betraying his worry and apprehension.

When Elizabeth came back with Livian, they had both the little girls with them. Belle was fussing a little bit so Livian held her close while Margaret stayed at her mother's side. Livian had her ear horn with her so if Dr. Livesey spoke clearly, she would have no trouble understanding him. Of course, she was an expert lip reader, so her gaze settled intently on Robert's mouth who began his tale when the group was together in the parlor.

"It's not good news, I'm sorry to say. Jim is sick with a fever. He came down with it yesterday and I rushed him to the Bristol Royal Infirmary where he is being cared for by Gwen, my nurse. We can't be sure what caused the fever, but two weeks ago Saturday, we visited the Bristol poor section and we treated a child who had a severe case of smallpox."

"Smallpox! Oh my God," gasped Elizabeth, clutching her hand to her mouth.

"Oh no. Not Jim, too," moaned Livian, the words coming from her lips with anguish.

"We don't know for sure. We just don't know. But Jim was here with us last Sunday before he went with me to the surgery on Monday."

"Are we all infected with the pox?" cried Elizabeth, pulling Margaret closer to her in an instinctive motherly hug.

"Are we going to get it, too?" said Livian haltingly, with a glance to Belle in her arms.

"I don't know. People who have been in the same room, in the same bed as a stricken patient have still not gotten it. It all comes down to chance, or luck, or God's plan. I don't know. I'm just as upset as you are, but I'm a medical doctor and need to take whatever steps I can to save Jim and anyone else. Tell me, do either of you feel the least bit feverish?"

"No," said Elizabeth. "I feel fine."

Dr. Livesey turned and spoke directly to Livian so she could read his lips. He had been doing this since Livian was a little girl, so it came naturally. "Livian, how about you? You were in the same bed as Jim over these weekends. I think the pox was in a dormant stage. His fever didn't start until yesterday when the pox would have been at its most infectious period."

Livian had been straining to hold the restless child and her ear horn in the other hand. She had developed this ambidextrous skill since Belle's birth, but still had to struggle to hear clearly. It had been fifteen months since her miracle, but her hearing had only improved to a certain fixed low level of clarity.

"I feel good," said Livian carefully. She began to shake ever so slightly with concern and fear for her husband's condition.

"And Belle? Have you noticed anything with Belle?" asked a concerned Dr. Livesey.

"She is fussing a bit," said Livian, feeling the child's forehead. "Her forehead is cool to the touch."

Livian was scared for her baby like any mother would be for a defenseless child against the ravages of a killing disease. She had lost her own hearing at age three to a fever, and the threat of something that would affect their precious Belle would be an unthinkable attack.

"She was all right this morning. I haven't seen any changes. She's eaten but hasn't had her afternoon nap. Perhaps that's the reason for the fussing," continued Livian.

"Well, all I can ask is that you keep a close watch on her. And at the first sign of a fever, prepare the yarrow root tea to flush out the fever as soon as possible. And keep her warm if she seems to have the chills," said Dr. Livesey. It was clear he was trying to remain calm even though his close family was potentially affected.

"Elizabeth, same for you. Please watch Margaret. I have to go back to Jim. I asked the driver to stay and wait for me. Margaret, honey, come to Daddy."

Margaret, the bubbly young four-year old rushed to Robert's arms where he held her with a hug he could not easily release, even though the little girl wanted down from his lap soon after the first loving embrace.

Livian spoke with a determination that could only come from a strong woman of the countryside. "I am coming with you. My mother can watch Belle. The two of them are fast friends. I have to see Jim. Have you given him an oatmeal bath? It's a country cure for the chicken pox—fights against the itching. Maybe cool the body down against the smallpox?

"Thank you for mentioning it. I forgot about it," answered Dr. Livesey.

"I'll bring a sack of oatmeal with us. If he has a fever, maybe we can take it down with this," said Livian.

"Are you sure you want to come? Jim may be highly contagious right now. I want to keep him segregated from anyone else. Gwen is taking a huge risk, but she said she had a mild case once as a child and that her mother said she wouldn't ever get it again. Is that more country folk lore?"

"It is what I know," answered Livian. "I had the fever as a child. Maybe it was the pox. Who knows? I might not get it from Jim."

Elizabeth sat listening intently. She couldn't offer any country herbal medicinal lore. Elizabeth was raised in a wealthy home in Bristol and could only nod in agreement to what Livian was saying.

Dr. Livesey and Livian left in the coach within the hour. Livian carried her ear horn, a small bag consisting of a change of clothes and a bag of ground oatmeal. It was late Saturday night and the driver was paid to stay and return his passengers to Bristol.

It was going to be a late night for everyone, but time was short and the peril of Jim's illness great. The driver had been able to get his horse some food and water but there hadn't been much time to rest.

When the two of them arrived, they found Jim lying in a pool of sweat being tended to by Gwen who grew increasingly wearied and worried by Jim's condition.

When Livian saw Jim, all she could see was her husband in a bed surrounded by blankets, alternating between sweating and shaking from chills. She leaned over him and said his name three times before he could open his eyes and acknowledge her. He couldn't talk much as consumed as he was by his worsening condition. Gwen had given him yarrow root tea and some apple cider vinegar tea which Jim had promptly vomited. The teas were meant to bring the fever out of his body, but when the fever broke, he would be weakened considerably.

"Gwen," said Dr. Livesey, "why don't you go home and get some rest. Livian and I will take over and see Jim through the night. You've been brave and diligent in your care, and I know Jim would thank you if he could. Mary should be here in the morning, so if you could relieve her around mid-afternoon, I would appreciate it."

"Thank you, Dr. Livesey. I can't say his condition has improved over the last few hours. He's had some convulsions, too. I keep putting the cold cloths on his head and it seems to help temporarily, but the fever is still with him."

"Yes, yes, I can see his redness and his flushed face." Livesey felt Jim's forehead. "There's only a slight reduction in his red-hot temperature." Dr. Livesey let out a worried sigh as he pulled back the covers. "There's the start of a rash on Jim's chest and arms."

Dr. Livesey turned back to Gwen. "Livian and I will put Jim in an oatmeal bath in a few moments. Before you go, could you run a bath? The water doesn't have to be hot, just room temperature will be fine."

The three of them gently pulled Jim from his bed, stripped his sweat-soaked clothes off, and threw them in a corner to be destroyed. There was no need for modesty at a time like this when a man's life was at risk. Even though he was delirious, Jim could stand and make his way to the tub. They helped the naked, sweaty, and shivering man step into the bathwater. While he lay soaking, Livian took the sack of oatmeal and found a roller in a cabinet to grind the meal into as fine a powder as she could so the oatmeal and water could mix more easily.

Livian took the oatmeal powder and poured a few cups of it into the bath and mixed it in with her hands. Livian was a country woman with a proud heritage of persistence and hard work. She had been raised on Livesey Farms doing any number of labor-intensive chores. Swirling her hands in a bath of oatmeal mush was nothing compared to some of the jobs she had done over the years.

Livian turned to Dr. Livesey who was watching Jim's face and feeling his forehead to see if he was cooling down at all. "We used this oatmeal bath on Dad once when he came into contact with poison ivy," said Livian. "And my mom put me in an oatmeal bath when I had a rash from bug bites. It helped."

"I hope when we take him out that when the boils and pustules surface, he won't be tempted to scratch them. I can see that the oatmeal you prepared is well dispersed in the water. That's good. It means any anti-itch property it has will get to his skin.

As Jim lay in the oatmeal bath, Livian propped his head up to keep it from slipping down into the water. She spoke to him with soothing words. Even though it was unclear if he could hear her, she persisted, telling him that Belle was well and she, too, was okay and for him not to worry about them but to take care of himself.

"Dr. Livesey is here with us," Livian continued. "Gwen just left, and Mary will be here in the morning. We will stay with you through this."

She whispered softly to him any words she could think of, as she swirled the oatmeal water around his body. If it worked right, the oatmeal bath would forestall or lessen the severe itching that was expected with any kind of rash or pox. They had to prevent him from scratching any rash or pustules for fear of spreading them all over his body, creating lifelong scabs and making the pox even worse.

CHAPTER 13

FEVER DREAMS

*I*n my fever dream, I saw a wicked queen. She was in a large painting on the wall with her horrified mouth agape, eyes scared and perilous.

The dreams flashed to me in seconds, changing from one weird, inexplicable scene to another. My delirium seemed to intensify, then suddenly ebb. My body shook involuntarily.

I saw people rushing the house at Livesey Acres. They were crouched down on all fours like apes, crab-crawling with mean vicious scowls on their faces. There was a little boy in the parlor, scared as he looked outside. Was it me? The house was bigger and older than it is. In an instant, I was standing at the bottom of a steep set of stairs looking up to the landing. I turned, and the door to the house was open and I was frightened. The crawling ape-men were trying to get in. I slammed the door shut on them.

Then I was fighting Ozzy in the shed and he was putting his knee into my side. I was tumbling over the shed's bench and Livian hit him hard with the clay pot. Then I hit him in the leg with the shovel, breaking his kneecap.

I was burning up and I was in Jamaica chasing down Long John Silver, the pirate cutthroat who would sell his mother to save his own skin. I had the musket at Ozzy's throat threatening to shoot him in front of a crowd of strangers.

There was a canopy of trees overhead as I ran, hobbled with a chain on my leg, running after Long John Silver. Then the canopy of trees cooled me, and I could feel the sweet breeze.

Suddenly, without warning, I and my shipmates were aboard the HMS Romney and we were fighting thieves who wanted to steal our boat. One of the shipmates shot his musket at a thief who looked like Herman Franks. All scattered away except Franks. He glared at me with hatred. I grabbed a musket and was ready to shoot Franks, but I didn't fire the rifle.

I saw a multi-level cargo barge sail right before us carrying what looked like hundreds of green uniformed soldiers who were on our side. They took me to a roughhewn underground bunker in the middle of a field. The underground bunker had slabs of rock with blankets on top, and there were open rooms on the side with rubble everywhere.

I found myself in the Bristol slums with children who were coming after me with hate in their eyes. I stopped them with my voice and told them I wanted to go back to my wife whom I loved dearly. I had a choice to go back or stay and fight them. They wanted to bite me. Then I felt as if I was in a big pool of water that was so soothing.

I was inside a prison that had huge, high rock formations where the men in it subsisted by stealing from each other. Men hung down from the ropes and slid down to the rock formations like monkeys headed for me. One of those men was Franks, and he slid down the rope and headed straight for me with a large sharp knife when the dreamscape changed.

People were in a room having bad, horrible fun with a bleeding man on top of a table. A blond woman, whose face was grotesquely full of makeup, and a man were fighting over a box which had money in it. She had a pistol and fired it into his face. My face was burning. I could feel the burning. Then I felt the cool breeze from the trees above my head. This blond woman with the horribly painted face was straddling the bleeding man on the table, her face just inches from his.

Now, I am cool again. I am not burning. There is no fire. There is no aggression. I feel smooth and wet. My head clears. My eyes open and I see Livian's face next to mine. Sweet, beautiful Livian. Auburn hair, green eyes—I recognize her smile. She is happy. All I ever wanted was to see Livian smile. I hear her voice. "Jim, Jim, it's me, Livian. Oh darling, you've come back. We thought we lost you."

◆◆◆

Throughout the night, Livian worked with Jim while Dr. Livesey slept for a few hours on a nearby bed. She had urged him to do so. He had been up all day, traveled back and forth from Livesey Farms, and just as importantly, was needed the next day to have the energy to confront the growing peril to Bristol. During the night, Livian scooped out the oatmeal mush water and filled the bath three times, adding cups of ground oatmeal with each batch of fresh water.

Toward dawn, Jim's fever broke, and he was able to speak to Livian through her ear horn.

"I am so glad to see you," said Jim. "You're a sight for my weary eyes."

"We didn't lose you, Jim. We were here with you all night. You were mumbling in your sleep. You had convulsions. The fever was bad, really bad," said Livian.

Jim clutched the side of the bathtub. "I'm so weak."

"If you can stand up, I'll get a bucket of water and rinse the oatmeal mess off you. Now do be careful. Dr. Livesey is sleeping."

Jim eyed Dr. Livesey on the bed. "I can see him. He looks restful enough."

"I made him sleep. He said he and Mac were going to the slums in the morning to seek out any more victims of the pox."

"That's dangerous. That's where I got it. Are you all right? How's Belle, Elizabeth, Margaret?"

"They were fine when Dr. Livesey and I left them at Livesey Acres last night."

"I can't believe you were here all night," said Jim, looking lovingly into Livian's eyes.

"Yes. We relieved Gwen. Gave you three oatmeal baths. Now listen, Doctor Hawkins, you must be a good patient and not itch anything. See the rash on your chest and arms? They will become blisters and boils. If you scratch them they will spread, and you'll be the worse for it."

While Livian and Jim were talking, she scooped out the oatmeal bathwater, threw it down a drain, then walked a few steps to the pump to put fresh water in the bucket to wash Jim and rinse the oatmeal mush off his body.

"I didn't think to bring fresh clothes for you, but I did find a hospital gown. You need to get back into another bed. Not the same one you'd been sweating in. We'll cover you up, and in an hour or so, give you another oatmeal bath. In the meantime, I found some winter mittens in the closet and you should put them on."

"Winter mittens?" exclaimed Jim. "What on earth for?"

"To prevent you from using your nails to scratch your skin. These red marks are going to itch and burn. You cannot, under any circumstances, scratch them. Is that clear?" scolded Livian. She continued with a kidding tone. "Didn't your school teach you anything. Or is good old country folklore too mysterious?"

"All right, my love, anything you say," said Jim, smiling. It was the first smile he had managed in the last two days before the fever put him down.

◆ ◆ ◆

When mid-morning arrived, Dr. McLaughlin made his way to the secluded section of the BRI where Dr. Livesey was awakening, and Livian had just finished rinsing the second round of Jim's oatmeal bath. She helped slip the winter mittens over his hands as he climbed back into bed.

"I see the fever has broken. Now you're in for the boils, pustules, and rashes," said Mac. "You're still contagious."

"Thanks, Mac, I needed that," said Jim sarcastically. He was not at all happy that the second phase of the attack was about to begin.

"Give them a week or more to scab off. Do *not* touch them."

"Everybody keeps saying that. I know, I know, Mac," whined Jim.

"Contagious, still?" asked Livian.

Dr. Livesey came back after being in the washroom. "Yes, he's still contagious. Let me look under your shirt, Jim." Dr. Livesey looked at Jim's chest and arms. "At this point, it looks like a mild case. The fever must have been something, though."

"I had dreams of the weirdest things, people, apes, guns, knives, underground caves, men climbing down ropes. Even Ozzy and Franks were in my dreams. Really crazy."

"I am sure we don't know what you are talking about," said Livian. "Hungry, Jim?"

"Like you wouldn't believe"

"Climb into this other bed. I'll cover you up where you can rest and then I'll get you something to eat. Remember, don't—"

"Touch them, I know, I know. Oh, and, Livian."

"Yes, Jim."

"Anything but oatmeal. And, Livian. You're going to have to feed me with these mittens I have on."

◆ ◆ ◆

It was late morning by the time Drs. Livesey and McLaughlin were able to pick up the fliers that the squire had gotten printed on short notice. Because of his standing in the community as one of the richest men in Bristol, the squire could command the printer to get out of bed on a Sunday morning and get the single-sheet fliers printed—fliers that would warn the population of a possible outbreak of the smallpox.

The two of them went door to door and handed the occupants the flier that warned of the impending outbreak, and to bring anyone suspected of having a fever to the hospital. It was a tedious task that took the entire afternoon. They continued until they ran out of the printed material. They only came upon two children whose parents said were running a fever, and one child who had severe pustules on his arms and neck.

Because the two men were on a mission to contact as many people as they could, they instructed the parents to take the three children to the BRI. To make sure they were admitted, Dr. Livesey wrote a signed note telling the BRI staff that he was seeing to their care and to place the children in a segregated ward away from other patients at the hospital.

They stopped by the house where Jim had contracted the fever and were told that the infected child had died. They asked the residents if anyone else had the fever, and no one there said they were sick. It was odd, but it was possible that the child had not infected anyone else. Just possible.

Exhausted, the two men reconvened at the surgery and checked their own vital signs. Neither was running a fever, but both were dead tired.

"I can't believe the living conditions in the slums," said Mac, nursing a glass of wine and wondering how Livesey and Hawkins could bear to work there on Saturdays. "It's the running sewage in the streets, the absence of clean water, the filth in the homes. What they do with food storage and garbage is positively hazardous," he said with a weary sigh of resignation.

"I can't solve all of Bristol's problems, but the industrialists whose factories loom overhead and uphill of these low-lying areas should do their part to contain the runoff. Good God, man, their filth runs downhill into these people's streets and homes," said Livesey, with a definite tone of anger. "I go to church at St. Nicolas's with these captains of industry. They sing the Lord's praises out of the hymnbook on Sunday and do the devil's work come Monday morning."

"You need rest, Dr. Livesey," said Mac. "Go home and check on Elizabeth and Margaret. I'll spend the night with Jim at the BRI. We'll take a coach over there and then you can take Livian back to Livesey Acres as well. She was up all night with Jim, wasn't she?"

Livesey responded, "Mary came this morning to relieve her so she could sleep. And Gwen was to come this afternoon."

"If Jim's fever is gone, he'll have to wait weeks for the pustules to fester, scab, and peel off."

"I don't know how long the pustules are supposed to last or anything else about this. That's why I am hoping Dr. Jenner gets here from London. I expect him by Tuesday or Wednesday. We need more information. But he is still contagious. And then there are those three children who should be showing up at the BRI. I can't expect the staff there to treat them. But we must isolate them and follow some sort of protocol. If they have the fever worse than Jim, they could die. You could see from their emaciated conditions that they don't have much reserve or stamina to withstand this virulent attack of the smallpox."

CHAPTER 14

It was Wednesday night at Squire Trelawney's home in Bristol. The Bristol Medical Group was meeting there to hear what the young Dr. Jenner of London would share with them about smallpox. While waiting, they murmured and questioned each other about any cases of the smallpox they had seen since the last time they met. None had. But none of them had accompanied Drs. Livesey and McLaughlin into the Bristol slums that previous Saturday, nor tended to the feverish Jim Hawkins.

Standing in the parlor talking to Squire Trelawney and Dr. Livesey was Dr. Edward Jenner, who was all of twenty-four years of age. The older physicians of the BMG were already skeptical of whatever he had to say since he looked so young. How could he possibly know something they didn't? The egos of this group seemed to raise the tension level in the room even before Squire Trelawney asked for quiet and introduced the young physician.

"I know what some of you are thinking. I can see it on your faces. Well, listen, gentlemen, and listen well. This young man from Berkley has been studying smallpox since he was stricken with it at the age of eight. That he survived is a godsend. Some of you may know Dr. Hardwicke of Sudbury where young Jenner apprenticed before going to London. Jenner is currently finishing his studies at the London Company of Surgeons, and with Dr. John Hunter, and will be returning to Berkley to set up practice. We may not have an epidemic on our hands just yet, but we don't want one. Anything Dr. Jenner can help us with will be worthwhile."

Squire Trelawney sat down and faced Edward Jenner. The seriousness and gravity with which the squire introduced Jenner reduced some of the pre-conceived misgivings among the physicians and quieted them for the time being. But the uneasiness among them was palatable and the room could erupt any minute in finger pointing and accusations as the last meeting did.

"Gentlemen, I just arrived an hour ago, so I must be brought up to speed. Since the squire has mentioned some of my personal history I won't try to convince you of my competency, other than to say that I have been studying and experimenting with cowpox and smallpox ever since I was stricken. Tell me, how many cases have you discovered?"

Dr. Livesey spoke while sitting in a corner chair. "Four for sure—three children and Dr. Hawkins, who attempted to treat one of the children who died."

"Do you know the incubation time? How long the fever has been? Were boils, rashes, and pustules present?"

"Dr. Livesey attempted to answer. "The child who died was riddled with the boils of smallpox and may have infected others. The three children currently have fevers with no skin signs. Dr. Hawkins has been in the segregated ward of the BRI—"

"BRI?" interrupted Jenner.

"Bristol Royal Infirmary for about five days now," answered Dr. Livesey. "We think he caught the pox a fortnight ago. We were able to break the fever and he is starting to show boils. He has nurses with him constantly."

"Have you seen the parents, siblings, and others whom the victims may have come into contact with?" asked Jenner. "I need to assess the potential spread of the disease. I could give you a spiel about the history of smallpox, but it's more important to know the condition of the victims and the potential spread of the disease in the city with a population of almost 40,000 people."

Dr. Livesey spoke up. "We asked the parents of the four children if anyone else had a fever, but most of them were not home at the time, nor were they expected to be home. Many roam the streets stealing food or begging." Dr. Livesey shook his head. "It was pitiful."

"So generally, we don't know any specifics about who the children have had contact with?"

"That's the sum of it," said Dr. McLaughlin sitting next to Dr. Livesey.

"And Dr. Hawkins?"

"Other than ourselves and his family, we don't think he had contact with anyone. He came down with the fever this past Friday evening. We checked with his wife, my wife, and the children, and all seem well to this point," said Dr. Livesey, trying to allay fears of the possible spread of the smallpox. He noticed a skeptical glance from one of the physicians sitting in the parlor. He wondered if that man thought he and McLaughlin had the disease. Sometimes, a strange glare could reveal more than any words.

"Well, let me share a little of what I know that may be of help. Incubation can be from ten to fourteen days. That's when the fever starts. Yarrow root tea, ginger root tea, and some have found a strong citrus drink—like tea with the squeezings from a lemon—will bring the fever out to full perspiration. Prolonging the smallpox fever, as you know, is not welcome. You want the fever to bring out the toxins, and quickly."

"What about the pustules? When they come, can we lance them? Break them? What do we do with them?" asked an impatient member of the BMG.

"My experience is that a mild case will result in only a few rashes, pustules, boils, if you will. A virulent case will have much more. It is imperative that you *do not*, I repeat, *do not* puncture the pustules. They itch like the devil, but do not allow the patient to scratch them. Scratching them will only make it worse. It will spread the disease throughout the body."

"That's what we saw in the slums," said Livesey, his face grim. "The poor boy had no control. He scratched them until they infected his entire body and killed him."

"Dr. Livesey is right," continued Jenner. "Also, the tendency will be for you to put some tincture, some mercuric chloride or other harmful substance on the pustules. I assure you, it will only make it worse."

"Then what do we do? When the fever stops, if it does, and the pustules appear," shouted one of the BMG members. He looked worried, nervous. "What if my own family comes down with it? What should I do?"

"When the skin itches from the pustules or rash, bathe the victim in goldenseal and flaxseed oil. It will help take some of the itching away," said Jenner.

"We used an oatmeal bath on Jim Hawkins," offered Dr. Livesey. "It seemed to help. Plus, his wife, Livian, put some mittens on his hands to keep his fingernails away from the sores."

"Excellent ideas. Both of them," said Jenner. "Listen carefully. The pustules will eventually dry up, create scabs, and the scabs will drop off. However, if they are treated improperly, that's when the pitting and pockmarks occur."

"That's all well and good for treatment of the ones who get the pox, Jenner. But what about those who don't have it. How can we prevent the spreading of the disease? Is it even possible?" asked a physician in a gruff tone.

"There's variolation," said Jenner. "I have been experimenting with it for a few years now—"

"It's been condemned from the pulpit," said an angry member of the group from the back. "You're not going to take material from a diseased patient and insert it into a healthy person. Not here. Not in Bristol, you're not."

"Sir, I have done this experiment successfully in Gloucestershire.

The patient who is variolated gets a less severe case of the disease, and after two or three weeks, will be healthy and will not ever get the pox again."

"You cannot assure this, Jenner. You cannot be certain," shouted this physician who was now on his feet and gesticulating toward Jenner as if he were a druid from a century ago full of black magic.

"May I explain variolation, sir? If I may."

Trelawney stood up and said, "Let Dr. Jenner speak, will you. Save your questions, gentlemen."

Jenner took a deep breath, looked over to Drs. Livesey and McLaughlin as if to say, *you didn't say this was going to be a hostile audience.* "Variolation is not new. It has been done in Turkey, China, and even in Africa before it came to Europe or England. You remember the Lady Montagu who in 1718 had Dr. Charles Maitland variolate her son. He recovered. Maitland variolated the Princess of Wales in 1722. I have studied this. It can work."

"Why hasn't it become standard practice? None of us were taught it in medical colleges, no matter which English college we studied at. You want to know why?" shouted a member of the group. "Because it's against God's will, that's why! Maitland was rebuked by the Church of England. Edmund Massey's speech in 1722 condemned variolation as an abomination. He called variolation dangerous and sinful, saying that people should handle the disease as the biblical figure Job did with his own tribulations—without interfering with God's test for mankind. That speech was sent to every vicarage in England. That's how we know variolation was eventually banished. It rightly condemned variolation as we should today. The healthy survive, Dr. Jenner, the unhealthy ones do not. It is God's will that some should perish."

"Now wait a minute," cried Dr. Livesey. "An epidemic will take the rich and poor, Doctor. It will not discriminate."

"Where did you find the disease, Dr. Livesey? You found it in the slums. The poor and wretched, who don't have the brains God gave a goat, live there. You wouldn't live there. I wouldn't."

Jenner spoke up. His own young spirit leading him to argue with older, more seasoned medical men. "I know variolation will work. We have to accept that it will take experimentation. But what is science without experiments? What is science without questioning the status quo of our established knowledge? What is science without some failures? That is how we learn. If it worked for royalty in 1718, it can work in Bristol in 1772."

"Surely you don't expect us to line up every citizen and inject a live disease into a healthy person?"

"Yes, yes, I do," responded Jenner.

From the back of the room, the man who had blustered his Old Testament quote yelled, "I'm leaving. I will treat those who present themselves to me, but I am not going to the Bristol slums to seek the disease. Good night, gentlemen." He left along with six to eight others. All that remained were a small handful of the members, Dr. Livesey, Dr. McLaughlin, and Squire Trelawney.

"Dr. Jenner, I apologize for your reception. I had no idea some of these men would turn on you like this."

"No apologies necessary, Dr. Livesey. But the evening is not lost. If you don't mind, I'd like to see Dr. Hawkins and see how he is doing. Perhaps the pustules have appeared and will shed some light on what we know, and perhaps tell us something we don't know."

With that, a group of eleven men called for their coaches and went to the BRI to see Dr. Jim Hawkins to examine him and the three children who were also in a segregated ward.

CHAPTER 15

"Well, Jim, you can see, you've become quite popular," joked Dr. Livesey, as eleven members of the Bristol Medical Group stood near his bed in the BRI.

The men took quick turns peering at Jim's sores and pustules. He didn't have many, which was a good sign that the pox hadn't ravaged his entire body. There were only a couple on his arms that looked like they would soon form the puss filled sacs associated with smallpox. The mittens he wore kept him from scratching the ones he did have.

"I still itch like crazy, Dr. Livesey," said Jim. He had gotten some of his strength back with Livian's, Gwen's, and Mary's careful, dedicated, attentive nursing care. The oatmeal baths had help soothe his skin and reduced, if not eliminated, the insane desire to scratch the pustules.

Dr. Edward Jenner spoke next. "Jim, all my research points to a longer stay in the hospital. You cannot leave and join the rest of the Bristol population until the sores have scabbed and fallen off. It could take weeks for that to happen. The good news is that once you have healed, you will never contract the smallpox again. From what I see here, you have a mild case."

"The fever didn't feel mild, Dr. Jenner. Not in the least. I thought I was going to die."

"And I thought so, too," piped up Livian, whose tired eyes revealed a woman who had been at her husband's side since early Sunday—three full days ago.

"He's still contagious," said Dr. Jenner. At that, ten men other than Jenner took almost involuntary steps away from the patient. "Yes, I would recommend no one touch this man until the scabs have started forming over the boils. By that time, the disease has run its course and he won't pass it along to others."

Jenner nodded at Jim. "We'll leave you in the hands of your nurses and doctors. You couldn't ask for better care." Dr. Jenner looked at Livian and asked, "Can you continue the baths? They'll help him avoid scratching and will soothe his skin. The baths won't take away all of the torment, but they'll help."

Livian nodded at Dr. Jenner, letting him know she'd keep giving Jim the oatmeal baths.

"Gentlemen, shall we see the children who were admitted? Dr. Livesey will you lead the way?"

Livesey took the group to another ward where there was a single nurse standing guard at the door to the ward. She had keys in her hand and only opened the door for the medical personnel who wanted to see the sick children.

"Nurse, I don't see anyone tending to the children, putting cold compresses on their heads, or anything."

"I'm sorry, Dr. Livesey, but the nurses I commanded to be here have rebelled. None of them have been exposed to the smallpox before and they were deathly afraid. I don't blame them."

"I see," said Dr. Livesey with a measured degree of disgust at nurses not wanting to do their duty. But he also understood that they didn't want to catch the smallpox and carry it back to their families.

"Let's see how bad the fevers are, shall we?" said Jenner, sounding eager to see the young ones.

As they surrounded the children's beds, they could see why the nurse was worried. Dr. Livesey felt the pulse of each, and it was obvious that one of the children had died since coming to the hospital.

"Nurse," said Livesey, trying to keep his temper. "When were these children brought here?"

"This morning, Dr. Livesey."

"Were they all alive when they arrived?"

The nurse wrung her hands, looking nervous. "I can't be sure. The parents brought them in here and left immediately. I hate to say it, but it was like they were disposing of them. They were afraid for their own lives. They left before we could ask them any questions. I'm so sorry."

"You should be," said Livesey, no longer able to keep calm. "This child is dead. Regardless of when he died, his parents and the hospital failed him miserably. Did they leave names, addresses?" He didn't wait for the nurse to answer. "We need to find them. Determine if they, or their other children are sick. Let them know about this child. Does he even have a name, good God, woman!" Dr. Livesey exploded, unable to contain his outrage. "Get an orderly to remove this dead child from this room, immediately!"

"Let's talk about what we can do for the three who have the fever," said Dr. Jenner, shifting the focus to the ones who could be saved.

"I'll ask Gwen and Mary to come to this floor and tend to their fevers," responded Dr. Livesey after catching his breath. "Both tell me they are not susceptible to the disease. At least I hope not. They have been brave and persistent with Jim upstairs and they can help here for a while. But they need their rest, too. I guess they could rotate their duties for a couple of days."

"Dr. Livesey, I hate to press you on this since you and Jim have been the locators of the smallpox in the Bristol community, but we need to find these children's parents and siblings as soon as possible. If we can, we need to find the children's playmates too and check them out."

Dr. Livesey was silent for a moment, trying not to get overwhelmed. "This is a bigger job than just Dr. McLaughlin and I can do, Dr. Jenner. We did not intend or want to be the public's full-time health service. We put fliers out. Don't we have to wait for the public to come to the BRI? Searching for them is almost impossible. The number of other children infected and passing on the disease could have already multiplied. We don't have the staff for an all-out epidemic. I doubt the BRI does either. We couldn't get cooperation from half of our medical group. They won't come here and tend to smallpox victims. It simply is not going to happen. All we can hope for is that the parents caught their child's fever early and that they brought them here before they could spread the disease."

Jenner looked skeptical. "That's quite a wish."

Livesey addressed the small group of doctors. "I'm going downstairs to administration and tell them what I've found. You gentlemen should go home, and in the morning, go to your surgeries. If you have anyone report a fever, send word to the BRI administration and get them here as soon as possible. Make sure to document name, parents, addresses, and associates that may have had contact with that patient so he or she may be checked out. You should check in with the BRI each day, if you can, and see if there are any new cases that were admitted. Don't rely on me or Dr. McLaughlin for that information. I will forewarn them of this potential influx. As of now, we only know of six cases: Dr. Hawkins and the five children, two of whom have perished. We'll have to wait and see what develops. Say a prayer that this is a small outbreak. If it gets larger, every one of us and our families will be in jeopardy."

As Dr. McLaughlin and Dr. Livesey walked Dr. Jenner back to his hotel, the three of them felt hopeless in the face of this potential disaster. As individuals they could do very little. Even as a group, they could do little more. If the disease spread, there would be little hope. Smallpox had killed thousands, even millions throughout history. This could be their undoing. As scientists, they knew there was a cause. But they didn't know exactly what it was, and exactly how to eradicate it.

Jenner spoke to break the tension. "I'll be going back to London tomorrow. I'll be finished with my studies in a month or so—probably the middle of June. I've already told Dr. Hunter I'll be returning to Berkeley to set up my practice, which as you know, is only 25 miles away. I prefer the country life where I can continue my work. Let London have its ways, its customs, its chaos, and its fashion trends. I can get more smallpox research done in the country. Count on me to help if you need me, will you?"

"Of course, Dr. Jenner," said Dr. Livesey. His demeanor had not changed since they had started walking from the BRI. He was solemn, serious, and downcast.

"Thank you for coming," said Mac. "We regret you didn't get as much acceptance from the medical group as we hoped you would."

"It's not the first time science has been scoffed at," said Jenner. "It won't be the last, I assure you. But we must press on. On the bright side, Jim's case looked mild. I expect him to be back to work inside of three weeks."

"We surely hope so," said Dr. Livesey as they stopped in front of Jenner's hotel. "We wish you God's speed back to London."

After the three parted ways, Livesey and McLaughlin didn't share another word until they got back to the BRI and went straight to the children's room where Gwen was putting cold cloths on the children's foreheads. They discussed the rotation with Mary for the next day and then went to Jim's room. He was asleep. So was Livian. They put their heads down on pillows on separate empty hospital beds and fell asleep until morning. Thursday was going to be another day full of fear and dread.

◆ ◆ ◆

When the group awoke in Jim's hospital room the next morning and had some light breakfast from the hospital's cafeteria, Dr. Livesey called for a coach to take Livian back to Livesey Acres. Then he spoke directly to Livian, so she could read his lips.

"Livian, please go back to Belle and check her to make sure she's all right, will you? And send word to us on Margaret. I have to stay in town. This problem may get bigger and I don't want to carry anything back to Livesey Acres that might hurt Elizabeth, Margaret, or anyone else. Mac and I will be fine. I'll stay here, at the surgery, or at Mac's place. We'll be here seeing to Jim's needs. You need some rest. We have Gwen and Mary to help us." He hoped Livian would take his suggestion and get some rest at home.

Livian spoke in a tired but upbeat voice, "I'll take your advice, but you must let me know each day how he is doing. I'll come back Sunday. Perhaps my father can drive me into town."

"Do one more thing for me, will you, Livian? Could you and Maye knit a dozen pair of mittens for these kids? I think we'll need them in a week or so."

"Robert," interrupted Mac, "don't ask Livian to do another thing. I have an idea for putting some mittens together. Let's have Livian stay away from Bristol for a bit, eh? I can take care of the mittens."

"Okay, Mac, we'll leave the mitten manufacturing to you. You Scots always have had a knack with plaid, haven't you," said Dr. Livesey with a weak attempt at humor.

The two men helped Livian pack up her belongings. She kissed her husband gently on the forehead and bade him goodbye for a few days. Jim's itching and torment would last for a week, until the pustules scabbed, dried up, and began to fall off.

◆ ◆ ◆

The two men spent a long day at the surgery on Thursday, and it was Friday before Drs. Livesey and McLaughlin checked back with the BRI to see if more children or adults were admitted to the hospital with a fever. When they arrived at the hospital, they had a conference with the administrator, Gaylen Jones, to check on the status of the children and to see if there were any new smallpox cases.

Because Drs. Livesey, McLaughlin, and Hawkins had been

volunteering at the BRI, they had a good relationship with Gaylen Jones. They had been giving of their time and expertise, and he reciprocated with blood sample slides for Mac to use with his microscope comparisons.

Allowing smallpox patients inside the already overburdened hospital and overworked staff was a stretch for the hospital administrator, but he didn't take lightly the potential for a real epidemic. These men had worked in the slums, and even though they brought the children here rather than let them die in their mother's arms, Gaylen Jones had limits to the number of rooms he could extend to the smallpox cases. He didn't want to endanger his staff and other patients. It was a tough call for him. If the number of cases ballooned, he might have to call an end to the space he provided. He was a practical administrator, and these were charity cases. They added costs to his operation without any hope of revenue.

"We had three more sets of parents drop off a total of three children with fever this morning. None of them left names or addresses. They're all frightened, and I don't blame them. We placed them in the same segregated ward as the other children and assigned some nursing staff to tend to them."

"Thanks for the update, Gaylen," said Dr. Livesey. "What kind of shape were they in?"

"I'll leave that assessment to you. What I need from you are nurses. Ours are too afraid to deal with smallpox."

"I have an idea," said Mac. "Let me contact Dr. Jenner in London. He has run across the smallpox or cowpox in his rural Berkeley community. He tells me that milkmaids who have had the cowpox tend to be immune to smallpox. Maybe he can send a few down here. If you pay them for their time, of course."

Jones looked relieved. "I'll do that. How soon can they be here?"

"I'll send a courier today. Maybe he can round up a few in a couple of days. It's a four-hour coach ride to Berkeley. If he can send a courier with a response by tomorrow, you might have help by Monday, but I can't promise anything."

"Let's hope the milkmaids will agree to come," said Jones. "We have one nurse who was brave enough to take these cases. She says she had the pox as a child. But she'll be worn out in a day."

"I can't ask Gwen or Mary to work with the children long term," said Dr. Livesey. "They've been with Jim Hawkins around the clock for almost two weeks. We'll go and see him now. I hope he's showing progress."

With that agreement, the two doctors went upstairs and saw Jim Hawkins. He was sitting up in bed while Gwen fed him.

"How's the patient, Gwen?"

"The itching is getting less demanding," offered Jim with a hint of relief in his voice.

"I asked Gwen," joked Livesey. It was hard to make light of this situation, but Livesey knew he could tease Jim a little bit.

"The pustules are formed. I've actually tried to count them, and their number has not grown," said Gwen. "They appear fully formed."

Livesey and McLaughlin took a careful look at Jim's sores on his arms and chest. "Jim, take heart, the toxin is leaving your body. Give it another week, these will scab, and according to Jenner, they'll fall off by the end of the next week and you'll be able to go home."

Jim's shoulder's slumped. "Two weeks before I go home? I don't want to stay here a moment longer than I have to."

"Remember how contagious this smallpox is. Please remember," said Dr. Livesey. "We have six children in another ward with only one brave nurse tending to their fevers. People are afraid, and I don't blame them. If we get any more next week, and you're rested and back to health, I may have to ask you to do nursing duties here at the BRI. I'll ask Jenner to send some milkmaids down here to help nurse these kids, but if they don't come, you're enlisted."

"Drafted? Impressed into service as it were?"

Dr. Livesey gave Jim a tired smile. "Afraid so. According to Jenner, if you survive the pox, you won't get it again. It's a rare characteristic that we'll have to take advantage of. But how do you feel aside from the itching?"

"All right, I guess. Gwen and Mary have been super to me. Really wonderful."

"Nothing like great nursing care is there?" opined Dr. Livesey. "Mac and I are going to take a look at the other patients. We've kept them away from you since you're in the later stage of the breakout and they're right in the middle of it."

"Robert, I want to take Jim's blood samples for our lab specimens," said Mac. "Perhaps take a very small amount from under one of the more advanced pustules. We can use the slides and compare Jim's to what the other patients have at a different stage of the disease."

"That's wise in one regard and questionable in another," said Dr. Livesey.

"What do you mean?"

"While it would be good to have the comparable evidence, I don't think we should break any of Jim's pustules for fear of spreading it. He's almost out of the woods, so I would hate to have him relapse because we wanted a sample."

"I see what you mean. Perhaps, I'll wait until the very end when the scabs are dry and breaking off."

Livesey nodded in agreement. "Much safer, I would think. Jim, we'll leave you in Gwen's hands for the moment while we look in on the children. Our hopes are not high. Not at all."

There were six children in various stages of the smallpox fever in the isolation ward. There was one nurse, soaking cloths in cold water and applying it to the children's heads. The moans of the fevered children filled the room, and the audible sounds of children in pain and feverish dreams was otherworldly. It was a haunting sound that might stay in the hospital ward forever should the children perish there.

The nurse greeted the two doctors. "My colleagues have left, Doctors. Perhaps Mr. Jones alerted you to this. They would rather quit than tend to these sickened children. I can't blame them, but I can only do so much. I'm only one person."

"Granted," said Dr. Livesey. "I'm sorry. What's your name?"

"Harriet."

Thank you for your bravery, Harriet. I'm sorry I yelled at you a couple of days ago. I was distraught. We won't forget your service. What have you been able to do for them?"

"They seem to be in different stages. Only one of the original three has started to break out. I have tried to give them some water, but they vomit it back up. They're not in very good shape."

"We're trying to get you help," Dr. Livesey sighed. "Some nurses may be able to join you in a couple of days. This is a dire situation we find ourselves in. I am just going to have to call Mary, our surgery nurse, to come and help you. She has tended to Dr. Hawkins in the other ward and knows what to do.

"We gave him yarrow root tea to bring out the fever faster. We think apple cider vinegar tea will hasten the end of the fever as well. It's difficult to keep down, however. The children may vomit it right up. If you run out of the yarrow root, takes some lemons and add it to some tea. That should help bring out the fever as well. We do not want the fever to lengthen. But there's a danger to this fever. If it spikes, we have a danger of losing someone."

"I'll get the kettle going, Doctor." With that, Harriet retired to the nurses' station and left Mac and Livesey to look at the children individually.

The two physicians changed the damp cloths on the children's foreheads, and when Harriet brought the tea, they tried to help each child take a swallow or two. One child had developed some early rashes. McLaughlin scurried to a cabinet, and with a scissors and thread, cut up a sheet and fashioned a pair of make-shift mittens which he tied around the child's hands. It was a minor attempt, but it could work to keep the poor child from literally scratching himself to death.

While he had the scissors out, he made three more pair. They were simple triple-plied mittens without thumbs that could be tied around the wrists. Whether they would work for children with an instinct to scratch, and no parent around to caution them against scratching the fiery pustules that were sure to form, was only a wish and a hope.

At Dr. Livesey's urging, Gwen went to the other ward to help Harriet. She carried a sack of oatmeal with her with the intention of giving the fevered children oatmeal baths. They would be doing this night and day for the next four days if all went well. By then, they might have reinforcements from Berkeley.

The two doctors bade Jim Hawkins farewell and left the hospital after checking back in with Gaylen Jones. Surprisingly, no new patients had been brought in. It was curious, considering how many other children the sick children upstairs in the ward may have come into contact with. The three of them wondered aloud about this, but knew that it could be just ignorance, ignoring the flier they had distributed in the slums, or dumb luck. They couldn't be sure.

They took a hansom cab for the ride to their surgery to see if anyone needed their help there. When they arrived, they sat in the office and went over their plans. They could go to the slums and try to ferret out new cases of the pox, but that could be more than laborious. It could be dangerous. Neither of them had any symptoms and they needed to stay healthy to help those who did come down with smallpox. They could go to Livesey Acres and see how the women and children were getting along. But with Livian there tending to them, the children and the rest of the clan were in good hands. They decided to stay at Mac's rented rooms for the weekend. They'd send a message via courier to Livesey Acres saying they would stay and monitor the crisis and return when it was feasible.

◆ ◆ ◆

On Saturday, they took a hansom cab to the BRI. To their astonishment, they found that no new cases—children or adults—had checked into the BRI. They talked to Gaylen Jones, who along with all the staff of the hospital, checked in for work for the weekend, except for the nurses who had quit rather than risk caring for the children with smallpox.

"I sent a courier to all the other Bristol hospitals, and remarkably none reported any cases being admitted. Have we dodged a bullet here, gentlemen?" offered Jones.

"I'm not willing to say," said Dr. Livesey. "Jenner said incubation is anywhere from 10 days to two full weeks. We know the children upstairs have the fever and the pox. When they contracted the disease, we can't be sure. They certainly can't tell us. Have you heard from Harriet and Gwen? Are all the children still alive?"

"Some. The fever has broken for one, but killed another."

"That's three dead that we know about. We'll do what we can. We're going to look in on the children upstairs. Please let us know if there are any more cases," said Livesey as the two of them rose and exited.

Upstairs, they saw the remaining children who were in the last throes of their fever states. McLaughlin found the mittens he had made and gave them to the children, with stern instructions not to scratch any of the rashes. He could only hope they would listen to him. The urge to pick apart the fiery pustules was so strong, it would take a huge effort to restrain from picking and scratching.

The nurses said they were giving the surviving children the oatmeal and goldenseal baths. The hospital had a limited supply of goldenseal. It would take a week or more to send in an order to LongAcre Supply to get more.

The remaining children could understand what Mac was trying to tell them. Dr. Livesey also took the time to speak to them about how dangerous and deadly it could be to scratch the pustules. "The disease killed three children almost the same age as you," he warned. "If you follow what the nurses tell you to do, you could be home in three weeks. Now won't that be good, eh?"

"I want to go home now," whimpered one of the children.

"I do too," said another.

"I know, but that's not possible," said Dr. Livesey. "You must wait until the scabs fall off. You don't want to infect anybody else, do you?"

"No," said one child.

◆◆◆

When the BMG met the next Tuesday, there were no new cases of smallpox reported. Livesey and McLaughlin were astonished. Happy, yet astonished that the children who'd died and the children who'd come through the ordeal had not spread the smallpox any further in their communities.

As the BMG milled around in Trelawney's parlor, Livesey kept thinking that the disease had gone underground. He speculated that nobody reported any cases for fear of being ostracized from their own communities. He couldn't be sure. If someone turned up at the BRI or another hospital, they would have to deal with it. For now, he could hope that the violent killer was dormant once again.

With deference to their own health and that of their families, they did not go door to door in the Bristol slums looking for additional cases of unexplained fever or the breakout of the smallpox disease. None of the BMG wanted to go and do what Hawkins, Livesey, and McLaughlin had done, to put their own lives at risk to save others. If Bristol was spared this time, they could only hope that smallpox wouldn't rear its ugly head again any time soon.

CHAPTER 16

The *William* took almost two full months to reach the East Cowes warehouse on the Isle of Wight. The *William* wasn't a big transport ship, and since she was laden down with hundreds of hogsheads of tobacco, rice, and turpentine, she was almost ungainly as she lumbered her way up the coast of the Americas. The sea current and the favorable winds pushed her at a speed of roughly six knots past Boston, and the British North American headquarters for the British Royal Navy in Halifax, Nova Scotia. When she went past St. John's at Newfoundland, she was in the open seas and kept a heading that would take her to the English coast and a rich harvest of British pound sterling for the goods in her hold.

Raven had spent the two months aboard doing his duties as Willy Reynolds whose "sailor protection papers" lay carefully tucked away in Reynolds' billy-bag which he had stolen when he took Reynolds' life with his sharp blade back in Yorktown.

Raven had taken a new name every time it suited him. He'd erased his past as Franks. For these two months, he was Willy the sailor to anyone who addressed him on board as the ship headed for Portsmouth, England.

Raven worked as directed and never once disobeyed an order. This wasn't easy at first. When he was Franks, it wasn't in his nature to take orders, because as surgeon back at Haslar Hospital, he practically ran the place and did whatever he wanted. But on board the *William*, he had to survive and get to the English coast without trouble, so taking orders—however odious or dangerous—was the rule of the day. He cleaned the decks, operated the bilge pumps on occasion, reefed and unfurled sails at eighty feet in the air (with nothing but a rope for a foothold), sewed netting for catching the fish that fed him and the crew, and drank his beer and grog with the rest of the men.

Although physically demanding at times, the work was brainless, and for a man with his intellectual cunning, was easy to accomplish. As long as he did his work, the rest of the crew and his superiors left him alone. Because the voyage only took two months' time, none of the sailors were looking to make friends. It was a paying job to them and nothing more.

The prevailing west by northwest winds off of Labrador and Newfoundland pushed them out into the Atlantic. It was an easy voyage for the slow-moving ship. The northern Atlantic was at its calmest in late May and early June.

A week before they would sight Falmouth on the southwestern edge of England, Raven prepared for the landing. Because he was on the prison ship, *Jonathan,* some fifteen months earlier, he couldn't be sure if anyone in Portsmouth would recognize him. He didn't want to take any chances. Even though the tobacco, rice, and hogsheads of turpentine would be unloaded into a warehouse in East Cowes, he and his shipmates would undoubtedly take a ferry for the seven-mile trip to Portsmouth where he had been convicted in open court and imprisoned. He worried he might be recognized. If found out, and the constabulary caught him, they would hang him on the spot. With this on his mind, he decided to radically change his appearance.

He had always worn his hair long at Haslar and in the colonies and thought that this and his full black beard gave him a certain disguise. But now it was time to change his look. He found out who cut hair aboard ship and got a close cut of his black hair down as far as was safely done with the rusted, worn out scissors used by the unsteady hand of the rum-drinking sailor. He finished the job privately. Taking soap and water, he lathered his scalp and used a razor to shave his head almost bald. One of his mates saw him doing this near their berth.

"What are you doing?" asked the sailor

"What does it look like I'm doing!" replied Raven who was known as Willy.

"Well, Willy, if I had to guess, I say you was either trying to look like you once did before you was in Yorktown, or you're trying to look completely different than you once did."

"Such a smart guy, you are," said Raven sarcastically. He didn't like personal questions and had not answered any during the two-month journey no matter who tried to engage him in conversation. He wanted to be known as someone who kept his mouth shut. He didn't want to know anything about anyone else, and certainly wasn't about to tell anyone where he had been.

After he shaved his scalp, he trimmed his beard down to mere stubble, then shaved everything except his black mustache. He looked at himself in the mirror and thought he needed an extra touch that would make him look different, so he attached a ring in his left earlobe. It was a small stroke of vanity, but it made the costume change complete.

◆ ◆ ◆

The *William* passed Falmouth and Plymouth and finally set anchor in the bay off of East Cowes. Within a day, the harbor master was rowed out to them, accompanied by three armed soldiers. It was the harbor master's responsibility to see that the ship was free of any overt diseases, and that the cargo on board matched the manifest. Then he made a surprise inspection of all the sailors. He wanted to see their papers. Each man filed in a straight line as the captain groused about the disrespect and indignity that a lawfully chartered ship flying the British flag was being subjected to. The harbor master told him to shut up, and that under British law, he had the right to make sure that all the sailors were freemen and not escaped convicts.

Raven stood with his papers in hand as did the others. Some had papers that were in shreds but at least had some writing on them declaring their citizenship and country of origin. When "Willy" handed his papers to the harbor master, he had determined to say as little as possible lest he get into an argument with someone with the brains of a pier post. The harbor master had soldiers with their muskets so there was no running for cover or diving into the Solent if he was found out. Thankfully, Willy's papers satisfied the gruff overseer of the laws of his Majesty, and the crew was approved to land.

The captain used minimal sail to carefully guide the *William* into the dockside port location that the harbor master had allocated it. It wasn't an easy or quick task. The harbor was full of ships with cargo. The late spring and early summer weather meant that there was a great deal of commerce, and the number of boats overwhelmed the available port stalls. The *William* had been given clearance to unload its cargo and all hands were on deck to work the sails and reef them as necessary to give the captain and the first mate all the flexibility they needed to get the ship safely dockside.

"Willy" had one more set of tasks to perform before he and the crew were released with their pay script that they could take to the paymaster ashore at Portsmouth to get their well-earned cash. The crew worked hard below in the cargo hold to rope off each individual cask—be it tobacco or turpentine—and move the heavy hogsheads individually to the opening in the deck. There, they would be hoisted by other crewmen on deck with a pulley system that was strung on ropes from one mast to another.

Once the cask made it above the height of the ship's side, dockmen would haul on another rope and gently bring each hogshead to the ground and roll it up a ramp to a horse-drawn cart. From there, a fully loaded cart would be taken to the warehouse. It was a time-consuming, labor intensive job and Willy worked as hard as anyone even though his head spun with anticipation for finishing this shipboard life and getting on dry land. He had survived prison ships, chains and shackles, and the disgusting life as an indentured slave. He wasn't about to do anything that would keep him from the revenge in his black heart that had been the sustenance on which he had fed for these many months.

The unloading process took close to three days, one hogshead of tobacco or turpentine at a time. The sacks of rice were easier to handle, although it still took manual labor to haul the sacks to a pallet that was summarily lifted to the deck, then slid sack by sack down a ramp from the boat to the dock where dockmen subsequently lifted them onto carts. Someone else owned the merchandise and someone else bought the goods and someone else was paid to store them until they could be transported to the mainland. It was none of Raven's concern. He just wanted to do his job and get off the boat.

Raven lined up with the other crewmen and received the script he could cash ashore for British pound notes. The first mate, Klug, said a few words to each man as he handed out the pay sheets.

"You worked hard, Willy," said Klug. "You didn't bellyache and did what we asked. You'd be welcome back here on the *William* if you choose. We sail in a month, once we get the goods delivered to us that we'll ship to the colonies."

"I'm not coming back," said Raven. "This was a one-way trip. I'm headed for Europe." Raven told the lie so if anyone in the future questioned Klug about him, he would point him in the wrong direction.

"Too bad to hear that." said Klug. "Good luck to you then."

Raven got on a small packet boat that the ship's captain had arranged to take the men to Portsmouth. The packet boat took about an hour to manage the Solent and make its way to the docks. When they landed, the other men led Raven to the paymaster where each cashed in their script. The amounts received were different depending on their years of service and their rank aboard ship.

Raven looked at the £60 he collected and mused that it was more than what his indenturement had been sold for fifteen months earlier. It wasn't much money. He had been paid £1 per day for his time on the ship. Scarce wages when compared to what he'd been able to stash away from his schemes at Haslar. But it would buy him room and board in a sailor's inn as he put together his plan for revenge.

Ashore at Portsmouth on a crowded wharf, he felt that he could blend into the crowd of sailors, merchants, dockmen, carriage drivers, and assorted day-laborers who flooded the piers. He kept to the sidelines as he walked and didn't make eye contact with anyone. He carried Willy's billy-bag with him and looked very much the sailor that he'd been for the last two months.

He was confident that his current disguise would prevent him from being noticed so he could stay in the background. He wanted to hunt his quarry on his time table and take his prey without rushing. He had to hunt down Bobby Axe and Bentley the crooked lawyer. He knew Bentley lived in Portsmouth, but he didn't know where. Once he finished with those two, he had to figure out how to get to the lying Q.J. Shaikh in Gosport who had betrayed him in court. He had killed without conscience in order to get back to England. Those killings had been to survive. These assassinations would be a pleasure.

Raven checked into an inexpensive sailor's room and board inn, and strolled down the shops where he purchased a Monmouth cap hat that would aid his disguise. It was a simple knitted cap that had originated in Wales. It was useful because he could pull it down well over his eyebrows if he needed to. His ever-present deer-skinning knife was in his boot, and in his belt, he carried another blade he'd acquired aboard the *William*. His scheming was in full sail, as the saying might go.

The fresh salt air on the docks helped him think, even though there was the bustle of goods being taken from ships and hauled away on carts by the dozen. He could blot out the cacophony from the street and think. Other doctors and surgeons used to admire him for his strength and calmness under pressure. He knew he possessed those qualities. It made his revenge more lethal. The killing would be easy, but the escape had to be thought out.

He felt that he had to take Axe first, get over to Bentley's house as quickly as he could, and get his money from Bentley before he killed him. He knew in his heart that if Bentley had gone over to Haslar to find one of his cash boxes, he would rip the floor apart to find the second.

He also needed to get Bentley to tell him where Hawkins was. He had a suspicion that Hawkins had gone to Bristol with McLaughlin, but he wasn't sure. He could extract that information from Williams or Shaikh over at Haslar Hospital—across the bay from Portsmouth at Gosport—but it might take too long. If Axe's and Bentley's bodies were found, there would be a man-hunt by the constabulary. And although at this point he could presume that the police wouldn't know who to search for, time would be his enemy. This would take more planning. His timing had to be perfect in order to escape Portsmouth and get to Bristol, if that's where Hawkins was.

He needed a boat. Escaping overland was out of the question. Too many people would see him. Too many people might see the scar on his hand. He could pass it off as an injury at an iron-forge to an American. But Brits knew exactly what it was and what it represented. There were too many people who had followed the court case fifteen months earlier.

CHAPTER 17

R aven spent the next few days waiting to catch a glimpse of Bentley. He hid in the shadows near the courtrooms and waited hour after hour, hoping to see him. He frequently changed his position from one alleyway to another, but always kept an eye on the main entrance. He couldn't take a chance and try to confront Bentley at his office wherever that was. It would mean asking for directions, and he didn't want anyone to remember him. He wanted to anonymously and stealthily, stalk his prey, accomplish his mission, and escape with his stolen money.

Although it was summer, Raven wore a sailor's coat. It may have seemed strange to some, given that the temperatures were warm during the day, but in a seafaring town, there were many sailors who wore their possessions on their back, ready to go "with the tide" if the mood struck them. Many sailors wore coats, so Raven blended in well. He kept his hat pulled down across his shaven head, and pulled a pipe out of his coat every so often and sucked on the stem, more as a part of his disguise than to smoke.

Raven's patience paid off. A small man with an oversize briefcase strode toward the courthouse, talking and gesticulating wildly with another man. It was that thieving, conniving Bentley. Raven's blood ran alternately hot and cold thinking about what the attorney had done to him. Raven wasn't close enough to listen and didn't care what they were talking about. All he wanted was right in front of him. Now, all he had to do was to wait until Bentley's courtroom business was over and follow him home. Then he would know where he lived, and he could take his vengeance when he was ready.

True to expectations, Bentley came out of the courthouse door about an hour later. It was late in the afternoon. He parted company with the man he'd entered the courtroom with and strode down the street. Raven followed him at a discreet distance taking note of the street names as they passed them. Raven planned to confront Bentley at night when it was dark and he wanted to remember exactly which streets he had passed and how far he would have to go to get back to the docks.

When Bentley got to a residential street, named Bailey Road, Raven hid behind some bushes to make sure he wasn't seen. He watched from a longer distance than was perhaps necessary, but was able to see the house Bentley walked into. Just to be sure he had the right one, Raven walked past the house, noted the house number, and kept walking, planning to return one evening soon. As he walked back to the main center of Portsmouth, he assumed the money Bentley had taken from him must be in his house. It was a large sum of money that he wouldn't keep at an office which might be prone to burglary.

Bobby Axe would be easy to find in one of the sailor's pubs next to the wharfs. The diminutive bilge-rat was a rum-sodden little thief who drank whenever the mood suited him, which was most nights. But before he made his move toward his prey, he needed to secure a boat for his escape.

As he strode along the docks of Portsmouth, there were mainly large transport ships and ships-of-the-line for His Majesty's Royal Navy. He walked the entire length, back and forth, looking at every boat that was docked. He walked the entire length of Clarence Esplanade and Broad Street and north past Harbor station until he came to the dockyards for the HMS ships being refitted. He could see the barracks for the soldiers and sailors and decided against going further, such was his apprehension about being spotted.

He needed a certain size boat that would take him past Plymouth, past Falmouth, up the English coast past Penzance, and up north to Bristol Bay and the Severen River, and ultimately to Bristol. He was looking for a single-mast boat, large enough to stay afloat in the open sea, yet fast enough and small enough for a single man to handle.

Smaller craft were docked together away from the large ocean-going ships. There were plenty of heavy wherrys that could handle thirty tons of cargo, but they would be too slow. He saw a small dinghy with a single mast that he knew he could handle, but it was only 14-feet in length and couldn't handle any heavy seas. Even though his plan was to travel close to the coastline to avoid the pounding heavy seas of the Atlantic, he wanted something a bit larger. He saw a large sail Bermuda Rig that looked like it would be fast, but it was just a bit too large for one man to rig and steer. Then he spied a cat-rigged boat. It had a mast forward of the center of the boat with a wide beam with high enough gunnels to keep the water out. This one was roughly 20-feet in length. It also had an extra attractive feature. It had a beam-wide cover that hooded a sleeping area for the skipper.

He didn't know exactly when he would need it. He hadn't located Bobby Axe as yet, so his double murder plan could not commence until he did. But he knew that the night he found him was also the night he would execute Bentley and then escape. He couldn't stay around Portsmouth once those deeds were accomplished.

If he stole the boat—presumably in the middle of the night—he could escape the docks and get underway into the Solent and sail westward down the coast toward Plymouth and sites west. But stealing a boat was serious business, and if the boat was discovered missing early in the morning, the constabulary would be in their boat or boats searching the coastline for it, since it was a small craft that would not be ocean-bound. That was a risk Raven did not want to take.

Raven saw the owner of the cat-boat named the *Compass* crawl out from the sleeping area and stretch.

"Ahoy, skipper of the *Compass*," yelled Raven from the dock. "Is your cat-rig for hire?"

"Might be," answered the grisly bearded, half-awake skipper.

"I might want to charter it for a trip. Would you be willing to take me to Plymouth?"

"Might, if the price is right."

"One-way trip," said Raven, determining that the skipper might be willing if the original destination wasn't too far.

"That's 150 nautical miles by my experience. Even though the *Compass* is a sleek cat-boat, we'd only average ten knots and we'd sail against a prevailing westerly. Take the better part of a long day. You'd have to pay for the trip and for my dead-heading it back to Portsmouth, you understand. Won't make anything on the way home."

Raven knew the man was bargaining by stating the difficulties he faced.

Even though he didn't want to know the man's name, he thought he'd ask just to ease the negotiations a bit. "They call me Willy. What's yours?"

"Folks know me by a single name, much like you. They call me Condon. What's your business in Plymouth?"

Raven knew that any lie would suffice, so he told him he had just gotten off the *William* from the Americas, had some time before shipping out again, and wanted to see his brother. Raven knew that Condon would never see Plymouth or Portsmouth again once they were out on the Solent and away from shore, but felt he had to keep up the charade.

"How much then?" Raven asked.

"I figure £40 for the charter," answered Condon.

"Too much. I'll pay you £30 in all. Half today and half when we sail."

Condon hesitated for a full minute, stroked his chin before agreeing to take the job. "All right, then, £30 it is. I'll take the half now, if you please. When do you want to go?"

"It will be early in the morning at daybreak some day this week. I'm agreeing to pay you this much because I have business in Portsmouth and cannot tell you exactly what day we'll go. Could be tomorrow, could be three days from now. You sleep on the boat?"

"You saw me get out from under the hood. You know I do."

"Then you'll be here when I want you to be here. It will be this week. Don't go anywhere." Raven took £15 from his pocket and gave it to Condon.

"If you're gone when I am ready to leave, there'll be hell to pay. You hear me?" Raven said these last words with menace, glaring straight into his eyes so Condon got the point.

"Understood, Willy, understood," said Condon as he blanched when he saw the fierce look in Raven's black eyes.

Raven spent the rest of the day prowling through each of the many waterfront pubs in Portsmouth looking for Bobby Axe. He didn't mention Bobby's name to anyone. He didn't want a single soul to know he was looking for him. He popped his head into pubs called the Black Swan, the Pack Horse, the York and Pier, Eight Bells, and The Parade Tavern. In each of them throughout the afternoon, he would sit in a corner, order a small rum that he barely sipped, and then watch everyone in the place for about twenty minutes before moving on to the next one. It was wearisome not being able to locate the little dock rat immediately, but he was confident that sooner or later, Bobby Axe would turn up. Bobby and his deceased partner, Julie Gore, were always down by the docks looking to steal something from someone.

When Bobby had testified against him, Raven knew Bobby would get a reduced sentence for the kidnaping attempt on Angeline and Dominique. He would squeal at the first opportunity. It was

Bobby's testimony that helped land Raven—then known as Dr. Franks—in prison, got him his burn scar on his hand, and ultimately transported him to the colonies. He would get what was coming to him and it wouldn't be long before he did.

It was late afternoon when Raven walked into the King's Arms pub and saw Bobby standing against the bar hoisting a beer and jabbering loudly at a companion. Without overtly making any motion towards him, Raven sat in a corner, and when the bar maid came and took his order, Raven made his decision. He gave a £5 note to the barmaid to give to Bobby so he could drink all night at the bar if he wanted to. He made her say that the money was from an anonymous sailor. Raven wanted Bobby to drink until last call. He wanted Bobby sodden and reeling when he took him at midnight, and he wanted to know where to find him. The money would secure both objectives.

After giving the money to the barmaid, Raven bolted upright and pushed out the door, not even waiting for his drink. He walked quickly to the docks and found the *Compass*. He woke Condon and told him that they were shoving off tomorrow morning. With that accomplished, he made straight for his boarding house. On the way, he bought cooked sausages and bread for what he was anticipating was an all-day boat trip tomorrow morning. He had at least six hours to sleep, if he wanted, before the bars closed.

It was hard to sleep. He let the revenge and the blood-lust darken within him and then settle. He had to think. There was a troubling decision he had to make now so his escape plan would go smoothly. He thought at length as to how to get to Shaikh inside Haslar Hospital over across the bay at Gosport. Hell, he could see it from his vantage point on the second floor of the boarding house. But there were too many guards, both inside and outside Haslar. Ft. Moncton was right at the tip of the bay with armed soldiers and a convenient and oft-used gallows.

Franks, now Raven, had worked at Haslar for over ten years. And even if he thought he could get into the hospital and assassinate

Shaikh, getting out, racing across the yard, avoiding the patrolling sentries would be too risky. As much as he didn't want to, he had to let it go. He had to concentrate on getting his money from Bentley and getting on the *Compass* the next morning without raising an alarm. Dr. Q.J. Shaikh would live for the time being, much to Raven's regret.

CHAPTER 18

A fter he napped a couple of hours, Raven left the boarding house with what gear and food he possessed and headed for the King's Arms. He popped his head in quickly, and sure enough Bobby Axe was still there, holding up an end of the bar. He was obviously drunk. Raven had waited this long, he could wait longer. He left and patiently waited in the dark alley, drawing his deer-skinning knife from his monogrammed boot.

Bobby stumbled out of the bar within the half-hour. He was alone which made him easier prey. Raven followed Bobby until he was out of the direct light of the oil-fueled street lamps that gave limited clarity to the streets near the docks.

Raven only had to follow him a couple of blocks when he came up right behind Bobby. He grabbed Bobby hard around his head with his left hand, then with his right hand, he slit Bobby's throat from left to right, pushing the knife a full half inch deep into his throat across the entire cut. Bobby struggled at first, but Raven held him firmly, twisting his neck and pulling him down to the ground. Blood was everywhere. It was not a clean killing. All that was left was to let Bobby know who had killed him.

Bobby lay on his back staring straight up, his hands around his neck feeling the life going out from him, his heart pumping blood from the six-inch wound that went from under his left ear to his right. Raven dug his knee into Bobby's chest to pin him down and accelerate the blood loss.

Raven put his face right up to Bobby's. Bobby couldn't talk—his short spasmic breaths alternated with the gurgling of blood from the deep wound. His eyes were wide open as he recognized his assailant.

"Can't talk now can you, Bobby? You talked quite a bit when you gave me up, didn't you? It's me, Franks. Yes, it's me. I wanted you to know as you breathe your last breath who did this to you. You deserve it, you squealing dock rat. This is what you get for testifying against me. You go to hell."

With a last breath, Bobby died, and Raven quickly hauled his lifeless body into a tight alleyway, shoved him into a corner, and wiped his blade clean on Bobby's coat. Then, he pulled a nearby canvas tarp over the body and quickly walked away.

Raven made his way up the hill to Bailey Road and Bentley's house. On the way, he paused and picked up some dirt and smudged his face with it. He took the Monmouth cap out of his pocket and put it on as well. He wanted his face to be as obscured as possible.

He figured he had five hours or more until daybreak. He made his way to the back side of Bentley's house. He tried to peer in through a window, but everything was dark. He went to the back door and shoved his long deer-skin knife between the door and the door jam, and with a strong move, he lifted the door latch on the inside. The door opened easily.

Raven walked through the back pantry area, then stopped and listened for any sound of someone on the stairs coming down to greet him. He opened a closet door and saw what he was looking for even without the aid of candle light. He saw the ropes and rags he needed to secure the couple he would soon meet. He strung the ropes around his shoulder and stuffed the rags in the pocket of his coat.

He found the stairs that led to the upstairs bedroom and carefully walked up, one step at a time. No use waking the older couple up until he could secure both of them and hopefully prevent any screaming that would alert the neighbors. There were two bedroom doors, and he opened the first to see the couple silently bundled in their warm bed.

He couldn't take any chances. Although both people were covered in the bed, he saw one body had long hair and quickly determined it was Bentley's wife. He grabbed an ornamental figurine that he could make out in the dark, and resolutely smashed the woman's head with it. He took one of his rags and crammed it in the unconscious woman's mouth.

The body on the other side of the bed stirred. He heard, a faint "What is it?" come from Bentley.

Raven quickly moved to the other side of the bed and hit Bentley on the side of his head with the figurine, which must have been made of solid onyx or jade because it hadn't broken with its first use nor its second. He pulled Bentley roughly to the floor, rolled him onto his stomach, and tied him quickly. As he did this, Raven was silently grateful for his time on the *William*. He learned all sorts of rope tying knots while on board. It made this job easier.

He didn't want Bentley talking just yet, so he put another rag in Bentley's mouth. Bentley wasn't out cold, but he was dazed and bleeding profusely out of the wound that he'd suffered. Raven thought the blood would make Bentley pay attention to the questions he'd have to answer to save his wife's life.

With Bentley secured, he went back to the other side of the bed and tied the unconscious spouse with the remaining rope. She was face down and hadn't seen who the attacker was. Perhaps it would be her saving grace. Raven had yet to decide her fate. Bentley's answers would hold the key to that decision.

The slightest hint of moonlight came through the brocaded drapes in the upper floor bedroom. With his prey secured, and the woman still unconscious, Raven opened the drapes to get a bit more moonlight into the room. He pulled his knit hat off his face, so when Bentley came to, he could see Raven's face clearly.

Raven wiped the blood out of Bentley's eyes with his own nightshirt so he could see. Bentley was coming around, but with his hands secured couldn't remove the gag from his mouth. Raven had him exactly where he wanted him.

"Can you tell who I am?' asked Raven coldly. "Nod your head if you can."

Bentley nodded his head up and down. His eyes, clouded with his own blood, showed how terrified he was.

"Good. Now your answers will determine if your wife lives through the night. I have killed many men to be right here in this room with you tonight to get what is mine. Do you believe that I'll kill your wife to make you tell me where my money is? Eh, Bentley. Do you? Nod your head if you believe me."

Once again, Bentley nodded.

"So the question is simple. Where is the money you stole from me?"

Raven removed the gag slightly from Bentley's mouth ready to insert it quickly if he cried out.

"I didn't steal your money. I don't have it."

Raven quickly replaced the gag and hit Bentley on the side of the head where the original wound was. Bentley squealed in pain, an almost inaudible yelp.

"Wrong answer." Raven grabbed Bentley's hair, pulled his head back, and brought his face as close as he could to Bentley's, and looked him in the eyes.

"Where is it?" With that, he could see Bentley's eyes move ever so quickly to the dresser bureau behind the two of them.

"The dresser is it? Which drawer? Come now. Make it easy on yourself. We have all night. If your wife wakes up before we're done, your options to save her are gone."

Raven partially took the gag out, and Bentley said quickly, "Second drawer in the back."

Raven shoved Bentley's gag back, got up from the floor, and pulled out the second drawer. He yanked a cashbox out and brought it back to where Bentley lay. He knew that he needed to stay close to the weasel attorney to constantly physically threaten him. Raven was suspicious that he'd given up the location fairly easily. Raven opened up the box and found £3000. That's less than half of the money that Franks, now Raven, had stowed away.

"Where's the rest?"

Bentley muffled through the gag. "That's all there is. I swear."

Raven pulled his deer-skinning knife from his boot, shone it in front of Bentley's face, and said, "Once more, where's the rest?" He removed Bentley's gag.

"I spent it, you bastard," said Bentley.

"Maybe this will help your memory." Raven stuck the gag deeper into Bentleys mouth, took hold of one of Bentley's ears, and deftly cut it off, slicing through it with the sharp deer-skinning knife like the piece of rough cartilage it was. Bentley's muffled scream didn't abate right away.

"Tell me now, or you and your wife are dead."

Bentley was breathing hard. He motioned for Raven to remove the gag, which he did. "Behind the books. It's all that's left."

Raven stuck the gag back and found the second cash box after strewing the books onto the floor. Bentley had been just like him, splitting up the savings into two different places.

There was £2,000 worth of sterling notes in the second box. He stuffed the money into his pocket along with the rest.

"One more thing before I leave. Where's Hawkins? I need to pay him and his wife a visit. Is he in Gosport? Portsmouth?"

Raven pulled Bentley's gag out to hear him say, "He and McLaughlin went to Bristol. I gave you what you wanted, now leave me in peace. I saved you from the gallows, damn it!"

"Fine. So Bristol it is." Raven ignored Bentley's plea and stuck the gag back tighter this time.

"Bentley, you little weasel," said Raven with a note of finality to his voice. He stuck his head even closer to Bentley's face so he could clearly hear Raven's final words to him. "You just saved your wife's life. But you, you wanted me to die in that hell hole of a prison hulk, or on the rotten transport barge the *Jonathan,* or in the tobacco fields of Virginia. Don't give me that 'saving my life' lie. Your wife will live to remember you. She'll say a real nice speech at your funeral."

With that, he spun Bentley to the ground onto his stomach, knelt with the full force of his knee on Bentley's back and plunged the deer-knife into the back of his neck, severing the spinal cord and ending Bentley's life without nearly the blood he would have spilled had he stabbed him in the heart.

Raven wiped the knife clean and placed it back into his boot. He walked calmly over to the other side of the bed, placed his head close to the nose of Bentley's wife to see if she was breathing and possibly awake, faking unconsciousness. Deciding that she was still out cold, Raven got up and made his way downstairs.

He raided the pantry for any salt pork, bread, and leftover brisket that he could find, wrapped it up, and put it into his billy-bag. He might not be putting into any port for a couple of days and needed extra provisions. The skipper of his escape boat, the *Compass*, might think they had a one-day destination to Plymouth, but Raven knew differently.

Raven bundled up, pulled his Monmouth knit cap over his head and down to his eyebrows, and as stealthily and quietly as he could, exited Bentley's house and made his way down the dim-lit streets of Portsmouth to the docks. He was wary of any watchful eyes. He didn't think there would be any patrolmen out, but he didn't want to tumble into any drunks either. That might cause a ruckus, and he didn't want any attention drawn to himself, not when he wanted to get on the *Compass* and sail away at the first break of dawn.

Raven found the *Compass* right where it was supposed to be. He quickly landed on the boat's deck from the pier and tucked himself into the covered space where Condon had been snoozing. Instead of sleeping, Condon sat there facing him with a blade in his hand, ready to use it.

"It's me, Condon, it's Willy" said Raven, not wanting a knife fight in these close quarters. He pulled his knit cap up over his head to show Condon his full face in the dim light. "Put the blade up. I've brought you some food." He brought out the brisket and bread, and the two of them munched on it for fifteen minutes. Raven's nerves were heightened. He wanted to cast off and get away, but they had to go by the book and wait until dawn lest somebody think there was suspicious activity.

"You lie back down and rest if you can," said Raven. "I'll do the same. I finished my business a little earlier than expected. We'll sleep and then cast off when you decide. You're the captain."

Raven wanted to allay any fears on Condon's part that there was anything to worry about. It wasn't in Raven's general disposition to cater to anyone else. But he'd learned in Virginia and aboard the *William* to bide his time. As Raven, called Willy, put his head down on the ship's wooden plank, he thought they had a couple of hours at least, if not a full half day before Mrs. Bentley would awake from her concussion, wiggle free from her bindings, and get help. *We should be well clear of the harbor by then.*

◆◆◆

When Condon rose two hours later, he immediately started to rig the sailing. Raven had been able to close his eyes but for a few moments, so his movements were slow. He didn't try to help Condon at first, but kept an eye on his movements. It wouldn't be too long before the boat was his and he was its only sailor.

Raven/Willy helped by unmooring the boat from the pier, and the *Compass* was on its way. There seemed to be fifty boats in the harbor, all up early and going about their business. Condon carefully navigated the *Compass* past the other boats, steering the twenty-foot catboat, or skiff, with a south by southwest heading away from Portsmouth.

They passed Ft. Moncton, and Raven took what he thought could be a last look at Haslar Hospital. Q. J. Shaikh was holed up there under armed guards. It galled him to think that his partner in the kickback scheme, his accomplice in the poisoning of Jim Hawkins, and the kidnapping of the two Jamaican women was able to testify against him and get probation while Raven suffered in prison hulks and prison ships. He might be able to sneak back someday and kill Shaikh, but it wasn't on this trip. He wouldn't forget. It might take a year or even two, but he would exact his revenge.

As they passed by Haslar Hospital on the shore of Gosport, he could see that Condon was enjoying skippering the *Compass*. They had a southerly wind this time of the year in early June, and the air temperature was warming. They stayed close to the coast, and Raven felt at ease knowing he had escaped Portsmouth with his money and his revenge assuaged for the time being.

"You have any maps I could look at to pass the time?" he called to Condon, who was at the helm.

"In the box under the hood," said Condon. "I don't need them for this trip. Done it plenty of times."

When Raven had fetched them and was looking them over, he called out, "How many miles would you say we had left to Plymouth?"

"Can you see the legend at the bottom of the map?" yelled Condon.

"Looks like we have roughly 110 miles to go."

"Sounds about right."

From that small bit of information and the legend, Raven measured with a piece of string the coastline distance to the mouth of the Severn River as it formed Bristol Bay. It was roughly three hundred and forty-five nautical miles from Portsmouth if he hugged the coast. A quick calculation meant that if he could make one hundred miles a day or more, he could beach the craft in three and a half days.

He didn't want any more of Condon. He could handle this cat-rigged skiff. But where to separate himself from Condon? They were still too close to Portsmouth. He would have to wait until well into the afternoon before he put Condon to sea. But which way would the body drift? He didn't want to be found out, so he went under the cover and luckily found a secondary anchor and an anchor rope. It was small, but it had the potential of holding a dead body down in the sea.

It was still early morning, so he announced to Condon that he was going to try and nap for an hour or more and went under the boat's cover and tried to sleep. For the first ten minutes, he devised a trick so he could attack Condon from the rear and not risk a full frontal knife fight in a relatively small space like the deck of a small twenty-foot skiff. He figured Condon knew how to handle himself in a knife fight, so he had to trick him into turning around without raising suspicion so he could stab him in the back.

Two hours later, Raven rose from the hooded cover with the maps in his hand. "Say, Condon, can you show we where we are relative to this map. I can hold the rudder while you check out the map."

"All right, here let me show you," Condon said as he moved forward and gave control of the rudder to Raven, now Willy. Raven slid aside Condon and took control of the rudder with his left hand and slid his other hand into his boot and quietly retrieved his deer-skinning knife.

Condon had his back turned to Raven for one fatal second as he looked at the map when Raven plunged the blade deep into Condon's back, held it firm, and twisted it before pulling it out and stabbing him one more time as hard as he could. The second blow was unnecessary since Raven, no longer called Willy by anybody, knew where the heart was on the front side of Condon's chest and was confident that the first blow had done its work.

Condon slumped to the deck. Raven found the piece of rope that was often used to secure the rudder in a fixed position, then tied it off so he could attend to the dead man. Raven climbed over Condon's body, got the spare anchor and its rope, and attached it to Condon's neck. No use taking chances. He dumped Condon's body overboard and watched it sink slowly into the deep blue water.

For the first time in over fifteen months, Raven was free. As he settled into the helmsman's seat aboard the *Compass* and adjusted the sail lines to maximum sail, he felt rich and free. But he wasn't done. He was a man driven by only two things: success and revenge. He still had Hawkins to deal with. *His time will come*, he thought, *and it will be soon.*

CHAPTER 19

By mid-June, the fear of the smallpox spreading had dissipated. Neither Drs. Livesey, Hawkins, McLaughlin, nor any member of the BMG had any clue as to why it had not spread. They felt relieved since the outbreak that had killed three children and affected Dr. Jim Hawkins so severely that the fever almost took him.

People from the well-to-do sections of town, as well as from the poorer sections, started to meet in their public houses, go to churches once again, and frequent the weekend open air markets. The markets were a big draw. There was one permanent location that covered a good ten acre spread on the south side of the Avon bridge. There were many other street vendors selling their linens—like Livian and Maye used to do—that drew in people from the countryside on the weekends. There were many other hand-crafted cottage industry manufactures that people liked to sample.

Squire Trelawney wanted to celebrate the beautiful weather and to thank Dr. Livesey and his team for their extraordinary effort to locate, treat, and stem the tide of the smallpox scare. Squire Trelawney had invited Dr. Livesey and his wife Elizabeth and their child Margaret, Dr. Jim Hawkins, Livian, and beautiful baby Belle, who was growing fast at fifteen-months and wanted to walk everywhere. He also included Dr. McLaughlin who had his own place in Bristol, and Mary Springer, his soon-to-be fiancé, if the talk among the women was to be believed. For the Friday night feast, at the urging of Robert Livesey, the squire also sent invitations to the Livesey Surgery nurses, Gwen and Mary and nurse Harriet, and their spouses.

The squire's house servants, Olivia Newsome and Monica Green, worked all week to get the townhouse ready for the expected weekend guests. In some quarters, it might have seemed traditional for city dwellers to relax in the countryside and escape the city. In this case, however, there was so much to see in Bristol, it seemed appropriate for the squire to invite Livesey, McLaughlin, Hawkins, and their loved ones to the city and attend the open-air market on Saturday.

Jim, Robert, and Mac were already in the city and could walk up the hill to the squire's place on Friday afternoon after closing the surgery for the weekend. Arnold and Maye Adams drove Livian, Belle, Elizabeth, and Margaret in the Livesey Acres carriage to the squire's house. They arrived well before the dinner hour, and since it was just a few days past the summer solstice—the day with the longest amount of daylight—Arnold and Maye had time after dropping them off to get back to Livesey Acres before the sun set on a beautiful evening.

The squire put on a huge feast that evening and invited a special guest, Nathaniel Newsome, Olivia Newsome's Jamaican free-born husband who worked as a warehouseman for the squire. At first Nathan, as he was called, was embarrassed to join in the festivities that evening, but seemed to loosen up with a few glasses of the squire's fine imported madeira wine.

After dinner, the squire got everyone's attention and let them in on the news of the day. It was the Somerset decision that had been handed down by the honorable Judge Lord Mansfield earlier that week.

"Listen, everybody, I want you to know that I have asked Robert here to make the announcement that many of you have been eager to hear. As a businessman, I am prepared to deal with the changes that are to come, but believe me, there will be a marked impact on Bristol and its citizens, I assure you. Robert?" The squire sat down and let Robert Livesey have the floor.

"Many of you already know my anti-slavery stance so I won't lecture anyone on what a terrible scourge I think it has been on English morality. The squire and I have debated its merits and demerits for years."

"It's made Bristol a very wealthy and important English city," piped up Trelawney who had been liberally indulging in his imported wines, and made the same debate point that he had pressed during years of back and forth with Dr. Livesey.

"Nonetheless," continued Livesey, "there has been a case in the English courts in London for the last two years that deals with a black slave named Somerset. Just so I don't get it wrong, I'm going to read you what the newspapers said happened this past Wednesday the 22nd of June.

"There has been for years a debate about whether black people living in Britain could be slaves or not. It was thought that they could only be slaves outside Britain in the colonies such as in Jamaica and elsewhere in the Caribbean. If they set foot in Britain and "breathed free English air," just that alone made them free. However, until this past Wednesday when Lord Mansfield ruled on the Somerset Declaration, most black and mixed-race servants in England would have had slave status. Yes, that's right. That is, they were not free.

So Judge Mansfield had to try the case between James Somerset, a slave who was abandoned in London when he fell ill, and his owner. When Somerset had regained his health, his owner tried to reclaim him and send him back to the Caribbean. The abolitionists, who campaigned against

176

slavery, took up the case on behalf of James Somerset. With their support the case went to court. The judge decided that owners could not force slaves who lived in England back to the plantations in the Caribbean against their will.

Slavery had never been authorized by statute in England and Wales, and Lord Mansfield's decision found slavery unsupported in common law. Lord Mansfield narrowly limited his judgment to the issue of whether a person, regardless of being a slave, could be removed from England against his will, and said he could not. Even this reading meant that certain property rights in chattel slaves were unsupported by common law. It is one of the most significant milestones in the abolitionist campaign.

This is the judge's statement: The state of slavery is of such a nature that it is incapable of being introduced on any reasons, moral or political, but only by positive law [statute], which preserves its force long after the reasons, occasions, and time itself from whence it was created, is erased from memory. It is so odious, that nothing can be suffered to support it, but positive law. Whatever inconveniences, therefore, may follow from the decision, I cannot say this case is allowed or approved by the law of England; and therefore the black must be discharged. Let Justice be done, though the heavens may fall.

Olivia Newsome looked confused by all the high-tone legalistic language of the newspaper, but immediately got the gist of what it had said. "But I am already a free-born Jamaican and the squire pays me. I am not a slave."

Her husband, Nathan, agitated by the article that Dr. Livesey had just read, rose from his seat and agreed with his wife. "Me neither. I get paid by the squire to work in the warehouse, but there are whites in the street who treat me like I am a slave. I am as free-born as any Englishman."

Dr. Livesey responded, "That may be so, but think of all the blacks from the West Indies and Africa who have been brought here by sea captains and merchants. As of last Wednesday, by being in England and breathing English air, Mansfield said they can no longer be treated as chattel. They're free. The newspapers said there could be as many as 15,000 of these people in England."

"There are a lot of people who are going to celebrate once they hear this news," said Jim Hawkins, who had for a time in Gosport, employed two Jamaican women who had been slaves of the hospital administrator.

"The newspaper article didn't say anything about slaves in the West Indies or in the American colonies," added McLaughlin. "They'll still be considered property, I would imagine."

"There's trouble in all this," said Abraham Gray, Trelawney's right-hand man, and bodyguard. As a former navy man, he was always looking to prepare for the worse. It's what made him so valuable to the squire and all his holdings.

"What do you mean, trouble?" asked Jim.

"Word of this decision will spread throughout England, throughout every city," explained Gray.

"As one would expect," added the squire. "The Bristol Gazette has it, the Leeds Mercury, the Newcastle Chronicle. They will all reprint the decision, I would think. This case has been brewing for almost three years now. And word will spread through every public house, tavern, and inn in the country, including here in Bristol."

"And the people like me who can't read will hear the story from others," said Nathan.

"And likely get the facts wrong," said Dr. Livesey, facing up to the potential for misunderstanding and potential violence.

"There's bound to be some backlash," responded Gray. "Nathan, did you hear anything near where you live before you came here tonight?"

"No, this is the first of it. But tomorrow could be different. Squire, didn't you say the Bristol Gazette printed the decision?"

"It was published yesterday," answered the squire. Now he'd probably have to hire more guards to watch over his warehouses full of goods, especially the imported wines from Spain and Portugal that could be raided in a street riot.

"Look at this from the Bristol workingman's point of view," continued Gray. "How many blacks do you think there are in Bristol? One-thousand at the most. Now they are no longer tethered to their masters. They'll go looking for work and compete with the white workingman for the same unskilled jobs, the same factory jobs."

"Tanners, brass workers, rope makers, textile workers, cotton movers, dock handlers, you name it," said the squire, who seemed to see all too clearly where Gray was headed with this line of thinking. It was entirely likely that the squire could reduce his overall costs of labor for all the material handling that he paid for. That could be a plus in the short run for a businessman like the squire, but the costs of labor unrest could be great if he replaced his current staff with lower wage newly-freed blacks. It was a clear dilemma.

"They'll bid wages downward willing to work for less, I would suspect," added Jim.

"Fearing that free slaves will take their livelihood away from them, I would think there will be some backlash against them. Before this, they were not a threat. Now they are," said Gray.

After a minute or two of reflection, the squire spoke, "Nathan, I think you and Olivia should consider going home before it gets too late. As you said, Nathan, although you are free-born, you may confront hatred just because of your skin color. I'll tell you what, Abraham will drive the two of you in my carriage and get you home safely. But I will ask you to do one small thing. You go to a tavern called The Hole in the Wall, do you not?"

"I do, sir, now and again," responded Nathan which elicited a heavy loud sigh and an over-acted rolling of the eyes from Nathan's wife, Olivia.

"Stop in there tonight and see if you can hear anything of a protest or anything of the sort," continued the squire. "If there is to be trouble I think it's our duty to warn the constabulary. Perhaps they can provide a united front and quell any disturbance."

"I can do that," said Nathan

"And for tomorrow, let us all at least enjoy the weekend. We're all planning to go across the Avon bridge and go to the open-air markets. Nathan, you can catch up with us there and let us know what, if anything, you have been able to find out. How's that sound?" said the squire, trying to put a worry-free attitude toward the potential problem. "We'll meet you on the bridge, say half past ten."

◆◆◆

In the morning after breakfast, there was quite the group that assembled to board the carriage at Squire Trelawney's home. Abraham Gray would drive seven others down to the base of the bridge, drop them off, and return to fetch them later. In all, the carriage included Jim, Livian, and Belle—with her pram tethered to the rear of the carriage—Dr. Livesey, Elizabeth, and Margaret, and the squire. Mac and Mary Springer had declined the invitation to join the group, and Monica Green stayed at the squire's house to do some cleaning up after the dinner party the night before. It was such a gorgeous summer morning, all of them wanted to stroll across the Avon bridge and experience the open-air markets on its south side.

The bridge over the Avon River had been newly rebuilt in 1768 and was both the source of wonderment, appreciation, and resentment. The old bridge had been there for many, many years and featured houses five stories high that hung over the river. These houses had been attractive because of the fresh air coming off the river. High rents were charged since the bridge had so much foot traffic, which partially explained the community of goldsmiths who could afford locating there. But this encroachment of the houses onto the bridge created congestion that often made pedestrian and carriage traffic hazardous. The new bridge removed all houses and left plenty of room for carriages and pedestrians alike on normal days. The days of the open markets were different, however, when much larger crowds developed, which made carriage traffic across the bridge all but impossible.

The resentment against the bridge stemmed from the toll that was charged both ways, north to south and then again south to north. It stung the pockets of everyone, especially since the open-air markets were on the south side, and on weekends, brought many people and piled the coffers high. But as the city fathers explained, someone had to pay for this bridge. It might as well be the ones who used it.

It was about half past ten when the squire and his entourage were dropped off at the toll house at the base of the bridge. Jim was helping Abraham Gray get the pram off the back of the carriage when out of the corner of his eye he saw Nathan and Olivia walking quickly through the crowd towards them.

"I believe that's Nathan and Olivia, Squire. They're moving their way towards us."

"Splendid, we'll find out if he heard of anything."

When Nathan got to them, Jim could see that Olivia was upset. She was a bit breathless since the two of them had been scurrying, trying to meet the squire's group at the appointed hour. What struck Jim immediately was the big welt next to Nathan's eye and his severely bruised and swollen lip. Neither had been treated and were already turning purple.

"How did you get your injuries, Nathan?" asked Jim, while he secured the pram and opened it up on the ground so Livian could put the baby in it. The squire and Dr. Livesey and Elizabeth came around the carriage to see what the fuss was about.

"The Hole-in-the-Wall tavern is what happened to it. I went 'round there as the squire had asked and hadn't been in there ten minutes when two of the Rooster Road gang jumped me, held me, and gave me a couple of you-know-what-fors, 'just for being black,' they said. They called me a black so and so...I can't use the word in front of the women here. But they were angry, and I didn't have a chance. I fought back as best I could, kicked one of them pretty good in his groin. He went down and stayed down long enough for me to wiggle free from the guy holding me, block one of his punches, and get in one or two of my own.

"I've been in bar fights, and the best response is a fast and sure one. I couldn't wait around to see if their friends were going to join in, so I beat it home and Olivia put a wet rag on my face, otherwise I think it would be worse than it is. I heard one of them yell out as I got out the door that they'd see me tomorrow and finish what they started on me."

Jim's sense of danger was heightened, and he wondered whether they should all get back into the carriage and make their way back up the hill to the squire's. There would be weapons at the squire's place to defend themselves, should the need arise. Jim's first instinct was to protect Livian and Belle. But that gang wouldn't chase Nathan all the way to the squire's house. That wasn't likely since the squire and Gray and his men had a reputation for shooting first and explaining later.

"You said it was the Rooster Road gang who jumped you?" asked Livesey.

"I know them. It was sure two of them," said Nathan. "They'd been in the tavern before."

"If the whole gang wants to get you, there'll be more than two," said Dr. Livesey, who once held the position of Magistrate. It sounded like it wasn't the first time he'd run into this gang. "They have eight to ten extended families that practically own Kingswood. They even demand a toll to get through the town. Even the constabulary doesn't like to go there. They're so emboldened by their hold over Kingswood that they're not likely to give up on you."

"Did you get the idea that there was to be any organized mob action in reaction to the Mansfield decision?" asked the squire.

"None that I heard of. But like I say," said Nathan, "I was only in the bar for a few minutes."

Jim knew that Squire Trelawney had faced many an adversary, and despite his girth and age, wasn't about to back down and let this threat spoil his plans for the day. To retreat up the hill to his house and forgo this planned trip to the markets, would be a humiliation. That word was not in his vocabulary.

"Well, we're here and it's a beautiful day and we're going to walk the bridge and enjoy the market. What do you say, everyone?"

Most everyone nodded in agreement.

"That's the spirit. We're come this far," said the squire with an optimistic tone that was infectious in a positive way. "Let's start walking. Gray, why don't you come back for us in two hours. That should give us plenty of time. Meanwhile, hand Jim a pistol that he can tuck in his coat just to be on the safe side."

Gray handed Jim a pistol which Jim stuffed into his belt. Although Gray was hesitant, he followed the squire's request and drove the carriage away from this small troupe of fairgoers.

Unknown to most people, the squire always went armed. He had two small eight-inch long, .42 caliber flintlock pocket pistols with wide cannon barrels tucked into his coat pockets. Normally, he gave off an optimistic aura of good fellowship, but with his wealth, he would always be a target. He hadn't been attacked recently, but then again, he usually had Gray with him to deter thieves.

Usually Jim didn't carry a weapon nor did Dr. Livesey. The crowds on this side of the bridge, on the bridge, and on the other side presented a problem. If someone wanted to start a disturbance, there would be confusion as to who or what started it, and perpetrators could get lost in the numbers and escape. And if a weapon was discharged, there would be further trouble since the man who shot the weapon was the one most likely charged with a crime, regardless of the circumstances. The constabulary usually chose that route because it made it simpler for them when they were determining who started what ruckus and who ended it.

They paid their tolls and their group of nine people started walking over the bridge. They paused in the middle to idly gaze at the Avon River on such a beautiful day with the wind blowing gently from the south. Some of their anxiety about potential trouble left them as they gazed downriver. They could see the people at the open-air market on the other side of the bridge. The market reminded Jim of the times the Adams family took Livian's linen and sold it to gain an extra £30 or so of extra money to tide them over until the next year.

The bridge was crowded with people. Perhaps too crowded for comfortable strolling. Dr. Livesey, Elizabeth, and Margaret led the way with Squire Trelawney next. Jim and Livian followed with Jim right behind Livian pushing the pram. Jim constantly turned around looking for any signs of trouble at their rear. Livian slowly pushed baby Belle in the pram and hummed a sweet little lilt to amuse the baby girl. Olivia and Nathan brought up the rear of the little group.

As they descended past the middle of the bridge, they heard a commotion up ahead. They could barely make out what was being said. But there were definitely people yelling with anger in their voices. The squire stopped walking, stiffened, and one hand went to one of the flintlocks in his pocket. He turned back to Jim and gave him a nod as if to say, "Be ready. This could be trouble."

Dr. Livesey was in the lead and the first to see a group of young men up ahead. They were yelling indiscernibly at everyone, obviously looking for a fight. Three of the young men crowded around a black man and his female companion. The one in front slammed his fist into the man's face with a powerful swing. One of the three pushed the black woman to the ground, gave her a single kick, and screamed, "Get out of Bristol!"

Five more of their little mob came onto the bridge and punched one man for no reason at all. Then they saw Olivia and Nathan, who were at the end of the Squire Trelawney party, and made straight for them, pushing others out of the way, almost dumping one person over the bridge into the river. It was clear that they didn't see Nathan and Olivia as real people. They just saw them identified by their skin color.

One of the men in the mob shouted, "Hey, you… you black bastard! Go back to Africa. Go to London. Get the hell out of Bristol. You're free now, ain't you? Get outta here!"

Two of the youths from the second part of the mob rushed up and came straight for Nathan as if they knew who he was. "Hey, we had a chance at this guy last night. He didn't get enough. I got a kick or two that I owes him!"

He rushed Nathan, but Jim and Trelawney stood in front of Nathan and blocked the thug's onrush. The young man plowed into Jim knocking him down, and as he did, he fell backwards into Trelawney and into the pram. Trelawney was down on the ground, but his body was between Jim's and Livian's. It was all Livian could do to keep the pram upright and protect Belle.

Rising to one knee, the squire pulled one of his flintlocks out of his pocket. He cocked the pistol but couldn't see clearly who to aim at. He kept looking and looking for a clear shot. The two toughs had others to help them. Now there were about eight to ten of them in all. They pushed Livesey and Elizabeth. Livesey fell, and one of the mob hit Livesey in the head with a rock to make him stay down. Elizabeth stayed down on one knee and hovered over Margaret to protect her.

These goons went to help their buddies attack Nathan. Jim tried to get up on one knee and tried to pull the pistol out of his belt, but he took another push to the ground with a kick that followed. There were just too many of them all at once. The gun went stumbling down to the ground. Nathan had been pummeled to the ground and three of the hoodlums were kicking him, screaming, "Black bastard" and other epithets as they continued to kick him. Nathan curled up in a ball to try and protect himself, but he caught a few of the blows in the head.

Olivia screamed at the top if her lungs for them to stop and get off. She was pushed backwards, reeling into Livian. Jim's pistol was on the ground and was accidently kicked towards Nathan. In an instant, Nathan reached out, picked it up, and without aiming, fired the gun in an upwards direction, trying to make the brutal kicking stop.

The loud report of the gun made everyone stop and look, including the attackers. They saw one of their own with a stomach wound from the .40 caliber flintlock. He was bleeding badly and groaned aloud that he had been shot. Nine of them ran away. Since they were by their very nature cowards, they left their injured compatriot there on the bridge to bleed while they scattered. After the mob left, Livesey, Trelawney, and Jim went to Nathan and saw that he was not shot.

"I shot the gun," said Nathan. "I had to. It was them or me."

The constabulary's whistle blew in the distance, signaling their arrival on the bridge. They had been maintaining a post in the market and only came running when they heard the gun go off.

While the three policemen came to them, Livesey checked with Elizabeth and Margaret and determined that they were all right, as were Livian and Belle. Jim was a little woozy, as was Dr. Livesey who held a handkerchief to the bleeding wound on his head. Bewildered, Trelawney stood there, gun in hand, looking ashamed that he hadn't been the one to shoot the thug who was rolling around on the bridge moaning and bleeding from the pistol wound.

"Who fired the gun?" asked Maxwell, the constable in charge.

"It was self-defense," barked Livesey, still holding the red-blood handkerchief next to his head wound, trying to stem the flow of blood.

"Who fired the gun?" repeated Maxwell. "I ain't gonna ask again or you'll all be going in."

"I fired it," said Nathan. "They was kicking me black and blue." Nathan showed the constable his bloody mouth and welt up against his eye.

"And your name?"

"Nathan Newsome." The constable repeated the name and wrote it down in his little pocket book.

"Constable, I'm Dr. Robert Livesey. I was once a county magistrate. I will attest before God and country that this mob of thugs came onto this bridge solely to do this man harm. We got in their way and took their blows to help defend him. Nathan shot the gun in self-defense."

"You a magistrate now?" said the gruff constable.

"No, I'm retired from that job. I am now devoted to my medical practice."

"So it is. Well, you'll have the opportunity to tell this story to the current magistrate. We'll get this sorted out sooner or later, won't we?"

Meanwhile, the other two constables held the injured man down and held a linen rag against his stomach to try and stop the bleeding. They weren't having much success.

"You say you're a doctor? We need you to treat this gunshot wound."

Trelawney, who looked beside himself with anger, said something he probably should have held back. "We'd sooner he'd just die here on this bridge."

Jim spoke up quickly. "What he meant to say is 'yes.' Dr. Livesey and I are surgeons and we will do what we can to help him. Our surgery is eight blocks from the bridge to the east. Can you transport him there? We don't have a carriage at the moment."

"And who might you be?" asked the constable.

"Dr. Jim Hawkins, partner of Dr. Livesey."

"We'll transport him to your surgery and we'll keep a watch on him as well. It would be in your friend's interest here that he be kept alive, don't you think? My men will accompany him. As for you, Nathan Newsome, I'm arresting you for the shooting of this man on the Avon bridge. Whether this charge turns into a capital offense and a murder charge depends on whether your friends can save his life. Turn around," said Maxwell.

As he put the handcuffs on Nathan, it became obvious that he was making a big show for the folks still on the bridge. His chest was a little too puffed up, his sideways glances too frequent to see the crowd's response, and his voice a bit too loud for the moment. His grandstanding did not go unnoticed by Trelawney. He looked like he could barely contain himself.

Trelawney barked at the constable, "We will have our day in

court and you will be embarrassed for what you are doing here. That man on the ground over there and his friends are to blame. Not Nathan Newsome."

Olivia screamed at the policeman, "He's done nothing wrong. He was the one being beaten. Can't you see that?"

The constable turned Nathan around and started leading him away. "He fired the gun, didn't he?"

One of the other constables ran and blew his whistle back in the direction of the open-air markets to alert the police wagon to come to this location.

Livesey and Hawkins walked back quickly after making sure Livian and Elizabeth and the children were okay to make their way back to the squire's house. The squire hailed a carriage, and he and the women and children jumped in and were driven back to his house.

Dr. Hawkins and Livesey made it back to their surgery and were opening the doors when the police wagon with the injured man pulled up. Jim, Robert, and the two policemen went to get the stretcher with the injured man.

"Let me check his pulse," said Jim, reaching toward the man. Jim gave Livesey a grim look. "Dr. Livesey, he's gone. He has no pulse."

Livesey repeated what Jim Hawkins had just done and confirmed the death of the young man. Both surgeons had seen battlefield wounds before and knew the often fatal consequences of gunshot wounds. It was a simple call to make, yet a difficult one under the circumstances. Not one of these four knew the man's name. They just knew that the gunshot wound at close range had led to extreme internal bleeding, and that even his young body could not sustain the heavy loss of blood. He was dead on arrival at the surgery, and now Nathan would have to face a murder charge or a manslaughter charge at the very least.

CHAPTER 20

CHAPTER 20

SEACOAST OFF BRISTOL
JUNE 1772

Raven spent the next three days sailing the cat-rig around the western tip of England and up the coast. He guided the small skiff close to land the entire length of his escape in the *Compass*. He passed St. Ives, Newquay, and Barnstable. Each night, before it grew too dark to see, he carefully navigated the twenty-foot boat to shore, avoiding rocks and shoals. Each night, he looked for a sandy shore, though these were scant along the rugged western coast of England. But he was able to find one every night so he could get to shore, beach the boat, and wait for the next morning's tide to carry him out into open water so he could continue.

He didn't want to be seen by anyone. It was difficult at one stage when he passed Plymouth Harbor. There was so much boat traffic leaving that harbor he thought someone would hail him and insist on stopping him to check him out, especially since he had Condon's boat. But he had some luck, and no one did.

He had some food left, and although it was a cold fare of leftover bread and sausage that he had stolen from Bentley's larder after he killed him, it would have to suffice until he was further away from Portsmouth and any pursuers. He didn't want to go searching for food even though he had plenty of money to pay for it. Remaining hidden was a top priority.

As the fourth day of his journey came to a close, he took a long look at the maps Condon had in the *Compass*. He took careful note of the coastline, trying to measure out the miles he needed to travel before going inland. He also took note of the distance between the coast of England and Ireland, his ultimate destination after he took care of Hawkins and slaked his thirst for vengeance.

If he set a westerly course right now and ventured into the Irish Sea straight for Ireland, he would avoid further bloodshed. But this was not the spirit that had led his black soul to this day, to this coastline. Besides, on the map, Ireland looked like two hundred miles of open sea, which could turn the twenty-foot, single-masted skiff, and him, into fish bait if a storm came up. No, it was best to continue up the coast and accomplish what he had set out to do.

He came to Portishead, England and found a relatively secluded beach to the north of town where he beached the craft and secured it. To his south, he could see the fishing village. It was near the mouth of the Avon River as it fed into the Severn River and Bristol Bay. After living in the boat the past four days, he needed a hot meal.

After securing the *Compass*, he grabbed his billy-bag with Condon's maps and headed to the docks, looking for an inn. He stopped at a tavern and ate a meal that was a warmed-over fish stew. He was so hungry that he couldn't complain, although he wanted to. While he ate, he decided against staying close to the shore. He had hunkered down in that boat for too many days to want to sleep there tonight, and if this tavern's beds were anything like its stew, they would be smelly, old, and a bit rancid. He asked the barkeep about other inns, and he mentioned one called the Admiral Benbow up the hill. "Quiet and out of the way. It backs up to a cliff with a good view of the ocean," the barkeep said. That was all Raven needed to hear.

It wasn't a half hour later when Raven came into the Admiral Benbow Inn and inquired about a room for a couple of days. The woman who clerked the front desk showed him a room, which he gladly accepted. He paid her for three days out of the stash of pound notes he had in his pocket, not knowing how many days it would take for him to gain his sea legs and his stamina back. He had been on short rations for what seemed like weeks and the fish stew hadn't helped. He wanted to rest and recuperate.

He slept through the night and most of the next morning. When he came downstairs and into the dining area, there was one other customer eating. Although the woman who brought him his large breakfast of eggs, potatoes, and a large slice of ham was friendly, he could not reciprocate. It was unlike him to fake charm when there was nothing to give. He nodded and accepted the food and devoured it. It was healthy, and it reminded him of the many days he had spent at Haslar Hospital eating like a prince whenever he wanted to.

The other customer tried to make small talk, but Raven would have none of it and told the man that he was sick and needed food, rest, and as little conversation as possible. The man took this as an insult, but when Raven shot him a glare with his black eyes, the man quieted down, slurped up the rest of his meal, and retired to his room.

When the innkeeper came to his table to clear his dishes, he asked how many miles it was to Bristol.

"Roughly ten to eleven miles depending which part of town you was looking for, Mister…? I didn't catch your name," the woman said.

"Because I didn't say it," snorted Raven. "Is there a carriage or coach I can hire to take me there?"

"Langley runs a coach service to town, stops here every morning to see if anyone needs to go into Bristol."

"That will suit me just fine. I'll be taking it day after tomorrow. I'm paid up through then, am I not?"

"Yes, yes…you are," The woman responded with some timidity. She picked up his dishes and walked quickly back to the kitchen.

After a small walk to clear his head, Raven went to his room and studied the maps as if his life depended on it. He tried to memorize every town, every port, every inlet. His plan of assassination and escape to Ireland had yet to take shape. But he knew he would have to make it back here after his business in Bristol was concluded. Although the twenty-foot skiff was small, he could use it if he was desperate to get across the Irish sea. It would be better if he was on a bigger boat however.

Raven sat on the edge of the bed looking at maps and his other possessions. He was forced to travel light, but he had the resourcefulness to utilize what few assets he had in order to get what he wanted. And what he wanted was the death of Jim Hawkins. He looked at the money, his pullover knitted cap, his two knives, his monogrammed boots, his maps, billy-bag, and Joey Cairnes' locket.

There it was—the locket he had carried with him all these months. Joey had told him on the deck of the wretched prison ship the *Jonathan*, *"If I dies, take the locket and tell me brothers what happened to me, will you mister, will you? Tell me you'd do that."* Those were Joeys last words.

Now where was Joey from again? Some place called Kingswood. Where is that on this map? How close to Bristol is it? Raven poured over the maps of the coastline for a half hour and didn't see it.

When he went downstairs for his evening meal at the inn, he asked the innkeeper where Kingswood was.

"You don't want to go there, mister," the innkeeper said. "It's full of a group of families that would sooner rob you than pour you a cup of tea. A right sordid lot, I've heard. Everybody stays clear of them."

"All right then, I'll be careful. But where is it? I don't see it on the maps I have."

"And you won't. The authorities refuse to even say it exists, but it does. It's a small village about five to six miles east of Bristol proper."

◆ ◆ ◆

192

Two mornings later, the coach that made the daily trip back and forth to Bristol stopped at the Admiral Benbow. Raven climbed aboard after paying the required fare to the driver.

"Name's Langley, sir. What's yours?" the jovial, way too cheerful fellow requested of his new passenger.

"Raven."

"Like the bird, the raven?" asked Langley as if he wanted to make a new friend.

"The same," Raven answered gruffly.

"Well, Mr. Raven, just trying to make a bit of merry on a fine summer day. It's going to be a beautiful day."

As Raven settled into the coach, he heard the driver call out, "We'll see you sometime this afternoon, Mrs. Hawkins. Shouldn't be too late for a gentle nip of your apple jack. If I don't mind."

Ravens ears perked up immediately. He had never asked the name of the owner nor the innkeeper of the Admiral Benbow. What was it to him when all he needed was food and shelter.

"Driver," barked Raven.

"Name is Langley, sir. Howard Langley, if you please." Langley was busy harnessing the two horses to the coach.

"Yes, Langley it is. Did you call that woman, Hawkins?"

"I did. She owns the Benbow and runs it with her sister, Maddie. Didn't you meet them both?"

"I didn't catch their names," admitted Raven. "So she has a sister. What did you say her name was?"

"Maddie."

"I didn't meet her at all."

"Must have been in the kitchen. She does all the cooking and does mighty well by it, I would say. Did you enjoy your meals, Raven? You should have. She has a reputation as the best around here. At least on my routes." Langley finished tightening the bridles on the two horses tethered to his rig and climbed aboard.

"Does Mrs. Hawkins have a son?"

"I believe she does. He's a surgeon in Bristol. Yes, sir. Dr. Jim

Hawkins been there for over a year now. Fine gentleman. Beautiful wife, partially deaf you know, and a new little baby girl."

"You know a lot about people around here."

"Kinda makes it my business. I'm like a newspaper. People climb onto my coach and I spread the news that I have. Don't know everything, of course. But I try to share the joy of the day, try to keep the sad news private. Know what I mean?"

"Sure, sure." Raven's head was reeling. This inn, the Admiral Benbow, was owned by Hawkins' mother. That could figure nicely into an escape plan. *This place can be a safe harbor with a potential hostage if I need one. The poor man's mother lives here at the Admiral Benbow.* The thought kept circling in his mind as Langley picked up the pace down the road toward Bristol.

Bristol is going to be crowded. That will help cover my identity, give me anonymity if I want it. But if I take Hawkins down with his friends around, I'd be doomed. That's it. I'll have to isolate him from them. And what a better reason to get him alone than to lure him to rescue his poor mother. That plan just might work. Lure him here to the seacoast and slay him without anyone around. If I had to kill his mother and her sister, they would just be collateral damage.

"Hey, Langley," yelled Raven loudly, so he could hear above the clip clop clatter of the horses and the carriage creaks.

"Yeah?"

"You ever carry Dr. Hawkins and his family around?"

"Yeah, sure," Langley yelled back. Since it was a summer's day, the windows were open and they could hear each other. "As a matter of fact, on my morning run into town on Fridays, I take the route past Livesey Acres and pick up Mrs. Hawkins. Her name is Livian, by the way, and her daughter Belle... and what a little sweetie she is, I tell you. I take them to the BRI where she works with the deaf or hard of hearing, since she is so afflicted herself. She's one heck of a lip reader. Practically doesn't need that ear horn she carries around. The patients love little Belle."

"What's the BRI?"

"British Royal Infirmary. She does volunteer work. I drop her off in the mid-morning, get a spot of lunch and a beer or two at the Pig and Whistle. I pick her up at three and take her and Dr. Hawkins home to Livesey Acres after his surgery is closed on Friday afternoon. Sometimes, if I've had an extra pint or two, I'll get another man to fill in for me. Sometimes, they'll hire another coach."

"You know a lot, Langley."

"It pays to know my customers' movements. I pick extra fares all the time because of it. Dr. Hawkins and Livian are very nice people. They pays me well for the service and I'm glad to provide it, I am."

Raven's plan wasn't set yet, but with this kind of information, he could put a hostage, assassination, and escape plan together. But if he was to use Livian to get to Jim, and not have the constabulary chase him, he would need a diversion. Send them somewhere else to keep them busy so he could do whatever he wanted.

Raven knew he had to get back to the Admiral Benbow to execute his plan. He asked Langley loudly as the coach moved five or six miles an hour. The roads didn't accommodate higher speeds.

"What road are we on if I have to get back to Portishead?"

"This is the Portbury Hundred, sir. You get on the Abbots Leigh out of Bristol to link up with it."

"That's good to know. By the way, I need to find a fellow in Kingswood. The innkeeper says it's east of town about five to six miles. I need you to take me there."

"You may not want to go there. I certainly will not."

"Why not? The innkeeper says it's a village."

"I'll drop you off a mile or two from the town if you insist on going there. But I tell you again, I am not driving my rig into Kingswood."

"I'll pay you more to take me there. What the hell is wrong with Kingswood?" shouted Raven.

"There's meanness there in all forms. They'll steal from you and leave you for dead, they will. I'll take you within a mile of it, and that's it. And then, if you please, I'm not waiting around for you. I'll go back to my stable yard in Bristol. No fare from you is worth my life. If you value yours, you won't be going there. I knows to stay away. So does everybody who lives around here, and best you do too. I got a pistol here in my box just in case. But it's only one shot. If there's more of them, I'll be done for. I haven't been held up by this bunch yet and I don't intend to.

"Who's in Kingswood that makes it so terrible?"

Langley abruptly pulled up the team to the side of the road so he didn't have to keep yelling back at Raven. Once he was able to settle the horses down, he came to the side of the coach and spoke directly to Raven trying to make his point as to how dangerous it was.

"I don't know your business in Kingswood, but it's nowhere you want to be. There are a number of families with cousins that run the place. The Cairnes, Bryants, Daltons, Rogers, Frys, Bakers, Hodges families, and more. They stick together. They gang up on anyone coming through town, demand tolls just for being on their street. And if you don't pay, there's a beating waiting for you. They're all highwaymen. Thieves. They've broken into peoples' homes and assaulted them coming home from church on Sunday. Assaulted folks coming home from market with a few quid in their pockets. Even the constabulary is loath to go into Kingswood to arrest anyone unless they have a full squad of armed men with them. The Kingswood gang will come into Bristol now and again just to cause trouble. They all belong in Bridewell prison, if you ask me."

"All right, Langley, you've warned me. Now just take me within a mile or so of the place and I'll walk into the town. Like I say, I have business with one of them. Here's an extra £10, just get me close. You did say Cairnes was one of the families, didn't you?"

"Yes, I did, and they're a brazen, tough lot. It's your funeral, mister," responded Langley as he jumped back up to the driver's seat, and with the lash applied lightly and sparingly, got the rig going again.

While they made headway toward Kingswood, Raven took his considerable money stash and stuffed it under his feet in the sole of both boots. He expected to be rousted as he walked into Kingswood. He believed Langley. Langley had stayed alive because he was cautious. Raven wasn't cautious, and what better villains to employ but those who think of themselves as above the law.

Langley pulled the carriage to a halt a little over a mile from Kingswood.

"If this is where you headed, I'm letting you off here," said Langley. "I don't know what your business is here in Kingswood, but I'll have none now nor in the future. Don't call me for a ride. No fare is worth dealing with these people."

Raven got out of the coach, grabbed his few belongings, and walked toward Kingswood. There were no words necessary between the men. Langley had said his piece and drove away, having used the whip more than once to hasten his getaway.

It was late morning. The trip took the better part of three hours over hillside rutted paths that could only loosely be called roads. Raven expected a greeting party from men who watched the roads looking for easy prey. As a single man walking without a horse or companions, he would surely be considered as prey for highwaymen.

He had walked about a half-mile when two young men, about half Raven's age, came running over a small hillock at him. They stopped right in front of him. The older one of the two pulled out a knife and held it up clearly where Raven could see it.

"What's your business, Mister?" said the one with the knife.

"I come to see a fellow in Kingswood. I have business with him."

"What kind of business?"

"That's for me and him to discuss."

"So you are cracking wise to us, now are you? You see, we need to know what you want. Maybe you're a constable, maybe you're a sheriff, although you don't look like one. In fact, you look like an old sailor away from the docks. Lost maybe."

The other young tough and the one making the remarks shared an instant moronic laugh at the other one's attempt at a jest.

Raven wanted to dispel this fellow's attitude and did not want to get into a knife fight with him at this point. It wouldn't suit his plans at all. The kid would most surely die and then he'd have an entire clan or two against him rather than working for him.

"I come to see a man who's a brother to Joey Cairnes."

"Joey! You know Joey! Why didn't you just say so? Where's Joey? We can take you to his brother. Everyone been sick with worry about Joey." The man stopped and gave Raven a suspicious look. "Hey, wait a minute. You could be lying. You have any proof you know Joey?"

Raven pulled the locket from around his neck and showed it to the kid with the knife, who had temporarily put it in his belt.

"Look, Billy," the older of the two toughs said. "It's Joey's locket—the one he took from Mrs. Prigg the night he got nicked. How did you get this, Mister... What'll I call you?"

"Raven...call me Raven. Joey gave it to me. He died of the typhus in my arms on the prison ship the *Jonathan*. Joey's last words were, 'Please tell my brother and me mother that I am gone to a heaven better than this earth.' I have to tell his brother that. Now take me to him."

◆◆◆

After making it to Kingswood, Raven was taken to see Joey's brother, Bennie Cairnes.

"So you saw Joey on the prison ship. What were you doing there?" asked Bennie Cairnes, the twenty-three-year-old leader of the Rooster Road gang. The family fathers and mothers ran the business, but the younger ones under Bennie's knuckle-jaw leadership did the stealing. Bennie kept turning the locket over and over in his hand, staring at it as if his little brother would appear if he rubbed it enough.

"I was sent to the Virginia iron-ore mines on a kidnapping charge. If you don't believe me, take a look at the scar they burned into my hand sixteen months ago." Raven ripped off one of the gloves he had been wearing to cover the scar and turned it palm up, so Bennie could plainly see it.

"I see it, I see it. If you was transported like Joey how come you made it here?"

"I escaped. Leave it at that. I made the trip here to do what Joey asked me to do." Raven carefully put the glove back on to his hand to cover the scar.

"I give you some credit for that, Raven. You didn't have to do that. The families recognize you went out of your way to get this locket to us and let us know for sure what Joey's fate was. If we can return the favor, we will. You say it was the typhus?"

"He was weak beyond help. It took him hard."

"But you didn't come all this way just to give us this locket, did you?" Raven could tell that as a leader of the gang, Bennie knew that everyone had an angle. Everyone was trying to get one up on his fellow, to take advantage of someone else. It was the way they lived.

"I came here to seek my revenge on those who testified against me. There may be a way you can help. But I can't be sure if this will work until I spend a little time in Bristol, find my quarry, and determine the best way to silence him forever and execute my escape. I don't mean to get caught."

Bennie leaned across the table where the two of them sat facing one another with five of the Rooster Road gang circling the table in case of any trouble. Then Bennie pulled a six-blade from his belt and lunged violently toward Raven, coming within an inch of his face. The other members of the gang stiffened as if they were ready to back his play.

Bennie's quick, aggressive move didn't bother Raven. He was always prepared for a fight. This wouldn't be an even fight, since he held his right hand low, beneath the table, mere inches from his deer-skinning knife in his monogrammed boot. And he could get three of them before they knew what gutted them.

"Didn't mean to startle you, Raven," Bennie chortled at his weak attempt to intimidate his guest.

"I wasn't."

"I see that. You have a killer's look in your eyes. I like that. You're a serious man and I believe that you mean to do what you say you'll do." Bennie looked at the rest of the gang. "Relax fellows. We can help this man, can't we? You want revenge. As it so happens, we want revenge as well. We lost one of ours in a street brawl a few weeks back. Bobby Baker was shot on the Avon bridge. He was shot and killed by a black bastard named Newsome. And we'll get him for it, believe me."

"So our interests may coincide," Raven responded. Raven was thinking quickly and could see that this thickheaded mob bent on revenge could provide an excellent diversion and keep the police away from him.

Bennie looked at Raven. "Of course, there will be a fee for our services if we help you."

"I expect nothing less," responded Raven. "This is what I need most immediately. I need to get transportation to Bristol, I need a place there where I can stay hidden and send messages to you. Once I have a firm plan in mind, you and I will need a way for us to agree on your fee and for me to get the money to you."

"You'll pay before we do any job…any job. Understand? No refunds if it doesn't come off the way you want it to."

"I have no fear of that."

"We have a place in Bristol. It's near the Hole-in-the-Wall tavern. Leave a message there with the bartender name of Lewis. He'll get the message to us. We're six miles out of the east end of Bristol, we can be there in an hour to an hour and a half."

"Bennie, I'll take that horse ride into Bristol now if you please. Introduce me to this Lewis fellow so he knows my face and takes me to my room. I have to start finding my prey."

Three of the Rooster Road gang drove Raven to within a mile of the city's east side in a rusted, beaten coach pulled by a single horse.

Raven saw the smokestacks rising in the industrial quarter and the houses beneath them.

The gang let him and one of the Hodges boys out of the carriage because they didn't want the constabulary to see them. They were well known and wanted for one crime or another. If they stuck together like a pack of wolves, they could win small battles. But they always followed Bennie's orders, and Bennie said drop them off a mile from town. And they did.

CHAPTER 21

CHAPTER 21

BRISTOL: JULY 1772

Raven and Hodges—from the Kingswood gang—walked the last mile into Bristol's east end and made straight for the Hole-in–the-Wall Tavern. After ordering beer, Hodges and Raven sat down, and Hodges motioned to Lewis the bartender to come over to their table against the wall.

"This here's Raven," Hodges said. "Bennie says to put him up in a room and help him where you can."

"If Bennie says it's all right, I suspect it is," Lewis said, acknowledging the brutal power that the Kingswood gang—and Bennie Cairnes in particular—held over Lewis and others of his criminal class.

"He needs a room and also he needs to send messages to Bennie through you—you being the messenger. Got it, Lewis?" said Hodges, seeming to gloat in his small molehill of temporary authority.

"I got it, Hodges, I ain't no stooge. Cooking something up, is Bennie?"

"For him to know and for you to be told what to do," Hodges said, sticking a bit of additional superiority to the barkeep.

"I need money up front," said Lewis, "for the room and the messenger service."

"Well, Raven, here is where you cough up a few quid to keep Mr. Lewis in your employ," snarled Hodges.

Raven had been quiet while Hodges and Lewis did their verbal sparring. But now it was time for him to pay, and probably give something to Hodges to keep him on his side. Things could go terribly wrong. The gang had seen his scarred hand. The gang who had allegiance only to themselves and a quick profit, had heard his general plan of revenge in the city of Bristol. If they went to the constabulary because he tried to avoid paying, they could turn him in for a reward and it would mean the hangman. This was not the time to take chances with villains.

He didn't want to reach into the soles of his monogrammed boots right there in the tavern. Not only would these two hoodlums see the amount of money he had, they'd know where it was hidden.

Raven offered a tone of acquiescence and minor joviality in order to get away from the table.

"Been a long walk, Lewis. Tell me where the gents is, will you?"

"Round back, you'll see the trough. It's in plain sight."

Raven went out the back door, found a hidden alcove with visual protection from the street and tavern, and pulled off one of his boots. He grabbed a few pound notes, slipped the boot on rapidly, and went back into the tavern.

"How much for the room for a week?" Raven asked Lewis, glaring at him with a grim smile as if to say, *if you gouge me, I will find a way to get back at you*. Raven's glare into Lewis's weak, rheumy eyes was enough to convince the bartender to ask only for the minimum.

"Five quid for the week, if you please."

Raven handed over the money. "Take me there. I need to rest. It's been a long day." Then he turned to Hodges. "Hodges, here's a five note for your trouble." He handed the five pound note to Hodges, and a greedy little smile took over his face. *I'll have to watch out for this one*, thought Raven as Hodges left the tavern. *He was born with larceny on his mind.*

Lewis got someone to watch the bar for him and took Raven next door, where he led him up the creaky old stairs to a room which was the opposite of fashionable. The bed frame was old pine, and when Raven sat down on the mattress, he knew it was old and rat eaten. He vowed to make his business as quick as possible so he could get out of this town and be off to Ireland.

As soon as Lewis left him, Raven slumped on the bed and went fast asleep. He would do his next prowling and information gathering once it was dark.

When he woke from his short nap, he looked into the cracked mirror and decided he needed a shave and a haircut. It had been days since he had either, and with his hair and beard growing back, he could be recognized. He had grown accustomed to his moustache, but the beard definitely had to be taken off and his hair shaved once again, or at least trimmed to minimal proportions. He went into his billy-bag and removed the razor and did what he could. Maybe he should get a real haircut at a barber. They were always a good source of information. A barber might be able to tell Raven something that would lead him to Hawkins.

Raven prowled the streets of East Bristol. Not wanting to make contact with anyone, he didn't engage in any conversation. He found a barber shop complete with the blood red and white pole that described their archaic brand of medicine. The red and white pole outside barber shops referenced a time when barbers were expected to perform bloodletting and other crude medical procedures. Even though Raven as Franks had been a surgeon, and presumably had a higher degree of medical training, the barber guild still had some clout. Raven would go there in the morning, but all he wanted was a haircut and a shave. And hopefully some information.

When he arrived back in the mid to late evening, he stopped at the Hole-in–the-Wall Tavern. He ordered some food and a beer and quietly, almost stealthily, listened for any conversation from nearby patrons that he could use. The one conversation he listened to intently came from men who sat two tables over from where Raven was sitting. These men had been drinking throughout the evening, and even though they didn't know it, they were talking loud enough for everyone in the tavern to hear them.

"Nathan Newsome is going to be in the dock on Friday. Mark my words, they'll hang him, sure as I'm sitting here."

Another voice said, "What do you know? You wasn't there. You didn't see him fire the gun that killed that Baker fellow."

"There's going to be a street riot, I can feel it. If the magistrate lets him off, him being the black man he is, the whites will terrorize every black man and woman in this side of town. Yeah, yeah, that's right. They'll be fires. I can only hope my flat doesn't get torched. I got the missus to think about."

"Like it's the last thing you'd think about, other than saving your own skin."

With a flash of anger, the man who had been insulted hit the other man flush on the side of the face with a haymaker. Raven didn't react other than to move his hand close to the knife hidden in his boot.

He could see Lewis step over with a well-worn cudgel that he kept under the bar and swacked the man who had started the fight in the back, knocking him over.

"You two, get out of here and sober up," said Lewis. He held the cudgel in a threatening manner and looked ready to bash one or both again if either came up swinging.

"You heard me. Go on outta here."

Intrigued by the loud claims about a riot on Friday, Raven asked Lewis what the trouble was about.

"You go to the city courtroom tomorrow. You'll find out all about it. I just hope this place doesn't burn. The source of all the ill tempers came from a court ruling a couple of weeks ago. The ruling made every black in England a free man. That's the core of it. We had a little trouble in here when the ruling came down. A couple of the Kingswood gang beat up a man name of Nathan Newsome who used to come in here, eat something, have a beer or two—even drank some rum once in a while. He works for Squire Trelawney, the wine merchant. They found Newsome on the bridge last week and tried to finish him off. They say Newsome shot Bobby Baker cold. That's how I heard it. The mob wants him dead, and the Kingswood gang would like to string him up. That's what they were talking about."

◆◆◆

The next morning, Raven got his hair shaved down to bare nubbins and his beard removed. He told the barber to keep the mustache. He had gotten used to its rough, mean look. It was early enough, and he found his way to the courthouse by asking a few people for directions. When he got close, he saw a crowd of people outside the courthouse milling about, intermittently yelling and cursing against the blacks.

Although he wanted to remain anonymous, he wanted to see the trial. There were a couple of people pushing up against the two musket-armed constabularies barring some people from entering. Some were able to squeeze by them and get inside. Raven was one of them. He settled in the back of the room and took it all in.

The mood in the room was tense, the anger palpable. There were a dozen or so black men in the upper balcony, but the crowd was mostly made up of white working-class men. From what he could hear, they were angry about any number of things. Some yelled out against blacks taking their jobs, some yelled about the murder of a white man by a black who never should have had a gun in the first place.

More people must have squeezed past the constabulary since more were coming in, leading to a dense crowd. All the chairs were taken, and any newcomers stood along with Raven. There were four more armed constabularies inside the room. They had now positioned themselves in the back and were guarding the closed door, refusing to let anybody else enter and make the crowded situation any worse.

If he strained his neck, he could see up to the front of the room. He saw the backs of some men's heads. One of them sitting between four white men was a black. Suddenly to his left near the door, the crowd outside tried to burst through the closed door. Despite the guards, the door began to heave open. It made a loud cracking noise as if someone on the outside was ramming something against the door. Everyone turned around to see if the door would explode. More of the outside crowd piled into an already chaotic, tense, and crowded room.

Raven kept his eyes to the front just as the four white men and the black man in the front of the room turned around in the direction of the noise. Raven almost swore aloud.

There he was. It was Jim Hawkins.

Raven's blood shot through his veins as he took careful note of what Hawkins looked like and the type of clothes he was wearing. This was the prey he had been stalking these weeks. This was the man he had sworn to kill for betraying him sixteen months earlier. He had been patient. He had been ruthless. But the evil in his heart, kept latent in the colonies, carefully deployed in Portsmouth, was now fully a boil in Bristol.

A man who must have been a magistrate came through a back door into the courtroom accompanied by two constables with muskets. They stood aside him and practically dared anyone to make a move in the magistrate's direction. There was a railing of sorts that separated the growing mob from the defendant, his defenders, the magistrate, and his guards.

It was as if the magistrate fully knew the gravity of the hearing. One of the guards loudly announced to the crowd that the hearing was for the alleged shooting of one Bobby Baker of Kingswood by Nathan Newsome, defendant, Magistrate Howard Gawtry presiding.

Someone yelled out, "Alleged shooting, my arse. The man's dead."

The compacted audience howled in response.

Gawtry quickly gained control of the situation with a stern warning. "There will be no further outbursts in my courtroom. If you do, you will be removed from the room, arrested for disturbance of the peace, and sentenced forthwith to six months in Bridewell prison. If you doubt my resolve, just try it."

The room quieted a bit and Gawtry continued. "We are here to hear witnesses of what happened on Avon bridge. Gawtry looked at his witness list. "The first witness is the arresting officer, Constable Harry Peyton."

Peyton went to the witness chair, swore an oath to tell the truth, and proceeded to relate the events that led to the arrest of Nathan Newsome. He didn't add much to what everyone already knew. There was a group of young men on the southern side of the bridge, they had gone past the constable's station. Five to ten minutes later, the constable heard the report of a pistol and rushed along with the constables under his command to the northern side of the Avon bridge where he found Bobby Baker dying of a gunshot wound to the stomach. He continued with his recitation of commanding Drs. Livesey and Hawkins to treat the wounded man back at their surgery where the young man died from the wound.

When Peyton was done, the magistrate asked a few simple questions about the weapon and how he knew Nathan Newsome had fired it. "He said he fired it," said Peyton. "When we came to the scene he was holding the pistol and confessed that he didn't mean to shoot anyone, but he had shot in self-defense because the group of young men had been kicking and beating him."

Gawtry then said, "Are there any other witnesses attesting to what they saw on the bridge, excepting for the moment those who are coming to the defense of Mister Newsome?"

A voice yelled out from the crowd, "We all know it was the Kingswood gang, magistrate. But none of them have the guts to be here."

This was followed by a timid, if vocal, crowd approval.

No one spoke up. If anybody had been on the bridge and saw the gang beat and kick Newsome, his wife, and the others, they weren't about to speak up. Any testimony against the deceased Bobby Baker, and the Kingswood gang of ruffians would get them a street beating.

Raven looked around the crowd and saw Hodges crushed between a couple of men. He didn't make a sound. He was there to report on what happened, not to come to the aid of his dead in-law, Bobby Baker. This was a gang that believed in street justice, not the justice of the law. Hodges couldn't raise his voice for fear of being arrested for past crimes or current misdemeanors.

"If there's no one who was a witness on behalf of the deceased, I call on Dr. Livesey who has registered with the court as a witness for the defense."

Dr. Livesey took his position in front of the magistrate, and facing the courtroom, swore to tell the truth. He recounted the mob scene that day on the bridge when the group of ten young men came up to Nathan, swore epithets at him, and started pushing, hitting, and kicking him and his wife, Olivia.

"I, too was injured," said Livesey. "One of the men in the group hit me with a rock. I still have the wound to show for it. Nathan was being kicked to death. He had the right to defend himself."

Jim Hawkins was next. He turned to McLaughlin sitting next to him and said, "I don't know why Nathan is a defendant. We were the ones who were attacked."

As Jim took the stand and swore to tell the truth, he said, "I can't see why Nathan is on trial at all."

Someone in the crowd yelled, "He killed a white man. That's why."

"Silence," bellowed Gawtry. "Or I'll have you removed from the court. Continue."

"The group of young men came and rushed me, knocked me down along with Squire Trelawney," continued Hawkins, pointing to the squire at the defendant's table. "My wife and baby were behind us and were almost knocked into the water. I tried to pull my pistol to shoot, but it fell to the ground and slid towards Nathan. He grabbed the pistol in self-defense and shot blindly. If Baker got shot, it was because he was standing over Nathan Newsome kicking him in the ribs and head."

Gawtry said, "So it was your pistol Newsome used?"

"Yes, that's right. The gun was knocked from my hand and slid on the bridge cobblestones. He picked it up for fear of his life. That's what happened."

The magistrate made a note on the ledger he kept of the witnesses' names, notes of their testimony, and events in case he needed to review them. "So Nathan Newsome did not bring a weapon to the bridge?"

"No sir," said Jim Hawkins. "The gun was mine."

While Dr. Hawkins testified, Raven kept his head low and watched carefully. Watching Hawkins on the stand reminded him of Hawkins testifying against what Raven (as Franks) had done back in Gosport at Haslar Hospital. It made him furious, but he had to keep his fury under wraps until he had the right moment. That would be a challenge.

"Squire Trelawney, I believe you're next to testify," announced Gawtry. "Do you have anything to add to what Drs. Livesey and Hawkins have said?"

The squire seemed to know the magistrate. It was as if a good friend was being asked if he wanted another cup of tea.

"I was on the bridge and was attacked by the same mob that rushed us, Hawkins, Livesey, Nathan Newsome, and our women folk. They included Olivia Newsome who works for me, Mrs. Livesey, and Mrs. Hawkins who had her small child in a pram. Those thugs were willing to push the pram into the river for their crude enjoyment.

"Magistrate Gawtry, it was chaos, and if I had the opportunity I would have shot one of them as well. We were under attack, pure and simple. And if I may, I want to testify to all here that Nathan Newsome is an honorable man. He has worked in my warehouse for over a year and has steadfastly performed his duties. He is an asset to my operation, and if he had to shoot someone to stop the mob from attacking us, then I believe he did it in self-defense and should be released."

When Trelawney spoke these words of defense, it was as if the mayor or governor had made a proclamation. Some of the anger, some of the hatred left the room as if air was expelled from the lungs of the crowd. The crowd was subdued for a moment if not completely silent. They had just heard a rich tory defend the honor of a black man in open court for all to hear. They hadn't expected it, and it caused a few in the crowd to murmur that maybe the shooting was justified.

Gawtry asked once more if there were any other witnesses who wanted to come forward. He let the question fill the room for a moment or two, then proceeded.

"According to the witnesses' testimonies of an attack by a group of men on another without justification—and the testimonies that Nathan Newsome was singled out and beaten and kicked by one or more of the attackers—it is the ruling of this court that Nathan Newsome fired the shot in justified self-defense. It is the order of this court that he is found innocent of any crime and be released from confinement. It is so ordered."

Cheers from the black men and women in the balcony rang out when the magistrate rendered his verdict. Rather than share the joy of the moment, the blacks' cheering only incited the white men in the crowd below them. Their hatred was incensed by the cheers above their heads. The crowd exclaimed against the verdict and yelled out:

"Black bastard got away with it!"

"Baker didn't deserve to die!"

"You'll still get yours, Newsome!"

These hate-filled shouts and others reignited the vehemence in the room.

Once the judgment was declared by the magistrate, two of the guards came to the table where Livesey, Hawkins, Trelawney, McLaughlin, and Newsome were sitting and removed Nathan's shackles. The other two guards led Magistrate Gawtry out the rear door and out of harm's way. The four other guards at the back of the room came up the center of the room and attempted to form an aisle for the defendant and his party to exit the building. It didn't work. There were too many people for the meager number of constabularies to keep back.

Although a few members of the crowd were mollified at Trelawney's testimony, many others didn't care about the verdict. They wanted their own brand of justice that came from inherent self-loathing, fear, and the transference of that fear to a black man they thought was their inferior.

A few members of the crowd kept yelling:

"Black bastard!"

"We should hang him anyway!"

"How can this killing be justified?"

"What should we care what the magistrate said?"

There were other slurs shouted against Nathan that were even uglier. The race hatred among those who wanted Nathan's blood quickly overwhelmed the room.

Jim saw that he and Mac had to get Dr. Livesey, Squire Trelawney, and most of all Nathan, out of the room. Then they needed to go down the street into Trelawney's carriage and back safely to Trelawney's house as quickly as possible. Trelawney had arranged for Abraham Gray to stay with his carriage and remain close to the courthouse, so all they had to do was to get down the street before the mob got ugly, senseless, and violent.

Jim got Mac's eye and said, "You lead Dr. Livesey and protect his right flank. I have the left flank with the squire and Nathan."

With his left hand, Mac grabbed Dr. Livesey by his belt and moved to the door, keeping his body between the crowd and Dr. Livesey. The four members of the constabulary held their muskets out in front of them, attempting to serve as a barrier, trying to keep the crowd away from Jim, Mac, Livesey, Nathan, and the squire. But there were only two on each side of a make-shift aisle down the middle.

The constables shifted from right to left towards the door, but it wasn't easy. Members of the crowd were yelling and trying to throw a punch or a kick at Jim and his party. Jim moved slowly, the pushing and shoving escalating. He tried to stay between the crowd and the squire who held onto Nathan's belt to keep them from splitting apart, which could have been deadly for Nathan.

The vehemence in the room rose with the passing seconds. One of the constables used the butt of his gun and shoved a crowd member in the stomach. Another constable butted a crowd member in the head. Now the crowd on that side of the ersatz aisle got even angrier, and one of them reached out and hit the constable in the head, knocking his hat off.

As Mac and Livesey moved, the crowd moved towards them yelling, "Traitors!" and "Turncoats!"

Trying to use his body to protect the squire and Nathan, Jim could tell that they were getting close to the back of the room where the door was open. But people on the outside of the courtroom now had open access to the melee occurring inside and wanted to get in on the action. They seemed to relish the physical contact. The two constables who had stayed outside tried to enter the crowded doorway to help their fellow constables inside.

Jim looked around and noticed—that because of his size and his willingness to strike back—Mac had Dr. Livesey almost to the door and out to relative safety.

The two constables on Jim's side of the phalanx were moving in tandem with him, the squire, and Nathan, but a couple people in the crowd tried to kick him. In an instant, one leg came at him, striking him sideways, then another leg appeared, and tripped him to the floor. He momentarily lost his hold on the squire who was using his considerable girth to pull Nathan forward toward the door at the rear.

Jim tried to get up, but before he did, he saw something in the blur of the action that froze his eyes, mind, and heart. He was on the ground but for a few seconds trying to get up when his eyes focused and he saw the HF monogram on somebody's boots that were close enough to kick him. Before the owner of the boot could strike, Jim got up and reconnected to the squire who still had hold of Nathan. Jim looked back to see if the person wearing the monogrammed boots was there, but he didn't recognize anyone. He needed to get away, and that was more important than anything else at the moment.

All four of Nathan's defense team as well as Nathan made it to the double doors and pushed and shoved away from the crowd. The constables with their muskets put their backs to Jim and his friends, raised their rifles, and were ready to shoot any of the mob that followed. There were now six constables with raised muskets protecting Jim and his party. Abraham Gray had drawn his pistol as well and stood at the carriage awaiting any trouble that came their way. He provided an extra layer of security when they needed it the most. They all made it safely to the squire's carriage and jumped aboard. Once all five of them were in the carriage, the squire urged Gray to get them away as soon as possible.

As the carriage made its way up the hill toward the squire's in-town mansion, Jim and the others took stock of any injuries. No one had been cut. No one was bleeding even though Mac especially had taken quite a few elbow hits and fist punches to his ribs. Dr. Livesey's head was bleeding again from the previous wound he'd suffered. Jim sat confused and shaken in the coach, adrenalin running through his veins, wondering if he was positive enough about what he has seen to mention the HF monogram and who might be in Bristol with blood-red vengeance on his mind.

When they got to the squire's house at the top of the hill and took some time and some wine to calm down, they were offered a bit of food prepared by Olivia Newsome and Monica Green. After they ate, Jim took Mac aside from the others.

"I swear he's in Bristol," said Jim, unable to keep his suspicions to himself any longer.

"Who's in Bristol?" queried Mac. He looked more closely at Jim. "I've known you for the better part of three years, and we've always had each other's back. I can tell you're worried about something, something serious. I don't think I've ever seen you look this worried."

"Franks is in Bristol," said Jim. "I saw his monogrammed boots in the courtroom when I was tripped and fell. I swear I saw the initials HF. Who else would have boots like this? Who else but the man who swore to kill me?"

"Jim, I have never doubted your word, but listen, Franks was shipped to the colonies. That's a world away. He can't get back here. Besides, if the prison ship didn't kill him, his slave masters in the Americas would."

"But Mac, the initials HF. They were clearly etched into the boots. There's only one man we know who would have the vanity and the money to get those exact initials etched into his boots. That's Herman Franks."

"All right, all right. We have both been through a lot this morning. We could both use a rest. But don't stay up at night worrying about him. If he shows up, and I sincerely don't think he will, we'll take care of him."

"Sure, sure. Maybe you're right. But just the same, I'm putting a pistol in my belt every day from now on. I'm making sure Livian carries one as well. You should too."

CHAPTER 22

AFTER RESTING THAT afternoon and putting a new dressing on Dr. Livesey's head wound, Jim and Dr. Livesey got a carriage to take them to Livesey Acres. They had decided to close the surgery on Friday. Even the Hippocratic oath wouldn't force them to be in the streets of Bristol if there was a race riot threatening their lives.

Squire Trelawney insisted that Nathan and Olivia Newsome stay the night with him. He was now determined to use his wealth and connections to help these two employees. The squire was full of complexities, but he always obeyed the law. King and country always came first. And if the high judge Lord Mansfield determined that blacks were not chattel and could not be forced to work against their will and could "breathe English air" as freemen, then so be it. But the squire was also a realist and understood the depth of hatred that flooded into the courtroom from which they had escaped. He knew it would take time and even tragic bloodletting to quell the unrest.

He had felt the pushing and shoving and heard the vitriol spewing from the full throttle throats of the crowd who wanted Nathan's head on a pike. Since Olivia and Nathan worked for him, the squire now had a personal interest in keeping those close to him as safe as could be.

◆ ◆ ◆

At Livesey Acres, Jim and Robert recounted the news of the day to Elizabeth and Livian at the dinner table. Thankfully the two women had stayed at Livesey Acres that day and weren't threatened by the mob action that had injured Dr. Livesey and frightened Jim Hawkins. As they told the story of what transpired in the courtroom, Livian could tell that Jim was worried. It was written all over his face. Robert did most of the talking and Jim just added a comment or two. Both were glad that they'd escaped with the help of Abraham Gray. Otherwise, it could have ended much worse.

When dinner was over, Livian was concerned about her husband and motioned him to join her outside on the porch to watch the setting sun. "I want to know what is troubling you," said Livian in her halting speech. Those who loved her unconditionally were patient enough to listen to her without interrupting. Livian spoke carefully, not always enunciating perfectly, but the people who were dear to her got her meaning.

"Jim, ever since you've gotten home, you've been distant, buried in your thoughts. Please tell me what is going on."

"I don't want to frighten you," said Jim, looking into his sweet Livian's face. She was an expert lip reader, but with Jim, she was also an expert face reader. She had bathed him in oatmeal and cold water when he had recently had a scare with smallpox. She had submitted to his seemingly crackpot ideas on using static electricity and crystals to reawaken her hearing. They had been through a lot in the few years they'd been married, but they both persevered despite the challenges that were thrown at them. She was an internally strong woman who would do anything to protect her family. So if Jim was worried, she had to know why. "You must tell me. We share everything. Everything, Jim Hawkins!"

"I think I saw Herman Franks at the courtroom this morning."

Her breath caught in her throat for a moment. "Not Dr. Franks from Haslar Hospital?"

Jim took the time to speak carefully into Livian's ear horn, which she always had with her in a loop around her neck. "The same. I saw his monogrammed boots, Livian. Mac doesn't believe me. He says Franks is dead or in the colonies and could not have possibly made it back to England. But I swear I saw those boots. I couldn't see his face. There was too much commotion in the courtroom. I looked around, but I didn't see anyone who looked like Franks when I last saw him."

Livian responded, "I believe you. You saw what you saw. Now what are we to do? We can't stay here at Livesey Acres like frightened rabbits. We are not cowards! You have a medical practice, rounds to make at the BRI. I have my Fridays at the BRI helping the hard of hearing."

"Yes, of course, you're right. But I will arm myself. I haven't wanted to carry a pistol or a knife, but until I know anything for certain, I am going armed. And you are too if you leave the confines of Livesey Acres."

She shook her head. "I don't want to carry a pistol."

"You have to. You know how to shoot, don't you?"

"Yes, Daddy showed me many years ago."

"And he taught you how to load powder and shot and reload if necessary?"

"Of course. Can't do one without the other."

"Then I am getting a pistol for you from Dr. Livesey's gun case and one for me. Franks means to do us harm. I will not let you be a victim. Tomorrow morning, we will tell Robert and take some pistols out away from the houses and practice."

◆◆◆

The next morning, Jim woke early and joined Robert for tea. He told him what he had seen in the courtroom. He told him of the threat and the real danger that he and Livian and maybe even Mac faced. He wouldn't be able to tell Mac until Monday when he went into the surgery. For now, he and Livian wanted to use Livesey's pistols to practice shooting and loading the weapons.

With Dr. Livesey's approval, they removed two of Robert's

flintlock pistols from the gun case in the study. Dr. Livesey had purchased them from His Majesty's Service after he served with the Navy. While Livian was waking up and taking care of Belle's early morning breakfast, Jim loaded the two pistols and took extra powder and shot from the gun case.

When Livian placed Belle in Elizabeth's care, she went with Jim and the weapons outside, away from any buildings. Their path took them by the cottage on the property where Arnold and Maye lived. Livian made a quick dash inside to tell her parents that if they heard gunfire to not be alarmed. She had another reason to talk to her father. Jim had asked her to see if her father, who was a master of many trades around the farm, to help Jim fashion a leather holster for Livian to carry the gun.

The guns they were going to shoot were a matching pair. They were Queen Anne flintlock pistols, .44 caliber, about ten-inches in length. They were made in the 1760's by Hutchinson's in London during the Seven Years war with the French. These were military pistols without ornate silver flourish.

When they reached a place that was safe to shoot, in the apple orchard, Jim placed a couple of rotten apples together on a tree stump about ten yards away. "Well, Livian, here's your chance to show me how well you shoot. I have already loaded the guns. Go ahead, cock the flintlock and shoot the apples."

Livian took aim and pulled the trigger, sending the flintlock hammer into the frizzen, creating a spark igniting the powder in the pan, causing the powder in the barrel to explode, propelling the shot toward the target. All of this occurred within about a second. The recoil from the shot was not unsubstantial, pulling Livian's arm up. The amount of shot necessary for the .44 caliber ball gave her some kickback.

"Did I hit the apples?" asked Livian. She didn't have the ear horn next to her ear but still heard a small amount of the report from the gun firing. Jim had been standing to her side and could see that her shot hadn't been anywhere near the apples nor the stump.

"No, you didn't," said Jim, looking at Livian so she could lip read. "These pistols are not accurate at ten yards. They are meant to be fired at close range."

"How close?" asked Livian.

"Three yards or closer and you will not miss. Aim for the bottom of the torso." Jim pointed toward his own lower stomach. "The natural recoil of the shot will lead to a travel of the trajectory in an upwards direction."

They both walked to within three yards of the apples. Jim handed Livian his pistol. "Take the shot from here. It's loaded."

"I am so close."

"You will have to be."

Livian stood, pulled the flintlock hammer back, and shot Jim's pistol. The apples exploded on the stump.

"I can hit something from this close."

"If you aren't this close, you will be wasting the advantage. You need to be close. Let me show you how to load these pistols. If you miss the first shot, you can load this pistol quite rapidly. These Queen Anne's have the advantage of having screw off barrels." He screwed off the barrel of one of the pistols, placed powder in the barrel, set the shot on top of it, screwed the barrel back in, placed a small amount of powder in the pan, and closed the frizzen. "These guns are special since you don't need a ramrod. The screw off barrels allow this. Now you load the second one."

Livian had been following Jim's loading procedure and carefully, and quickly loaded the second pistol.

Livian and Jim both took turns shooting apples off the stump and gradually improved their marksmanship until they could step back to about five yards and still hit their target.

Jim cleaned the barrels of unexploded powder in both pistols and spent the rest of the day working with Livian's father fashioning a pistol holster for her to wrap around her waist in a concealed way. Livian didn't want one that was so obvious. She said she couldn't possibly conceal the pistol if it was in the small of her back. "Make a smaller belt, Dad, would you? I'll hide it under my skirt around my thigh."

The men looked at other with a bit of wonderment but acceded to Livian's demands. They made the holster so there were two simple pockets, one for powder and one for a few shots. When it was done, Jim and Arnold were quite proud of their creation and let Livian tie the holster around her leg. Livian was glad for the weapon, but silently hoped she would never have to use it.

◆ ◆ ◆

The riots continued sporadically throughout the weekend. White men spending their time drinking in taverns would bumble out into the street, spy a black man or woman, and rush over to harass, punch, and kick until the wounded party was able to get away. Then like a pack of cowards fearing the constabulary, they would stop the abuse and huddle back into a tavern pretending rage against freed blacks and patting each other on the backs for the fear they put into the poor victim.

Raven watched the small mobs all day and night—first from his window in the boarding house, then on the street as a silent observer, then in the tavern. He thought about how he could use them. The alcohol consumed certainly allowed the assembled to lose their inhibitions leading them to do something they would never do otherwise. The people they attacked were no different than them other than the color of their skin.

These people were upset all weekend over the magistrate's decision to free Nathan Newsome. But there was something more. It had to be the threat they thought the freed blacks made to their own livelihoods. These were unskilled men, mostly dockworkers, rope makers, coopers, dray haulers, and common manual laborers with nothing more to offer than their brawn. A mob could be exciting and powerful, and it could make people feel part of a huge group that they could hide in because they didn't think they'd be detected or held responsible for their actions.

What he saw on the street was inherent cowardice. The mob

usually followed a single man or two men, and if stoked up enough, would do whatever the leaders asked them to do. But the violence couldn't be sustained in one place. It only lasted for a short time because of their fear of being arrested. Being tossed into the pit of a British prison could mean a slow death if you didn't have the means to bail yourself out or to pay a hefty fine. He should know. It wasn't too long ago that he had suffered such deprivation.

Raven thought he would employ Bennie and his Kingswood gang and direct them to start multiple attacks from multiple taverns so they could get the drunken mob to follow like sheep.

That part of the plan was taking shape. He needed to act fairly quickly so the heat of the moment wouldn't be lost. If he could fund Bennie Cairnes' buying of drinks for a tavern full of louts, they might follow him despite the drivel that would come out of his mouth.

If the mob fever was high enough, the mob might be led to burn down a couple of places where the blacks lived. If multiple members of the Kingswood gang would start trouble in at least three different areas, he could get the Bristol constabulary fully engaged. That way, the constabulary wouldn't bother him with what he was going to do to Jim Hawkins and Hawkins' bride. He needed a time and date, then get a message and money to Cairnes.

Raven stalked the streets of Bristol trying to work out how to lure Hawkins away. He didn't want to talk to anybody. He kept his head down as he walked up one street and down another. It took him an entire day of walking. He found Livesey's Surgery. They had even put Hawkins' and McLaughlin's names on the nameplate. He was trying to think of a strategy to get Hawkins isolated from his English and Scottish friends. Then he remembered what the carriage driver, Langley, had said about Livian helping all day on Fridays at the British Royal Infirmary. *That's it. Friday. That's the day. Three o'clock is the time.*

Raven went to Lewis at the Hole-in the-Wall Tavern and instructed him to get a message to Bennie. "Tell him to meet me here tomorrow night at ten o'clock."

Lewis was too inquisitive. "What's this about then?"

"None of your damn business. Just get him the message."

"I'll need some money."

"No you won't. I've already paid you for this." With that, Raven glared at Lewis and the bartender meekly turned away and went back to the bar.

◆◆◆

The next morning, Raven went to an apothecary and bought two bottles of tincture of opium. He wanted to know the concentration, and therefore the strength of the drug. Opium could be distilled and added to a small amount of liquid to get the liquid form he needed. He had a long talk with the apothecary who never questioned Raven's motive for wanting so much of the drug. And Raven didn't produce any.

He knew this sleep inducing drug better than anyone. He had used the weakness of Duncan—the former administrator of Haslar Hospital—and his addiction to implicitly get control of the hospital's finances. This was Raven's drug of choice to knock his victims out. He knew from his experiments at Haslar Hospital that he would need to use a good deal of the liquid to knock his victim out. The effect would not be immediate, so he planned on there being a struggle which he had to do out of sight of the general populace.

◆◆◆

The next night, he met with Bennie Cairnes, Hodges, and Bobby Baker's younger brother in a back room at the Hole-in-the-Wall Tavern. If the constabularies had known Bennie was in town, they would have arrested him on the spot. He was the suspect in many former robberies and assaults. He was known by sight to them and that's why he would only come into Bristol at night when the darkness might shield him from suspicious eyes who might report him just for a reward.

"Let's get down to business," said Bennie. "I can only stay a short time. The sooner I'm back with my kin in Kingswood the better." Bennie sat with his back to the wall so he could see the whole room through the doorway. If he had to run, there was a back door not far away.

Raven revealed his plan to Bennie. This coming Friday, three to six of his gang would take the money Raven would give him and buy drinks from noon until two in the afternoon at three different pubs.

"As benefactors of this alcoholic largesse, your men will have everyone's attention when they speak. Rile up the louts with race hatred. Use the release of Nathan Newsome. Use the loss of jobs these men will likely suffer if the blacks take them for cheaper pay. Use any damn excuse you want, but rile up the crowds and lead them to the streets. Find out where some blacks live, ransack their homes if you want, and burn the houses. Once you lit the flame, clear out and head back to Kingswood, fast as you can. Let members of the mob be arrested. Your men will have already made their escape with as much loot as they can carry. That's all you have to do."

"That's all we have to do...is to have a drinking fest, yell and scream a bit, get a mob aroused to a fever pitch, and go out to the streets and torch a few houses. You're not asking much, except we'll be exposed out on the streets."

"You can find an escape plan to Kingswood. Have your wagons waiting at the edge of town. It's a short run for it."

"What will you be doing?" asked Cairnes pointedly.

"That's not your business. It's mine and mine alone."

"So if you won't be with us, we're a diversion, aren't we?"

Raven kept silent and just stared back at Cairnes. Raven slowly moved his hand down to his boot and put his hand on his knife handle. This was the moment in the negotiations where if Cairnes wanted to rob Raven, Cairnes would nod to Hodges, and Raven would get a thumping on the back of his skull. Raven looked for any telltale nod from Cairnes as their eyes met each other—stare for stare, villain to villain.

"It'll cost you a lot of money for this little operation. It may seem like a jolly old time to you, but it's possibly jail or the hangman for us."

"How much?"

"You got the money with you?"

"I can get it. How much?"

"No promises. No refunds."

"How much?"

"I have to pay my cousins for their efforts, I have to buy drinks for a crowd of sots. That's expensive. I'll need it all tonight. We may never see each other again."

"How much?"

"£100 sterling."

"No. Too much. £50." Raven knew if he didn't bargain the money side of it, Cairnes wouldn't think it was a true deal.

"You forget who you're talking to. You want this done? It will cost you. But bargains can be struck. We'll do it for £75."

Raven paused. He could go further with this, but the project might collapse.

"£75 and I better see smoke in east Bristol on Friday at 3:00 p.m., or I'll come looking for you."

"A threat now is it? Well, you know where to find me, don't you? Surrounded by eight families who will protect me with their lives. Come now. You'll see the smoke. My lads need a bit of fun. Now to the money."

What Cairnes didn't know was that Raven had already secured an alternative sleeping room at a sailor's boarding house closer to downtown. It was in no better shape than this one, but if Cairnes and his fellow thugs were to try and rob him tonight when the money was exchanged, he wanted to be somewhere else other than the sleeping room Lewis had so cleverly arranged for him. After this meeting, Raven planned to go to the other place and leave the Hole-in-the-Wall behind him for good.

"I'll go to my room and get it." Raven left the bar and planned to return in a suitable amount of time. He made sure he hadn't been followed, but had his knife in his hand anyway the entire time he was out of the bar.

Raven never went to the room. He carried all the money he had—several thousand pound—in his boots as normal. He stopped in a dark alley, retrieved the agreed upon sum from one of his boots, and returned. All three were there sipping their beers. He handed the money over to Cairnes who counted it carefully.

"£75. You drive a hard bargain."

"It must be worth it to you. We'll have some fun Friday, won't we boys."

And with that bit of cheerio, Cairnes nodded, got up, and left with the other two not offering a handshake or "been glad to know ya" to Raven.

CHAPTER 23

BRISTOL

R aven had a couple of days to scout the area. He walked the streets of Bristol from the Avon Bridge up the hill about a mile until he found the British Royal Infirmary. He sat outside and imagined what he had to do to overtake Langley and abduct Livian. It wasn't hard, but he wanted to do it with an absolute minimum of noise or detection. He needed to know the streets well enough to get out of town without attracting attention. That might be difficult to do, especially since he wanted Langley and Livian alive.

He followed the carriage traffic for hours as they traveled up and down Victoria Street to the bridge that would carry him across to the southern side of the Avon River and the roads to the Admiral Benbow. He hadn't written down Langley's instructions as to how to get back to the Admiral Benbow except he had to follow Abbots Leigh Road out of town and meet up with the Portbury Hundred. That shouldn't be too difficult to remember. Driving the roads for the first time might be, except he knew time would be on his side.

◆ ◆ ◆

Friday at noon, Raven put all his possessions in his billy-bag, including a leg of a chair he fashioned as a club. He left the small sailor's room in the boarding house and walked over to the Pig and Whistle Tavern. It was about a half mile walk to the West. The BRI was another half-mile or so directly up the hill.

He had prepared a note to leave with Langley with instructions to take it to Hawkins. What was in the note should lead Hawkins to come after him as soon as he could get a weapon and transportation. As he walked to the tavern, Raven's scientific mind tried to count the number of minutes it would take for Langley to get to Livesey's surgery and for his pursuer to give chase. Depending on how long it took for Langley to awake after Raven knocked him out, he would have a good hour head start on whoever would chase him down. It was all he needed.

When he got to the Pig and Whistle, he saw Langley's coach with the horses parked outside. The coach driver was obviously inside eating and drinking. Raven waited outside and found an alleyway where he could remain undetected. Despite all the traffic on the street no one bothered him. No one asked what he was doing outside the Pig and Whistle in the early afternoon. He was there for at least an hour, and not a single constable strolled by. If Langley was to get to the Royal Infirmary in time to pick Livian up, he would be coming out in a half hour or so.

When Langley came out, Raven yelled to him before Langley could get to the street. "Hey, Langley, remember me?"

"Who's that calling my name?"

"I was one of your fares a week or so ago. It's Raven, it is." Raven put a light sing-song in his voice trying to put Langley at ease. Langley was bigger than Raven but, had obviously been drinking and seemed a bit unsteady on his feet.

"Raven. Oh yes, I remember you. You're the bloke that wanted to go to Kingswood. And you're still breathing to talk about. I would have wagered anyone that you wouldn't make it out of that village alive that night."

Langley took a couple of long strides toward Raven who was visually protected in the alleyway. "I can't bother to chat long, I have to pick up a fare. I believe I told you about Livian Hawkins. What have you been up to while you've been in Bristol?"

"Walking everywhere, Howard Langley. Walking everywhere. Just look at the wear I've put on my good boots."

Langley bent his head down, and his rum soaked eyes glanced downward toward Raven's boots. In an instant, Raven pulled out the club he had hidden and hit Langley as hard as he could on the back of the head. Langley went down and fell to the brick and dirt covered pavement. Raven quickly looked up to see if anyone on the street had witnessed the clubbing. None had. Raven put his body between Langley's and the street and dragged him over to the side of the alleyway.

Raven stashed the club back under his coat, took the note he had prepared, and put in on Langley's body where he couldn't miss it when he regained consciousness. Raven put his finger to Langley's neck and determined that he was still alive. He then took Langley's hat, placed it on his own head, and made his way as quickly as he could to Langley's coach. The hat helped others identify him as a coach driver.

He cautiously drove the two-horse team up the hill another half-mile to the Royal British Infirmary and parked the rig directly across from the hospital. The timing had to be right. If Langley woke up and ambled up the hill, he could easily spoil Raven's plan. From his elevated position, Raven turned around in the driver's seat, keeping a firm grip on the reins, and looked backwards toward downtown Bristol. His heart was lifted when he saw towers of smoke from three different places. From what he could see, the fires were coming from the direction of Newgate prison and Wine and Castle streets where the poor of Bristol lived.

The money he'd paid Bennie Cairnes had been a good investment.

◆ ◆ ◆

The Rooster Road gang was having its idea of grotesque fun. They and their drunken cohorts had been drinking for hours, and at the urging of a couple of the gang, led three groups of thugs from three different pubs out to harass and brutalize black men and women in the East Bristol slums.

It didn't take much to incite riotous mobs. The minor riots of the last week were small melees compared to this day. All any of the Kingswood gang had to say to the drunken louts was:

"Those blacks need to be taught a lesson!"

"They don't belong here!"

"They'll take our jobs."

"Let's find Nathan Newsome, he killed Bobby Baker! Avenge Bobby Baker!"

These mobs were trumped up on booze. Their narcissism, self-righteousness, and their anger needed an outlet.

One of the groups found out where Nathan and Olivia Newsome lived. They broke down the door of their flat, and not finding them at home, ransacked the rooms, stole what they could, and torched the place before leaving. It took a few minutes for the fire to spread, then the rioters left that street and went on to the next.

As instructed, the Kingswood leader of this particular mob left the group and ran as fast as he could to a hill outside of town where a wagon was waiting to take him and his other Kingswood instigators home before the constabulary arrived. Bennie's plan had worked so far. The wagon didn't leave for Kingswood until the other two Kingswood instigators made it to the waiting wagon.

◆ ◆ ◆

When Livian came out from the hospital around 3:00 carrying baby Belle across the street, Raven saw her pause for a moment when she noticed him in Langley's coach. He remembered Langley's story about sometimes being too drunk to drive, so seeing a different driver hopefully wouldn't concern Livian.

"Where's Langley?" Livian shouted up to Raven. She then held the ear horn up to her ear to hear the answer.

"He's had too much to drink, Milady," said Raven. "I was hired to take you home."

"Are we picking up my husband?" Livian shouted.

"No madam. Langley said that Dr. Hawkins told him he would be late and would get another carriage, but I was to take you home immediately. Look, there's fires in the city."

Livian took a step back from the coach and saw the smoke rising from the east side of Bristol.

"I think we need to leave before there's danger," said Raven. "We can get across the bridge and to the south side of the river before the fires spread. Best be on our way."

With that, Raven jumped down from the driver's seat, opened the door, and gave Livian a hand as she grabbed ahold of the handrail while holding Belle, and settled into her seat. Raven took careful note of which side of the coach she was sitting on, closed the door, got up to the driver seat, untied the leather reins—and with a sneer on his face and anger in his voice—told the horses to move it.

Langley's coach made it down the hill in short order, across the Avon Bridge, and onto York Street. From there, they'd go east by southeast until they came to Abbots Leigh where the right fork would take them to Marcombe Road and Portbury Hundred which would lead him to Hawkins' mother's inn.

Raven could see the black smoke on his left as he traveled down the hill to the bridge. *The firemen and constabulary will be busy. They won't pay any attention to Langley or to Hawkins even if they take my note to them. They'll be too busy with the fires and the mobs.*

He was smugly proud of the way his plan was working. He had spread a little money around to people who wanted to destroy things, and he got what he wanted. A little chaos always helped if you wanted to escape in another direction.

He wasn't necessarily traveling very fast. Abbots Leigh Road was where he planned his first stop. The left fork would be the road that would lead to Livesey Acres. It was at this fork that Raven would have to take action if Livian was to be subdued for the rest of the journey to the Admiral Benbow.

◆ ◆ ◆

Langley had come to and regained his senses about a half-hour after Raven had clubbed him in the alley. The combination of the rum and ale with the hard knock on his head kept him out longer than just the attack would have. When he was totally conscious, he noted three things: he had a splitting headache, his coach was missing from across the street, and he had a note stuffed into the breast pocket of his coat. Once he read it, he walked toward Livesey's surgery. He couldn't move very fast, but he ambled as best he could, trying to get to the surgery as fast as his shaky legs would carry him. He looked desperately for a constable on the streets, but he didn't see one of them.

◆ ◆ ◆

At the fork in the road that would lead him to Abbots Leigh Road—before Livian would notice they were on the wrong road to Livesey Acres—Raven stopped the coach for a moment, stuffed some leather reins from the driver's box into his coat, pulled the liquid opium from his pocket, and poured the entire bottle onto a handkerchief. He wasn't about to get into an argument with her that might attract attention from passing rigs. He jumped down from the driver's platform, opened the coach's door, and abruptly entered the passenger area.

He needed the element of surprise for this attack. He noticed that Livian held the sleeping baby in her arms and that she may have been dozing herself. He pushed himself onto Livian, grasped her hair with his left hand, yanked it backwards and shoved the opium-soaked rag onto Livian's mouth and nose.

Livian tried to kick him but his body weight prevented her from raising her leg high enough to get any leverage. Belle had slipped out of her arm and onto the seat. Livian tried to scratch his eyes and face. Although she was losing strength from the effects of the opium, she succeeded once and was able to draw blood on the left side of Raven's face. He held the rag tight. He wanted her to breathe the drug into her lungs, so he let her gasp for air a few times. The drug wouldn't take effect immediately, so he held the rag in this position for a good three minutes. He stared directly at her, using his entire body weight to hold her down. He waited for her eyes to tell him that she was going unconscious. Livian finally ended her struggle, went limp, and slumped into the seat.

Raven listened to the any sounds on the road that would indicate he'd been detected, but luckily no one had passed by. He looked at the baby on the seat, and without hesitation, put the opium-soaked rag on the baby's mouth and held it long enough to see that the baby girl was unconscious. He tied Livian's hands in front of her with the leather reins, left the coach's passenger seat, climbed to the driver's station, and whipped the horses to get moving.

◆ ◆ ◆

Langley reached Livesey's surgery, burst through the doors, walked past the nurses' area, and right into Dr. Livesey's office where Dr. Hawkins, Dr. Livesey, and Dr. McLaughlin were discussing next week's allocation of duties. They were unaware of the fires in the slums.

"Dr. Hawkins," said Langley breathing heavily, "I was hit over the head an hour ago before I left to pick up Livian. The attacker, a man who calls himself Raven, hit me over the head, took my livery rig, and gave me this note." He held the note out to Jim. "It's for you."

"Here, Langley, take my chair and sit down," said Jim as he rose from his chair and opened the note. Jim read it aloud for all to hear.

> *"You took my life from me, Hawkins. You saw to it that I suffered. Now you will too. I have killed Bobby Axe and that thief of a lawyer I had. I have your wife. If you want to see your mother, wife, or child alive, come to the Admiral Benbow alone or they will all die. Bring £500 and I may let them live."*

Jim's face went white. "It's Franks. It has to be him," he gasped. Livesey and Mac were already out of their chairs. Mac spoke first. "You were right, Jim. You did see him in the courtroom. I'm sorry I didn't believe you."

"I need a horse," said Jim. He went to his desk in the surgery, pulled a loaded flintlock pistol from the drawer, and stuffed it in his belt.

"Jim, hold on a minute. You're not facing this killer alone," said Livesey. "It's too dangerous. We'll get a rig."

"I have to go. I have to go now!" said Jim as he put on his coat. He now had two pistols, the one he pulled from the drawer and the smaller Queen Anne which he carried in his outer coat pocket.

"Don't be rash," said Dr. Livesey. "He's going to wait for you, isn't he? You're the one he wants. Why go there without us backing you up? That's playing right into this trap."

"You heard what the note read. 'Come alone.' If he spies a group of us, he'll kill Livian, maybe even Belle. And if he's at the Benbow he could kill my mother too. I have to go now! Don't try and stop me!"

"We're all going," insisted Livesey. "We'll get a livery to take us to Trelawney's house, and get Abraham Gray to drive us to the inn with all speed. Let's take a street livery right now up the hill, get our weapons, and if you insist on saving time, you can ride another horse there. We'll be bringing up the rear in due haste."

"What about me? He stole my rig," punched in Langley.

"You have something more important to do for the moment," instructed Mac. "Find the constabulary. I suspect you know exactly where it is. You tell them what we're doing and why we're doing it. Tell them to send some men to the Benbow. Don't listen to any argument about jurisdictional nonsense. Even though the Benbow is in another county, the constabularies help each other and that's all that matters."

With that, the men rushed out the surgery locking the door behind them. As they boarded a livery coach that would take them up the hill to Trelawney's, Jim saw the smoke rising to their south and east.

"What's the smoke, driver? Are there fires?" asked Jim.

"Riots and mobs attacking black people, sire. We best get up the hill as soon as we can before the trouble spreads to here," said the livery driver.

"Then by means whip those horses," said Livesey. "We're in a bit of a hurry ourselves."

When they arrived at Trelawney's, they paid the livery driver. They frantically knocked on Trelawney's door's. Olivia Newsome opened the door, and the three men rushed past her to the office where Trelawney and Gray were sitting.

After hurriedly telling them the story and their plan, Dr. Livesey insisted that the squire stay there because of the danger of the rescue mission.

"I don't want to slow you men up," said Trelawney. "Abraham, drive them there and get those women out of this fiend's clutches. I'll be all right here."

Just then Nathan appeared at the doorway. Trelawney continued, "Besides I have Nathan here to protect me. Go, go…with all speed."

They ripped musket, powder, and shot from the gun cabinet. The muskets were always loaded. Trelawney thought unloaded muskets unable to fire immediately were almost useless. The four men went back to the carriage house. They saddled Trelawney's youngest and fastest horse. As soon as he was saddled, Jim tucked his hat on tight and checked that his pistols were secured.

"When you come, stay back from the inn and spread out so he doesn't see you," barked Jim. "You don't want to spook this crazed monster. If he makes a run for it, shoot him down like the mad dog he is."

"What about the money he asked for?" asked Mac as he gave Jim a boost up into the saddle.

"I'm not giving him any money. He wants to kill me; he doesn't want my money. Besides, I'm going to shoot him first for stealing Belle and Livian."

Jim pulled the horse around and bolted out the carriage house door to the street.

Gray, Livesey, and McLaughlin all pitched in to harness and saddle their horses as quickly as possible. Trelawney had four horses in all to power his coach and had two spares. They didn't want to be that far behind Jim. Once their horses were saddled, they secured the muskets, made sure their pistols were loaded, and rode towards the Avon Bridge as fast as traffic would allow them. Jim was already fifteen minutes ahead of them.

◆◆◆

Raven arrived at the Admiral Benbow about an hour later after he had assaulted and drugged Livian. When he pulled up alongside the front door, he made sure that Livian and Belle were still knocked out. He had given Livian a full loading of the drug. She could sleep for hours. He needed control of the inn, because when Jim came, he wanted to humiliate and torture him in front of his wife and family to show them what domination Raven had over Hawkins.

He went into the inn and saw Sara Hawkins at the front desk. Thankfully, no one else was around. She recognized Raven as a former guest, "I remember you. What are you doing driving Langley's coach? Where's Lang—" Before she could say another word, Raven rushed up to her, pulled his club from his coat, and hit her on the head as hard as he could. She went down in a clump.

Reacting to the noise, Maddy came out from the kitchen and saw Raven standing over her sister. She screamed, "What have you done?" and ran back into the kitchen looking for a knife to defend herself. Raven ran faster. Before she could grab a blade, Raven clubbed her as well. She went down.

Raven pulled a rag from the kitchen basin, soaked it in opium from the second bottle he'd purchased, and held it over Maddy's mouth for a couple of minutes. After checking her pulse to make sure her heartrate had slowed down as a result of the drug, he tied her up with twine that he found in the kitchen closet. He took the rag, tore off a six-inch by six-inch square, put a bit more opium on it, and stuffed it into Maddy's mouth. He didn't want any interference once Hawkins came after him.

He went back to the reception desk area and saw Sara Hawkins still knocked out. He did the same thing to her that he had done to Maddy. He wanted them all to be where he could keep an eye on them, so he dragged Sara first, then Maddy into the dining area where there was a small fire going. This time of day, there was no one else in the dining area. Raven thought the women looked so serene, propped up against the wall, drifting into opium dreams.

He went out to the coach and decided to keep Livian and the baby with the other women. It meant lifting Livian without waking her. He had a bit of rag left, so he used the rest of it, poured some opium on it and placed it as a gag for Livian. What did he care if she never woke up? He didn't care about her—he just wanted her husband and he wanted him dead.

He hoisted Livian out of the coach, onto his shoulder, carried her into the dining area, and placed her next to the fireplace aside the other two women. He went back out and got the little girl and placed her right next to her mother. All of the women were now in front of him so he could see if they were awake and they could see him for his finale with Jim Hawkins.

Confident that Hawkins was at least an hour behind him, he had some time. He could leave the women alone, drugged and tied, and see to his boat. When he was finished here, he planned to steal food from the Admiral Benbow and escape to Ireland on the skiff that he had beached over two weeks ago. *Damn, that boat better still be there.*

He was sure he could make it to the beach, move the boat a bit closer to the water's edge, untie the sail, make sure the lines were all set, and get back before Hawkins would show up. If the boat was ready, all he had to do was shove off the beach, raise a sail, and be out of the reach of anyone following Hawkins. It felt like a perfect plan. He was feeling more than a bit smug since the fires had been lit in Bristol by hired thugs. He had executed a perfect kidnapping and had a near perfect plan for killing one of his betrayers.

◆◆◆

While he was busy with the boat, at least a quarter-mile away from the inn down at the shoreline, Livian came out of her opium coma a little bit. The powerful drug had given her a terrible headache and her vision was blurred. To her left, she could see Jim's unconscious mom with a bleeding head wound. Maddy was propped up beside Sara. Belle was to her immediate left, fast asleep.

With an insatiable fury, Livian's anger let her see a bit straighter, think a bit more clearly. She had always been strong under pressure when defending Jim or anyone else she loved. And she needed to think clearly now.

Her hands were tied tight in front of her, but not behind her back. "That, you fiend, was your big mistake." She didn't know where her attacker was, but knew if she was going to free herself, she'd better be quick about it.

She got up on one knee, edged closer to the bricks surrounding the fireplace, and rubbed the leather reins as hard as she could until they tore. It must have taken her ten minutes to accomplish this. She stopped every few strokes to listen for anyone coming. Once she was free, she knew she needed a weapon. She noticed the iron fireplace poker. She was just about to pull up her skirt and take the pistol out when she heard footsteps at the door. She quickly sat down, put her hands in front of her, pretended they were tied, and bent her head as if she was still sleeping.

The door opened sharply, and Franks walked in. He walked up to the women and looked at them closely, even coming within a foot of each of their faces to see if they were still unconscious. He seemed satisfied that he didn't have to drug them anymore and went into the kitchen.

While he was in the kitchen, Livian could hear him rustling around. Since the kitchen was physically separated from the dining area, she was able to move, and remain unseen. She got up quickly, and without making a noise, fetched the iron poker from the fireplace and hid it beside her out of sight. She went back to her slouched position, still pretending to be under the influence of the drug.

She knew the distance from Bristol to the Admiral Benbow and figured she must have been out for a good hour or more. The drug was wearing off, but not completely. Everything was a bit blurred, and her mouth and nose felt terrible. She had to keep the rotten opium rag in her mouth to keep up the pretense. It smelled and tasted like dirt.

Franks returned from the kitchen wiping his mouth. Out of a corner of her eye, she saw that he was briefly startled by the sound of hoofbeats outside the inn. She heard a horse breathing heavy and the noise of someone getting down from the saddle.

Franks pulled a big shiny knife from one of his boots and hid behind the main door of the inn.

With a loud crash, Jim kicked the door open, probably suspecting that Franks might be hiding behind it, waiting to attack. It was the right thing to do. The door swung back hard and hit Franks.

Livian pulled the gag from her mouth and yelled, "Jim. Look out!" as loud as her vocal cords would let her.

Franks turned his body to the entrance and slashed at Jim who had moved to his left to try and avoid the knife. But Franks made a strong downward slash with the deer-skinning knife and caught Jim on his right arm, making a deep gash in his flesh even through his coat. Jim yelled in pain and his pistol fell to the floor.

As Franks drew back his knife to plunge it into Jim, an iron poker came down hard on his right arm fracturing his forearm. Livian had bolted upright, grabbed the poker, and brought it down as hard as she could. She'd aimed for Franks' head, but with her blurred vision, had missed her target and merely struck his arm.

She was ready to pull back the poker and hit Franks again when Franks tackled Jim and drove him to the floor, the two them spilling over the dining table sending chairs crashing. Neither could use their right arms. Jim's arm was bleeding heavily and was nearly as useless as Franks' fractured arm. With his left hand, Franks tried to choke Jim. Jim struggled and put his own left hand in a death grip around

Franks' throat. Neither had an advantage, although Jim tried to kick Franks off of him so he could grab his gun on the floor.

The entire time the two men were fighting, Franks howled through his constricted throat. Nothing came out but a hateful, grotesque, almost otherworldly litany of swearing and death threats to Jim. He yelled about how Jim had betrayed him that Jim was the one who sent him to that hellhole of a prison ship and that Jim was the one who had put him in bondage in the colonies.

Jim was finally able to push Franks off of him. The two rolled around on the floor, both crawling and fighting for the pistol lying on the floor. Neither gained an advantage as they pulled each other back.

Livian circled the two men, looking for an opportunity to bash Franks in the skull. Although it was dangerous in her fuzzy-headed condition, she put down the poker, lifted up her skirt, pulled out the Queen Anne's pistol, and took two steps toward the men fighting on the floor.

Without hesitation, she took one more step to make sure she was within three yards, pulled back the flintlock, aimed the pistol five inches lower than her target (as Jim had taught her), and pulled the trigger. The loud report from the gun shook her and woke up Belle who started to cry.

All went quiet except for Belle's cries. Maddy and Sara woke up. Livian went to her toddler and picked her up, cradling Belle in her arms. She stooped to the floor, picked up Jim's pistol, pulled back the flintlock, and was prepared to shoot again when Jim said, "He's gone. He's dead. You blew a hole in the back of his evil brain. Give me the gun, Livian. You did it again. You saved my life."

Without her ear horn held up to her ear, Livian only heard some of what Jim had said.

Jim took his pistol from her with his left hand, and aiming the gun at his enemy, pushed Franks' dead body over with his boot. Blood covered the floor, and Jim was still bleeding.

Livian said, "Let's go to the kitchen and get some water to wash that wound. It's deep. It will need stitches."

At that moment, Dr. Livesey, Abraham Gray, and Dr. McLaughlin rode up, hitched their horses and burst through the door with their pistols ready. Gray had the larger musket cocked and aimed.

Jim spoke first. "Livian shot him while he and I were fighting. Franks is dead. He will never be a threat to anyone again."

Dr. Livesey went to Jim. "You seem to be bleeding pretty badly. Let's get that wound looked after," he said.

Livesey, Jim, and Livian went to the kitchen to see to Jim's wound. McLaughlin and Gray untied Sara Hawkins and Maddy and got them some water to drink to try to wash the opium taste and smell from their mouths and noses. They were both pretty shaken up by the trauma they'd suffered, the bashes on their heads which needed medical attention, the gunfire, and the blood all over the dining room floor. It would be difficult to wash the floor and the memories clean, but they would do it, eventually putting this day behind them forever.

When Jim's wound was stitched and bandaged, and Mac had seen to Maddy's and Sara's head wounds, the group stood in the dining area and stared at the lifeless form of Franks, not knowing what to do. Jim and Livian stood with Belle in a loving embrace, joyously happy that they had survived this nightmare.

Livian spoke up, "I heard him say he had a boat on the beach that he was going to escape in."

Abraham Gray who had always been a man of action, said, "I'll take care of the body. Dr. Livesey, as a former county magistrate, if you contact the local constabulary and tell them what happened here, I think they'll release the body to us."

Jim was next to speak in the somber room. "Dr. Livesey, if you do that, I'll notify the constabulary in Portsmouth. In his note, he said he killed Bobby Axe and a lawyer there. They ought to know what happened here in Bristol."

Gray said, "At that point, I will take the wretched soul, wrap him in a weighted, sewn sail from his boat, and dump him in the harbor like His Majesty's Navy does. Because this was an evil man, he will not get a Christian burial by my hand."

"Nor mine," said Jim

"Or mine," said Mac. "He truly lived like a demon. He thought he could do whatever he wanted, hurt, and even kill whomever was in his way. No. He'll take his Godforsaken soul to a watery hell where he will never be found, never be visited, and never be missed.

EPILOGUE

W hile Jim and his mom, Sara, got their wounds stitched and bandaged, Dr. Livesey rode his horse down the hill to the Portishead constabulary. While there, he explained what had happened, who the assailant was, and what his motives were for attacking the women in the Admiral Benbow, Dr. Jim Hawkins, and his wife, Livian.

Two constabularies came back to the Benbow with Dr. Livesey, surveyed the scene, then left, granting the ones there permission to bury the body as they saw fit. They would write up a report—and at Dr. Livesey's urging—write a letter to the Portsmouth Constabulary telling them what happened and the disposition of Franks' body. This would be in addition to the letter Jim Hawkins would write to the Portsmouth constabulary explaining what Franks had said in a note about killing Bobby Axe and a lawyer in Portsmouth.

Mac, Gray, and Livesey hauled Franks' body to the Benbow's wagon that would take him down to the beach where Gray would prepare his canvas burial casket. Jim couldn't help because of the deep, painful wound to his forearm, but he accompanied the small procession to the wagon.

Once they got Franks' corpse lying flat in the dray, Mac took one long look at Franks' expensive boots. "For all the money he spent on them, they didn't do him much good," said Mac.

"I know when I spotted the HF initials, it was him," answered Jim. "They still look like they have some miles left in them, somebody should wear them."

"Not me. I wouldn't have this scoundrel's leather touching my feet," commented Livesey.

"Maybe we could give them to someone," suggested Gray. "Someone like Langley. He could use a good pair of boots, and the monogram on the side of them would be something to tell his children and grandchildren about."

"There's a good idea," said Mac, who reached down to take the boots off. When the calf length boot was off, a roll of pound sterling notes fell to the ground. Mac picked it up and undid the twine that kept the roll wadded up.

Jim looked over Mac's shoulder as Mac casually thumbed through the large roll of money. "There's a couple thousand pounds in that roll," said Mac.

Gray immediately pulled off the other boot and another thick roll of notes fell to the ground. Picking it up, he echoed what Mac had just said. "I think we'd better count it. But I'll be damn sure we won't bury this loot with him."

"I wouldn't be surprised if it was the money he stole from Haslar Hospital for all those years," suggested Jim.

"I think you're right," echoed Mac. "He was trying to take his revenge and escape with the money he stole in that kickback scheme."

"Kickback scheme?" asked Gray.

"It's a long story, Abraham," said Dr. Livesey. "Jim will tell you all about it when we get back to Bristol."

They used the horse drawn dray to haul Franks' body to the boat he had stolen. Gray ripped down the canvas sail, and with the sewing kit he found aboard the *Compass*, stitched Franks' body into the crude burial crypt together with some heavy stones. Then Mac and Gray rowed the catboat out a couple hundred yards and unceremoniously threw Franks into the Portishead Harbor.

When the four men arrived back at the inn about an hour later, they put all the money down on a table, counted it, and stared at it like it was contaminated.

"It's the law of the sea," said Gray. "It's salvage, and we have a right to it without guilt."

After a moment or two of reflection, Dr. Livesey decided that Gray was right and that it would be impossible to return it to Haslar or to anyone else. "As a former magistrate, I rule that we divide it up according to the harm he caused others," said Livesey.

He counted out one thousand pounds and handed it to Sara and Maddy. "For the injuries which he caused, ladies." It was more than they could have earned at the inn in ten good years.

"Jim, Livian, here's two thousand pounds. Jim, you suffered significantly as did Livian. You both deserve it. Anyone say different?" said Dr. Livesey.

No one spoke up.

"Mac, Gray, and myself will take £500 each for our troubles, and we'll see to it that Langley gets £200 and the squire receives £300 for the use of his horses and guns. They'll both be happy with that," offered Livesey.

"And Langley gets the boots," responded Jim.

"Aye, Jim," said Mac. "And Langley gets the boots."

ABOUT THE AUTHOR

Richard A. Yach is a retired teaching economist and corporate trainer. He has written, produced, and published over 300 training videos, manuals, and technical magazine articles. He has also written five plays, four of which have been produced. These include: One Way, Brave New World Revisited, The Bard of Beale Street, A Round with the Boys; Golf is a Four-Letter Joke, and Daggett, Dag-nabbit! In addition to his plays, Richard has written *The Destiny of Jim Hawkins* and *Discovery!*, two novels in the Jim Hawkins series. Richard lives with his wife, Linda, in West Des Moines, Iowa with children and grandchildren in the Midwest and California.

Made in the USA
Columbia, SC
01 February 2019